BONE BY BONE

Sanjida Kay is a writer and broadcaster. *Bone by Bone* is her first thriller. She lives in Bristol with her daughter and her husband.

BONE
BY BONE

Sanjida Kay

CORVUS

First published in trade paperback in Great Britain in 2016 by Corvus, an imprint of Atlantic Books Ltd.

10 9 8 7 6 5 4 3 2 1

A CIP catalogue record for this book is available from the British Library.

Trade paperback ISBN: 978 1 78239 688 8
E-book ISBN: 978 1 78239 690 1

Printed in Great Britain by Clays Ltd, St Ives plc

Corvus
An imprint of Atlantic Books Ltd
Ormond House
26–27 Boswell Street
London
WC1N 3JZ

www.corvus-books.co.uk

To Jasmine

PROLOGUE

It wasn't until the train went past that she saw the small body lying in the long grass by the side of the wood.

She couldn't tell how long she'd been searching for her daughter. It was dusk, but it had seemed darker as she ran through the wood, tripping on hooked tree roots, her feet crunching through crisp, curled ash leaves. Around a tight bend, she stopped. Blocking the path was a dog. It was looking directly at her, as if it had been waiting for her. The dog was built like a wolf, but white with uncanny blue eyes. In the twilight, its ghostly fur seemed to glow. A woman, all in black, with dreadlocks bound by silver coils, jerked its lead; the dog's pink tongue lolled over its sharp teeth. She hauled the animal ungraciously out of Laura's way.

At the edge of the wood, Laura paused, trying to catch her breath, wondering which way to go, where to look next. This part had once been an orchard and was now overrun by sycamore saplings with diseased leaves, but there were a couple of crooked apples left with a few remaining fruit on the uppermost branches, small and hard and a poisonous green. Out of the shelter of the trees she felt the rain, light and cold, sweep across her face; the wind rustled through the leaves. Somewhere overhead, a crow cawed.

She ran blindly across the meadow, through puddles of freezing mud. There were ranks of rosebay willowherb, the last seeds clinging to the desiccated stems, and clumps of hemlock, architectural against the clouded night sky. The white underbelly of wheeling seagulls reflected what little light was left.

She kept catching the image as if out of the corner of her eye: a small girl with a tan satchel and a red coat, running, running through the grass. Autumn had been missing since school had finished. No one had seen her nine-year-old daughter after she'd left the classroom.

At the meadow's edge, she followed a concrete path that led across a bridge suspended over a railway. There were bars all the way around to prevent people falling onto the track. She was more exposed to the elements now: the wind and rain howled through the metal cage enclosing her. It seemed impossible that someone could fall or be shoved from the bridge. She forced herself to look down. She had to prepare for the worst.

There was no sign of her daughter, no sign of a small body crumpled by the railway. She pushed her damp hair out of her eyes and turned back towards the darkening expanse of grass, the skyline dominated by bare-knuckled branches, stark against the orange glow of the city. In her haste, she hadn't thought to bring a torch. She turned her mobile on and used the frail light from the screen to comb the ground. After a few moments, the phone chirped. She hoped against hope that it was a text from Mrs Sibson to say that she'd found her, that Autumn was safe. There was an image of a red flashing battery. She turned her phone off. If she didn't find her daughter soon, she would need enough charge to ring the police.

She ran up to the peak of Narroways' one sharp hill. The tiny, urban nature reserve, bisected by three railway lines, spread below her, an unfolding of black shapes: choppy grass, thorny shrubs, spear-tipped metal fences, the dark bulk of the wood and, straight ahead of her, a chasm through the stone cliffs to the train tracks below.

The lines began to sing, a shrill, electric song, and then the cacophony of the train roared out of the darkness. The carriages were almost empty and painfully bright as they hurtled along the tracks to the heart of the city. In the fleeting light she saw the meadow, dotted with stunted hawthorns, their twisted limbs dense with red berries, and then a shape: achingly familiar, child-sized, shockingly still.

She ran down the hill. In the blackness of the night and in the rain and the wind, it felt as if she were falling, falling towards her daughter. She found the satchel first, in a thick clump of clover. And then there was Autumn, abandoned below a tangled briar. She was wearing the red coat her grandmother had bought her a week ago. Laura knelt next to her and cupped the child's cold face in her hands and felt her hair, wet against her wrists.

She switched on her phone and, in the last few seconds before it died and the screen went blank, in that one moment lit by the eerie electronic light, she saw that she was kneeling in a circle of grass where every blade was coated with red. Autumn's hair was sticky with it; her face and neck were bright red. Only one small, pale spot on her cheek was visible where her skin, free of blood, gleamed, as polished as bone.

FRIDAY 26 OCTOBER

LAURA

It sounded as if someone was trying to open the front door. *Matt*, she thought; he must have forgotten his keys. She frowned. That was something she was likely to do, not him. And then she remembered. It couldn't be Matt, it wasn't his weekend to look after Autumn. She rolled over and looked at her bedside clock. It was 4 a.m. The door shook in its frame again.

She rose, wide awake now, and flung on her dressing gown. Although her room was at the top of the house, she always slept with her bedroom door open so that she could hear if Autumn needed her in the night. Who could it be at this time? The house was old – at least Edwardian – and the floorboards seemed to wince under her weight even though she tried to walk quietly down them so she wouldn't wake Autumn and Vanessa.

She hated how vulnerable she felt, a single woman in her early thirties with a young child and her mother asleep in the house. There was nothing secure about their front door – it opened straight from the hall onto the street; there was no spy hole and no chain on the inside. Like everything else in the house, it needed replacing. Now she'd reached the door, she could feel the draught stealing around the warped edges.

'Who's there?' she said, but quietly, so that she wouldn't disturb her family.

There was no answer. She looked through the narrow hall window but all she could see was her own reflection, sharp and bright, in her white dressing gown. She rested her forehead against the glass and cupped her hands around her eyes but she couldn't make out anyone on the street and her view was obscured by the branches of the fig tree she'd planted in a pot and placed right in front of this sliver of a window. In any case, the angle was wrong to see who it was if he was standing right by the front door. She assumed it was a he. It always was, wasn't it? She moved away, in case he could see her reflection, and stood directly in front of the door, listening for breathing, for the scrape of shoes against the pavement. Nothing.

She turned the key in the lock and opened the door a fraction, and then pulled it wide open. A blast of damp, icy air hit her. There was no one there. She leant out to look further into Wolferton Place. The trees in the small park opposite tossed in the wind, the branches of the old pines creaking, and the rain came in hard gusts. Her hair was instantly whipped into a tangle. The short cul-de-sac they lived on was deserted.

She closed the door softly and locked it. For a moment she stood there. Had she imagined the noise? Or had it been the wind? Their house in London had been modern and she wasn't used to the sounds this one made, the way the wind moaned around the chimney and the odd groans and sighs and hisses as air sifted through the gap in the sash windows. Now that the adrenaline was starting to leave her, she became acutely aware of how cold her feet were. The thought of her bed, still vaguely warm, was appealing. She crept back up the stairs, hoping she hadn't woken Vanessa or Autumn. She assumed Vanessa would go for a run if she was already awake. Her mother had no patience with lying in. Laura, on the other hand, felt drained.

She pushed open the door to Autumn's bedroom and peered inside. After a moment her vision adjusted to the gloom. She was startled to see two large eyes staring at her, gleaming in the dark.

Autumn was sitting up in bed, pale and still. She was wearing her white pyjamas, the ones with the rose pattern, the flowers now faded.

'Autumn? Are you awake?'

Laura went over and sat on her bed. She folded her arms around her daughter, feeling the child's thin arms and ribs, the chill of her limbs. She must have woken ages ago.

She'd been worried about Autumn for weeks – almost since the start of term. Her daughter had been miserable and not like her usual sunny, quirky self at all. At first, Laura thought she was missing her dad and finding it difficult to settle into a new school – Autumn had never had to change schools until this summer – but her daughter's mood had only worsened over the past few weeks.

'What is it, love? Did I wake you?'

Autumn shook her head.

'Is there something bothering you?'

Her daughter's shoulders shook and she felt hot tears drop onto her collar bone. She stroked her hair and hugged her.

'What's happened? You can tell me, sweetheart.' She tried to peel her away – Autumn's face was pressed tightly against her neck – and wiped her tears with a crumpled tissue from her dressing gown pocket.

Autumn sniffed. 'It's a boy. He's been saying mean things to me.' She dissolved into tears.

'A boy in your class?'

Autumn shook her head. 'He's in the year above. He calls me names.'

An older boy in the final year of primary school: it somehow made it worse, a child of that age preying on her daughter at a time when children were still supposed to behave like children.

'Oh, sweetheart, I'm so sorry. How long has this been going on for?'

'A bit after I started school.'

'You mean, in September?'

Autumn nodded and blew her nose loudly.

'But that's ages ago, Autumn. Why didn't you say anything?'

'I didn't want you to worry. I thought he'd stop.'

She squeezed Autumn's shoulders. 'And has he done anything else to you? Apart from calling you names?'

Autumn dropped her head. She hiccupped as she tried to speak. 'Slugs,' she wailed and started to cry again.

It was hard to tell what she was saying, but Laura finally got it out of her. Autumn had opened her drawer in class and it had been full of the creatures, packed on top of a layer of rotten apples. Laura thought of those writhing, slimy bodies, the malice it would have taken to collect them all and press them onto her child's books.

'Try and get a little bit of sleep before we have to leave for school.'

Autumn reluctantly lay down and closed her eyes.

'I'm going to talk to your teacher this morning,' Laura said. Her feet were now really cold and she felt tired. She shunted Autumn over and slid into her narrow single bed alongside her. 'It's not acceptable, what that boy is doing. What's his name again? Lenny?'

'Levi,' muttered Autumn, as if the word left a bad taste in her mouth.

Autumn rolled onto her side, curling up and snuggling into the duvet. The child's face relaxed and her breathing slowed. Laura's feet started to tingle. The heating clicked and rumbled into life, the radiators gurgling as the water within them slowly warmed. It was still cold though. Laura knew she should get up but it was so rare to be able to watch her daughter fall asleep.

It felt as if hardly any time had passed since Autumn had been a baby and yet here she was, looking down at a nine year old whose long, thick, light-brown hair was spread across her pillow. When Autumn was born, it was as if she recognized her, as if she'd always known that it would be her, this little person who had come to live with her and reside permanently in her heart. It was a love unlike any other: fierce and powerful. It was a shock to Laura, who had never felt anything so all-consuming in her life.

She couldn't bear the idea that Autumn was being teased.

'There is nothing I would not do for you,' she whispered to her daughter in the darkness as she stroked her hair one last time.

They'd moved from London to Bristol late that summer, once the divorce had been finalized and their house sold. Laura had chosen to live in Montpelier because the school was so good: Ashley Grove Junior had excellent Ofsted grades, the teachers seemed nice and they could walk there. Compared to Autumn's school in Hammersmith, it was calmer and quieter – there were only two classes in each year.

When Autumn had first started at Ashley Grove in September, Laura had been as nervous as her daughter. She'd been worried about Autumn – if she'd make new friends, if she'd fit in – as well as for herself – would the other mothers like her? It had felt, as she'd walked to school that morning, her mouth dry and her stomach churning, as if it were her first day too. Autumn had gone to one school all her life and Laura – probably because of her peripatetic childhood, being shuttled between Namibia and London when her parents were working overseas – hated change.

School started at 9 a.m., but the pupils were expected to arrive five minutes early, so there were normally a lot of children and their parents milling around in the playground beforehand. For the first couple of days, a few of the other mothers openly stared at her and Autumn but no one spoke to them. It wasn't until the third day that, to Laura's eternal gratitude, Rebecca came across to talk to her. It didn't take long for Rebecca's friends – Amy, Lily and Rani – to follow. Rebecca was an alpha mother and being accepted by her had made Laura's life a lot easier. It didn't stop Laura feeling lonely and isolated though. Her own friends were in London but so far none of them – not even her best friend, Lucy – had had time to visit. She couldn't remember a period in her life when she hadn't been surrounded by a network of people: she'd stayed in touch with all the mothers and their children from her NCT group, and then there were the odd assortment of gardeners, whom she'd seen once a week at her allotment and often in the pub later, as well as the friends she'd made on her horticultural course. Still, she thought, it was just a matter of time. They hadn't been here for long and it was absolutely the right decision to move to Bristol and make a fresh start.

Today Laura looked around for Rebecca's black Range Rover and her two blonde, beautifully dressed little girls, Poppy and Tilly – Tilly was in Autumn's class – but there was no sign of them. They were still a couple of minutes early, though.

As they were crossing the yard, Autumn moved closer to Laura so that she was pressed against her side.

'He's there,' she said in a small voice. 'Look.'

She pointed to a group of boys who were lounging around the climbing frame. A couple of them were hanging from the bars.

'Which one?' asked Laura.

'By the swing,' Autumn said, and half turned towards her mother so that she could no longer see the gang.

Laura didn't know what she'd expected: a small podgy boy with mean eyes, if she'd been pushed to describe the image in her mind; a kid on free school meals and benefits with a tattooed father and his shirt tails hanging out. But not this boy.

'He's in the year above you?' She couldn't stop herself from saying it.

'Don't stare!' said Autumn, her cheeks colouring.

'Sorry.'

She started walking again and Autumn continued leaning against her, keeping time with her steps, her face resolutely turned away.

So that was Levi. She could hardly believe it. The most obvious thing about him was that he was beautiful. Stunningly good-looking, in fact. He was tall, at least as tall as Laura. He appeared older than ten, although she guessed he could be eleven already. And then there was the fact that he was black. Not dark or blue-black though, but a warm, golden-brown. His hair was in corn rows, ending just below his collar and his large, dark eyes were fringed with thick eyelashes. He had an aquiline nose and bow-shaped lips. He looked neat in his white shirt, blazer and black trousers. The uniform was quite relaxed at Ashley Grove but he'd chosen to wear the most formal clothes he could and they were spotless. Propped casually against the metal post of the swing, coolly regarding the antics of the other boys, he seemed older, wiser, superior. Laura found it hard to believe he'd even noticed Autumn. Levi looked like a teenager; you could see in his face the young man he would become. In comparison, Autumn looked like a child with her round cheeks and bony knees, her gap-toothed smile and her plaits.

'Where are his parents?' asked Laura, looking around the yard.

'I don't know. I've only seen him walking to school by himself,' mumbled Autumn, stepping away from her.

Laura felt the sudden chill where Autumn's warm body had been. Unable to help herself, she glanced over at Levi again. To her surprise he was staring directly at her, as if he were calmly appraising her. She ducked her head and hurried after Autumn.

She took a deep breath, walked into the school and knocked on the open door of the Year 4 classroom. Autumn trailed unhappily behind her.

Autumn's class teacher, Mrs Ellen Sibson, was tall, in her late fifties, with an angry rash across her chin and severely parted hair streaked with grey and dotted with a few flakes of dandruff. She wore an ankle-length pale-blue cord skirt and a long-sleeved top and cardigan in a matching colour. A necklace made of round green plastic beads hung across her bosom and rested on her stomach. Laura thought she was intimidating, not like the jovial George Wu, who'd taken Autumn's class last year in London.

Laura found any kind of confrontation difficult and had been rehearsing what to say to Mrs Sibson all the way to school, so that their walk had been in near silence. She realized, with a fretful pang, that she hadn't even tried to reassure Autumn.

'Could I just have a quick word?' she asked Mrs Sibson, who frowned and then attempted a smile.

Laura immediately felt at a disadvantage. Mrs Sibson was readying herself for her class and would hardly want to have an extended chat right now. But it was for Autumn's sake; she had to do it. She pushed the door shut and clenched her fists, her nails digging into her palms.

'What can I do for you?' Mrs Sibson asked.

'It's about Autumn. I'm not sure she's settling in that well.' She gave Mrs Sibson a small smile, trying to look friendly.

'I think she's doing remarkably well, considering how difficult it must have been for her, moving here and transferring to a new school.'

'Well, it's more than that. More than simply starting at a new school.'

'She is quiet,' said Mrs Sibson, glancing at Autumn, 'but she's been working hard, and she's very gifted artistically. Our PE teacher is particularly impressed with her gymnastic ability.'

'I'm not worried about her school work,' said Laura.

'We all think Autumn has been doing better than we'd anticipated by this stage in the term. But if you have any concerns, by all means come in when we have more time and we can discuss it further.'

'I am concerned, Mrs Sibson, that's why I'm here. Autumn is being bullied.'

'Bullied?'

'A boy – his name is Levi – is bullying Autumn. I'd like you to speak to him and make sure it stops. Yesterday—'

'The slugs,' interrupted Mrs Sibson. 'I'm sorry Autumn found it distressing but it was just a prank.'

A prank? Laura looked at her in disbelief.

Mrs Sibson glanced down at Autumn as she leant against one of the desks and scuffed the linoleum with her toe, staring intently at the floor. Her cheeks flushed scarlet and she closed her eyes, an old childhood trait she'd developed when she was a year old if anyone apart from Laura or Matt spoke to her. Mrs Sibson looked rather pointedly at the clock on the wall.

'I wouldn't call stuffing a child's drawer full of slugs a prank,' said Laura.

'I think it was a one-off,' said Mrs Sibson. 'I haven't noticed any of the children in this class teasing Autumn or playing tricks on her before this occurred. And I cancelled the children's Halloween treat because no one owned up.'

So as well as being bullied, her whole class would be annoyed with her, thought Laura.

'Autumn says Levi was responsible,' said Laura. 'He's been bullying her virtually since the start of term. She's only just told me now or I would have come to see you earlier.'

Ignoring the charge of bullying, Mrs Sibson said, 'Levi is in the year above.' She turned to Autumn for the first time and asked, 'How could he have done it?'

Autumn screwed her eyes closed even tighter and said nothing. Laura wanted to shout at Mrs Sibson to stop this child, this Levi, whoever he was, from speaking to Autumn ever again.

'It's not up to Autumn to work out how Levi could have got into the classroom!'

Both she and Autumn still had on their winter coats and the room was hot. She felt uncomfortable, a minor tremor running through her torso because of the heat, the awkwardness of the situation.

Mrs Sibson said, 'I appreciate you coming to me about this matter. We don't tolerate bullying in this school. Every child here is taught a respectful attitude to others.' She added, 'We adhere to our stringent, anti-bullying policy, Mrs Baron-Cohen, so we do take your concerns seriously. I can't say I've noticed Levi speaking to her. But I will take it up with Mr Bradley, Levi's class teacher. The teachers are generally not outside during the lunch break, so I will also talk to the dinner staff who monitor the playground. I do wish I had more time to discuss this with you, but I have a class to teach. I'll let you know what Mr Bradley says and we'll keep an eye on Levi, particularly at break-times. Perhaps you could make an appointment for next week,' she said, looking at the clock again.

She's saying she doesn't believe Autumn, Laura thought.

Autumn opened her eyes and looked over at her, her face set in a hurt expression. She moved towards her daughter but, at that moment, the bell rang and Autumn's classmates, who'd been pressed against the door, flooded noisily into the room. Autumn moved away so that Laura couldn't kiss her goodbye in public and shrugged off her coat with her back to her. Laura forced herself not to help her. She stood in the doorway, jostled by the incoming children, and then made her way slowly out of the school.

As she walked across the playground, she saw Rebecca standing near the gate with a small group of parents. Rebecca, as usual, looked like a mother in a catalogue. She had long, wavy chestnut hair and was wearing white jeans and knee-length dark-brown boots, a grey cashmere coat and had an elegant scarf wrapped around her neck.

How can she wear white jeans in winter? Laura wondered.

She was talking to Amy, a petite woman who was half Vietnamese and was also always immaculate. She wore retro-chic dresses with cinched-in waists, emphasizing her tiny frame and her flat stomach, in spite of having had three children. Laura didn't recognize the other two mothers or the man they were with.

Rebecca waved her over. 'Now here's someone you really must meet. He's an absolute genius at sorting out computers – he does the IT at Ashley Grove and doesn't charge us a penny.' She flapped her hand between the two of them. 'Aaron Jablonski. Laura Baron-Cohen.'

If Laura had been asked, she might have come up with some nebulous image of what a man who worked in IT might look like: pot-bellied, pale, sandy-haired with poor dress sense, perhaps. Nothing like this man. He was tall, handsome, with a straight jaw and chiselled features. He exuded masculinity in an understated kind of way, like a woodsman, a log-cutter, someone from the forests of North America. Beneath his coat he was wearing a white shirt and black waistcoat with jeans. A messenger bag was slung over his chest and the hand that held the strap had a silver charm on a woven leather strap around the wrist; no wedding ring.

'Aaron,' he said and held out his hand. His voice was deep.

Laura felt as if she was reaching out to grasp his hand in slow motion. He squeezed her hand firmly. She realized she'd been staring and blushed and stepped back.

'Are you new to the area?'

She nodded. 'We've just moved here. My daughter started school this term.'

'I've just dropped my son off. I hardly ever have the chance. It's my one small pleasure in life. But he's at that age where he's embarrassed to be seen with his dad so when we get within a few hundred metres of the school, he hares off so I won't – God forbid – try and hug him in front of his mates.' He smiled and Laura could see the other mothers leaning in, imperceptibly drawing nearer, hanging on his every word.

'Oh, my daughter's the same. She's already told me I'm not allowed to hold her hand or kiss her in front of any of her school friends.'

'A bit different from when we were growing up,' he said, looking at her as if the two of them existed in some private universe that no one else had access to. 'Our parents never bothered walking us and to and from school. Am I right?'

Laura nodded, feeling her cheeks begin to glow again.

He straightened and looked around at the small group breathlessly waiting for his attention. There were so few fathers at the school gates it was no wonder Aaron was attracting so much attention, she thought, and then, of course, he was ridiculously handsome...

'Ladies, I must dash. Laura, if I may...?' He took a small leather wallet from his pocket. 'My card. Just in case. I do home visits.'

'Oh, he's a godsend,' said Rebecca, 'the amount of times Aaron has come over at a moment's notice to fix my Mac.'

Laura took the card, still faintly warm from where it had been pressed against his thigh. The mothers watched Aaron stride away, his long, dark coat flaring behind him.

'Is everything okay?' asked Rebecca, turning to her. 'I saw you talking to Mrs Sibson.'

Laura hesitated. She was still angry at being dismissed so summarily by the teacher, but she forced herself not to rant about it. She didn't want to upset the fragile balance of her relationship with Rebecca.

'Autumn is finding it a little difficult to settle in,' she said.

Rebecca pursed her lips sympathetically and said, 'That's such a shame. The girls in her class are so sweet, though, I'm sure it won't take long for her to make friends. Why don't you come over for afternoon tea tomorrow? Poppy and Tilly would love a play date with Autumn, and we can have a gossip.'

Laura nodded gratefully and felt a surge of pleasure in spite of the circumstances. She'd gone for coffee with Rebecca and her coteries of mothers, but she'd never been to her house. She knew that Rebecca and the other women sometimes met for drinks, or for an afternoon in the park at the weekend, the one with a café that apparently sold amazing coffee, hand-roasted in Bristol, and gluten- and sugar-free cakes and cookies. Laura had not been invited so far and was not certain enough of Rebecca to ask if she could join them. Tilly had invited several girls, including Autumn, for a sleepover, but it wasn't for another week and she knew Autumn would love the chance to have Tilly to herself for a short while.

'That would be wonderful, thank you.'

She glanced down at herself. Next to Rebecca and Amy she looked dowdy and badly dressed. She was wearing her work clothes: mud-stained army trousers, cracked hiking boots, an ill-fitting fleece and a flannel shirt. Her hair was scraped back from her unmade-up face.

Rebecca smiled and kissed her on the cheek. 'Three? At my house? I'm sure I'll see you both before then.' She gave a little wave as if dismissing her, and then bent to speak to Amy.

Laura crossed the road and headed down Briar Lane. That had gone badly, she thought. Autumn was upset and embarrassed, Mrs Sibson hadn't taken her seriously and she hadn't managed to put a stop to the bullying. She didn't even know who Levi's parents were – perhaps if Mrs Sibson did nothing about it, she could speak to them? She shivered at the thought of confronting them; she knew they'd be horribly defensive and angry. And, on top of that, she was going to be late for work. She half jogged, annoyed with herself for becoming so unfit.

The lane, which ran directly opposite the school behind the terrace of houses that lined the main road, led to a miniature nature reserve created between the intersection of three railway tracks. You reached Narroways nature reserve by crossing a thin bridge suspended over the lines. It had high corrugated metal barriers on either side that were scrawled with neon-bright graffiti, and it was encased by wire bars, so that the whole bridge was like a cage, preventing anyone from accidentally falling onto the train line.

The path from the bridge skirted a scrubby meadow that had been carpeted with wild flowers when she'd put the offer in on the new house in May; the sight had lifted her spirits, but it was now pock-marked with the burnt embers of fires and scattered with beer cans and crisp packets. It led to a peak, the highest point in the area with a startling view over the red-brick terraces of Easton and St Werburghs, and beyond to green fields and hedgerows in the distance. In spite of the upheaval coming here, Laura loved the fact that from her neighbourhood you could see the edge of the city. It was unfeasible to be near the centre of London and see where that vast metropolis neatly, clearly and sharply, ended. It was one of the reasons why, after she and Matt had split up, she'd wanted to move to Bristol. Now Autumn could grow up somewhere with fresh air and countryside nearby, but still have all the benefits a city could offer.

On one side of the meadow was a cliff of exposed red earth and gritty stone with stunted ash trees clinging to it that led down to a railway track. The path divided and you could either walk up and over the peak or around it and then down through a small wood. Laura, because she was in a hurry, chose the shorter route.

Her mobile rang. She looked at the screen and saw it was Matt.

'Hello,' she said, in the new, chirpy voice she'd taken to using when he called.

'Laura. Just checking you haven't forgotten about Nepal.'

Nepal? For a moment she was confused and then she remembered.

'No, no, of course not, it's today, isn't it?'

There was a pause. She could tell he knew she'd forgotten and was weighing up whether to use it as an opportunity to have another dig at her.

'That's right,' he said. 'I'm at the airport now. I still want to speak to Autumn tomorrow night. I'll Skype at the usual time, okay?'

'Yes, that's fine,' she said.

'I've emailed you a copy of my schedule. I'll try and Skype the following Saturday as normal too – we should be back in a village that has Internet access by then. The satellite number is on the schedule if there's an emergency. With Autumn,' he added, in case she was not absolutely clear that any emergencies concerning her were no longer his responsibility.

Like her parents, Matt had trained as an anthropologist and originally specialized in making films about tribal peoples for the BBC and *National Geographic*. As audiences had grown accustomed to more light-weight entertainment, he'd turned his skills towards the reality-TV market. He was currently making a series featuring athletes competing against tribes in a traditional rite, such as a wrestling match or canoe race. This was his first trip for the series and he was heading to the flanks of the Himalayas to film an endurance race between a Buddhist tribe and a team of five female athletes.

Typical of Matt, she thought, to surround himself with toned, beautiful and sporty women in the guise of work. She wondered what Leah, his new girlfriend, felt about the trip and then realized that, since Leah was his researcher, she'd probably be with him.

Nothing to do with me, she reminded herself, taking a deep breath to steady herself. That was the trouble with being divorced and having a child – you could never truly get away from it all. Moving to Bristol had been her way of putting as much distance as possible between her, Matt and Leah. And even though Bristol wasn't that far from London, Matt was still annoyed with her, as if she had done it deliberately so that he couldn't see Autumn as much as he'd like to.

She wondered whether to tell Matt about Autumn being bullied and then decided not to. She could handle it by herself.

'Talk to you on Saturday,' she said breezily and hung up.

The wood was really an orchard that had gone wild, and Laura had been delighted to find apple, pear and plum trees. The plums had all been picked, but there were a few apples left, tight and shiny in the ragged branches. From the wood there was a path that led into the allotments, which bordered the lane at the bottom of their house. It meant that their day started off with an almost rural feel.

Fortunately, Bronze Beech, the landscaping company Laura was working for, was currently redesigning a garden in Montpelier, on the other side of the nature reserve, so Laura could walk to it after dropping Autumn off without being too late for work. Her boss, Barney McLoughlin, was a rugged, burly man with wind-burnt cheeks and an Oxbridge accent. He wore a singular combination of tweed jackets with elbow patches and combat trousers for work.

As well as Laura, Barney employed Ted, who had dreadlocks so bleached they were white – he even bleached his eyebrows. Throughout the early weeks of autumn Ted had taken his T-shirt off most days, exposing badly drawn Maori tattoos from an old trip to New Zealand, and beer-blurred muscles. Laura thought he was a particularly toxic combination of misogyny and sycophancy. Her agreed hours were 9.30 a.m. to 3 p.m. but Barney and, more often, Ted, frequently made comments about her arriving late and leaving early; today Barney would be furious because she actually was going to be late. She sighed. She was going to have to put Autumn in an after-school club so she could work for longer.

AUTUMN

It was why she hadn't told her mum about Levi before. She didn't want her mum to feel worried or upset. Because then she'd try to help and she wouldn't be able to.

She squeezed her eyes shut and felt again the excruciating embarrassment as her mother had blurted out, *Levi is bullying Autumn*.

It had sounded... belligerent. She'd learnt it in Literacy. Her mum wasn't normally belligerent, but she did get upset easily. It was her reaction – like a frightened mouse might bite because it doesn't know what else to do. Or else she became quieter and quieter. Autumn knew the feeling – sometimes when Mr Wu, her old teacher, had called her out in front of the whole class, she literally couldn't say a word, couldn't even open her mouth or make a sound. As if she'd never known how to speak.

The name-calling had begun just after she'd started at the new school. Of course she'd noticed Levi before – who hadn't? He was good-looking and all the boys in her class thought he was cool. Some of the girls said they fancied him – whatever that meant. She'd noticed him watching her a couple of times when her mum picked her up from school. And then it happened.

'Autumn?' he'd said, and she'd said, 'Yes?' in a tiny voice.

She couldn't believe he was talking to her. But he wasn't. He was talking *about* her.

'Autumn. What kind of dumb name is that? Who'd call their kid that? It's like saying, "Hey, November, come in for your tea."'

He'd turned his voice into a high-pitched falsetto and the group of boys that always hung around with him burst out laughing.

'Oh, darling February, time to go to bed now.'

As he continued, calling her more random and ridiculous names, the boys in her own class started to laugh too, and some of the girls put their hands over their mouths and smirked.

Later on that day, Tilly tossed her long, blonde hair over her shoulder and said, 'Come to think of it, it is a weird name. Why are you called that? I mean, it's not like you're some kind of celebrity or anything.'

A couple of the girls nearby sniggered and shouted out the names of stars' children: Blue Ivy, Princess, Brooklyn, Harper Seven.

'Hey, isn't there some film star called, like, January?' one of the girls said.

Molly put her hand on Autumn's. Molly, like Tilly, was *thinking* about being her best friend. Her real best friend, Cleo, was in London.

Molly whispered, 'I like your name.'

It had continued. Some days Levi didn't seem to notice her, at other times he'd taunt her, whistling through his teeth at her, calling her bizarre things: Toilet Cleaner, Andrex, Equinox.

Recently he'd moved on to the gap in her front teeth and how ugly it made her. That was the first time she'd cried, by herself in the toilets. Because he was right. She *was* ugly. Her teeth stuck out, with a wider gap at the bottom than the top and she was missing two more teeth, where the baby ones had fallen out but the big ones hadn't come through. If she didn't smile, perhaps no one would notice. She started to keep her top lip over her teeth when she opened her mouth so other people couldn't see them. Levi saw, though.

'Look,' he shouted, 'that psycho kid, Canada, or whatever her name is, she's doing a fish impersonation. She thinks we can't tell she's got wonky teeth.'

He started imitating and exaggerating her attempt at smiling and his friends held their stomachs, almost crying with laughter.

At break-times her hands would grow clammy and her mouth dry, her breathing became shallow. She wanted to stay indoors and it was only with the greatest reluctance that she followed the others outside. She wished she could hold Molly's hand, as if Molly could protect her. She tried to make herself take deep breaths.

It's going to be okay. I won't always be the new girl.

She kept wondering what Levi would do when the name-calling was not enough. And then she found out.

Yesterday afternoon they had Art and Design, her favourite part of the week. There was still the sleepover with Tilly and some of the other girls to look forward to the following week. She was feeling upbeat, hopeful, safe: all the things she hadn't felt for what seemed like a long time. She wasn't prepared for it.

Mrs Sibson said that today's project was going to be to draw some natural objects with an autumnal feel. She walked around the class putting conkers and scarlet maple leaves and hazelnuts on each table. She handed out large pieces of sugar paper and trays of pastels and coloured pencils. Autumn liked drawing the outlines first in black ink and then shading the picture in. She'd brought her special pen to school, the one her mum had given her, and she'd put it straight in her drawer at the start of the day. She'd checked it was there before and after break and again before she went for lunch.

She almost skipped over to her drawer and pulled it open. She recoiled and gave a little shriek, then clapped her hands over her mouth.

'What is it, Autumn?' asked Mrs Sibson, frowning at her.

The pupils fell silent as the teacher strode over to her. Autumn couldn't move. She could feel the blush spreading across her cheeks and blazing up to her hairline. The odour seemed to creep like something living into her clothes, crawling across her skin. A few children came to see what she and Mrs Sibson were staring at, and within minutes, the class was in an uproar, children screaming and shouting, some of the girls pretending to gag, a few boys laughing.

The drawer was full of slugs. At least a hundred of the creatures writhed and twisted over each other; some were fat, others thin; there were tiny black ones, thick beige ones, a few the colour of stewed tea and two enormous beasts, pale and covered in jagged spots. This pair were in the process of devouring one of the smaller slugs; its entrails, pale as putty, oozed across Autumn's Literacy notebook. The rest were voraciously consuming the bed of rotten apple that had been packed into the drawer, which stank of mould and sour cider. Released from their dark confinement, several of the slugs, eye stalks stretched to their limits and quivering, started to pour over the edge of the drawer and drop in a pulsating mass to the floor.

Mrs Sibson rested her hand on Autumn's shoulder for a moment. Autumn realized she was trying to comfort her, but Mrs Sibson's hand felt heavy, like a weight pressing down on her collar bone.

The art lesson was abandoned. When the mess was finally cleaned up and order restored to the classroom, Mrs Sibson declared Autumn's books *quite ruined*. They were stained with decomposing apple and covered with slime. Autumn watched as the teacher dumped them all in the bin. Since no one owned up, Mrs Sibson said there would be no cupcakes for anyone on Halloween. There was a collective groan. Autumn was sent to the stationary cupboard with the school receptionist and given an entirely new set of exercise books. She was nearly crying as she returned to her silent, resentful class.

LAURA

There were ten of them stuck to the wall with Blu-tack. Each one a vibrant miniature, the outlines in fine black pen, coloured in with vivid inks. She'd used such a fine brush, thought Laura, remembering Autumn painting the first one. They were childish but charming – and Autumn was so proud of them. Laura particularly loved the one of a thin, spiky woman with a big smile, carrying a giant harebell that bobbed above her head like a lantern.

Laura suddenly had a vision of Autumn as a tiny child – about eighteen months old – sitting at a child-sized table with a set of felt tips. She neatly took the top off one, drew great arcs of pink across the paper, before replacing the lid, then chose another colour – red this time – and repeated the procedure. Orange was the last one she'd picked. She would always follow this pattern – three colours in the same tonal range, creating these stylish mini rainbows, putting the tops neatly back on the pens after she'd used each one. Autumn still loved drawing and painting and always had some form of self-generated project on the go. She was such a quiet, shy child; it was as if art was her way of communicating. *No, that's not right*, thought Laura, Autumn was nothing if not articulate – it was her way of expressing how she felt.

Laura had spent the day wondering if Autumn was okay. She left Autumn's room and went downstairs into her mother's. That was how powerful her mother's influence was, she thought; it was no longer the spare room, even though Vanessa had only slept in it for a night. She'd left Laura's dad working in London and arrived the day before to give her daughter a bit of *moral support*, as she put it. The bed was neatly made and Vanessa's clothes were folded and had been placed in a pile at the end, her shoes lined up beneath them. She'd gone out running.

Since they'd moved to Bristol, Autumn had started walking home by herself. Laura worried about it – particularly as the clocks would change on Sunday and it would be dark when she was on her way back. But it did give Laura an extra fifteen minutes to return home from wherever she was working with Bronze Beech. Laura checked her watch once more. It was three minutes to four. School finished at 3.30 and it only took twenty minutes to walk home through the nature reserve – fifteen if you were quick. Even allowing for Autumn leaving her classroom late and dawdling... Laura couldn't bear it any more. She ran downstairs to the hall and pulled on her coat, wound a scarf around her neck and crammed a hat on her head. She grabbed her trainers and sat on the bottom step leading into the kitchen to put them on. Now that she'd decided to do something – go and meet Autumn on her way home – she was filled with urgency. Vanessa had taken a key so she could let herself in. She thought about leaving a note for her and then decided against it. She wouldn't be long.

She flung open the kitchen door. Directly below her, crawling through the long, damp grass next to the path, was a large slug, five inches in length. Laura tried to push it away from the house with her toe but the slug only writhed a little, exposing its pale underbelly beneath an ominous orange-lined mantel. She shoved it again and this time it wound across her trainer, depositing a thick trail of slime. Laura shuddered as she finally knocked it off her foot and back into the grass.

It was still cold enough for her breath to freeze in clouds, and with a fine drizzle, the kind that falls so gently you barely notice but, in the end, chills you to the core.

Vanessa had sent her two texts complaining about the Internet today. The second one had said

Given up. Gone to a café with Wi-Fi.

Laura had immediately seen her mother's comments as a criticism – she was failing to keep the house together and she lacked the right kind of mind to sort it out. She knew it was irrational and that her mother was probably only annoyed at the delay to her work. But her mother did have a point: she'd need to make sure the Internet was working properly so that Matt could speak to Autumn via Skype on Saturday – plus it was crucial for those nights she worked late, setting up her garden-design company and studying for her degree. Barney didn't believe in taking long breaks and he also hated her making calls during work hours. She'd ignored his frown as she'd dug out Aaron Jablonski's card and texted him. He'd replied almost immediately to say he was free this evening. She'd felt a slim tremor of excitement as she'd slipped her phone back in her pocket and resumed digging in a row of espaliered apple trees.

Now she locked the garden gate behind her using the key code and then walked down the lane towards the allotments. Autumn was a dreamer, an ambler, just like Laura. She could easily have stopped to pick a bunch of the last wild flowers of the season, or to examine an interesting seed pod. But still. Laura had a horrible feeling of foreboding. Her stomach felt as if small lead weights were being slowly dropped into it.

Laura loved the allotments: the quirkiness and individuality of each one, how some were wild, brambles and ragwort and Michaelmas daisies threatening to overrun them, and others were neat and orderly, the grass shaved, vegetables in raised beds – rows of leeks and onions were all that were still growing, their blue-green leaves glistening in the rain. The last allotment before the path turned sharply into the wood was like an extension of someone's garden: a line of pink dahlias, their dying flowers decaying ball gowns, a slate-grey shed, an iron bench trailing tea-roses, several gnomes standing guard over the vegetables, and an iron stand with bird feeders dangling from it. There were no birds today. Laura normally felt wistful as she walked through the allotments, thinking of the productive plot she'd left behind and how long the waiting list in Bristol was. But today she hardly noticed them. She almost jogged into the wood. It was a steep hill and she panted as she walked quickly up it, sliding in the mud. It reminded her, yet again, of how unfit she was, and she thought of her mother, twenty-six years older than her, running effortlessly, gazelle-like, around the streets of Bristol.

She stopped briefly at the top, screened by the branches of a tree, trying to work out which way to go. If Autumn had reached the meadow with its mini peak in the nature reserve she could have returned home along either path.

I should have seen her by now.

Laura decided to take the lower path that skirted the hill and keep looking upwards in case Autumn had decided to go over the top.

A magpie alighted on the grass in front of her, bouncing on both feet, head cocked on one side to regard her.

One for sorrow...

She tried to remember what Autumn had been wearing today. She had a vision of her in white knee socks, already falling down – so she must have put a skirt on – and her black winter coat, which wasn't waterproof. Plus the coat was last year's, cheap and growing threadbare and too short for her. No hat, Laura remembered now, but there was a hood on the coat. She should have insisted Autumn change into trousers or wear tights. She felt guilty again.

She set off, walking briskly, taking in lungfuls of chill air to steady her breathing. What if, she thought, she walked as far as the end of the nature reserve and she still hadn't found Autumn? There was only Briar Lane left, stretching steeply upwards, before it bent sharply behind the houses lining the road opposite the school. Suppose she reached the end of the lane?

Her heart was banging painfully in her chest. Could something have happened to Autumn?

I couldn't bear it, she thought wildly.

Autumn was her life. There was nothing more important to her, or that she loved more dearly, than her daughter. She'd given up everything for her – though she'd never seen it as giving up. When Autumn was little, learning to walk and then to run, and she fell, Laura would gasp and call out as if she had been wounded as well and would rush to comfort her child, her baby, and kiss her hurt knee, her grazed elbow.

Over-protective, her mother said.

Laura tripped over a tussock of grass and almost landed in a mud-filled hollow, black with ashes left from some fire, surrounded by cans of cider. She stood up straight. She'd pulled a muscle in her calf and it twinged when she tried to walk. Laura wiped the rain from her face and looked anxiously up towards the hill. Nothing. Only dense, grey rain clouds blocking out the sun, heralding dusk. She took a couple of experimental steps. It hurt but she could walk. She would have to, she thought grimly. She did a quick calf stretch and winced.

As she started to round the curve of the hill she heard them. Childish voices. Laughter. Some deeper voices.

Is there an adult with them, she wondered?

The thought of an adult in the midst of a group of feral children was immediately comforting. A shout. More laughter. It was definitely darker now. *Gloaming*, her father would have said: that moment when it's not quite dusk, when the darkness has not started to fall, but because of the lateness of the hour and the season and the banking clouds ranked across the sky, there was a dimness to the day. The drizzle started to grow heavier. In her hurry, she slipped in the mud again. As she righted herself, she saw them.

Her heart skipped a beat. They were not children, you couldn't call them children – youths perhaps. They were boys, young boys, but tall. Older than primary school children. Secondary school kids. There was something intimidating about running into them here. No one else was around. Not even a dog walker. Their noisiness, boisterousness, lack of control – as if they'd grown too swiftly for their bodies, like over-large toddlers – made her anxious. She dipped her head and hurried on. They fell silent and watched her. How did they view her, she wondered? A woman as old as their mums, uncool in her unfashionable coat and maroon woollen hat? A figure to be derided, who had nothing in common with them?

Something drifted across her path and she stepped over it.

So much litter. All these crisp packets and cardboard boxes left lying around – *it's a nature reserve!* she thought, averting her head from their intense gaze. Just get past them. She felt like running but how ridiculous would that be? You're a grown woman, she told herself. They're children.

She stopped. The litter – it had not been rubbish as she'd first thought. The image was half-formed, almost imprinted in her mind: white paper, a picture. She started to turn and then she saw them drifting all around her, lying in the raw, red, wet earth, strewn across the thick, coarse grass, jewel-like colours, broken butterflies, the ink bleeding in the rain.

Autumn's pictures.

She spun around. And that was when she saw him, casually standing to one side of the group, with his hands in his pockets, a black hat pulled tightly over his skull, his corn rows poking out the bottom. He was smirking at her.

Levi.

She took a step towards them and a couple of the boys moved slightly and stood aside. In the centre of the group was a girl, tiny in comparison to them. Her white knee socks were streaked with mud, her bare legs red from the cold, her hair plastered to her head. Her face was white, her pale-grey eyes bright with unshed tears.

Autumn.

She ran to her daughter and held her tightly. Autumn was shaking. Laura wiped the rain and hair from her face and pulled her hood up.

'Are you hurt? Have they hurt you?' she asked.

Autumn shook her head.

Laura had rushed out so quickly, she hadn't even brought her phone. They were alone here. There was no possibility of help.

'My pictures,' whispered Autumn, and started to cry.

The sound tore at Laura's heart. It wasn't like the crying of a child; it was harsh, guttural, dry sobs without tears that wracked her whole body. Laura bent to grab some of the pictures out of the mud but even as she managed to rescue a couple of them, she realized they were beyond saving. The ink had been washed off, they were stained with earth and, worse, they'd been torn into scraps. Autumn snatched them out of her hand and threw them away.

One of the boys laughed. A single bark. Laura's head snapped up. The group were starting to slouch back towards Briar Lane.

'Did you do this?' she shouted at Levi. To her shame, her voice quavered.

He turned towards her, his mouth twisted in a half smile. 'Wass it look like?'

Laura swallowed. Levi took a step backwards.

'Why?' said Laura. 'Why would you destroy her pictures? Why are you doing this to her?'

'Because,' he said, still walking backwards, his hands in his pockets, 'she's a stuck-up bitch, innit.' Behind him, his cadre of mates laughed and he smiled. 'Thinks she can draw. This is rubbish. Waste of paint.' He jerked his chin towards the fragments of paper.

'How dare you?' she shouted. 'How dare you do this to her? She's done nothing to you.'

Levi shrugged and turned away. He started to whistle. Laura was trembling with anger at his callousness, his insouciance. She ran towards the boy and grabbed his jacket, yanking him around to face her.

'Don't walk away when I'm talking to you,' she said. It sounded more like a plea than a statement or a threat.

She wanted him to acknowledge her, to show some contrition. He shrugged her off easily. She stood in front of him, panting. Part of her registered how tall he was – about five foot four, the same height as her. He was on a slight rise in the hill and he looked down at her steadfastly, his eyes large and lighter than she remembered, tawny, with murky-green streaks.

He still had his hands in his pockets but he leant towards her and said quietly, 'Don't never touch me.'

He was so close his breath grazed her lips. He smelt of fried oil and tomato crisps. She recoiled, stumbling back. Behind her she was aware of Autumn, shivering, small, vulnerable. Behind Levi stood the six older boys, lined up, watching her.

'Don't you ever go near my daughter again,' she said. She was shaking.

'Or what?' Levi asked, glancing at his audience.

He laughed and the boys, closing in alongside him, inched nearer to her and Autumn.

'There is nothing,' she shouted, 'nothing I would not do to protect my daughter.'

She reeled, surprised at herself, at her bravery. It was such a strong, firm statement, ringing with conviction. Surely that would be enough? He would know she meant it. He must back down now.

Levi made a face at her. 'You one stupid bitch,' he said, and took his hands out of his pockets.

He took a step towards her. She could have reached out and touched his face. The boys behind Levi jostled and pushed against each other, like dogs straining at a lead.

'She is worthless. She is a piece of shit,' he whispered.

The boy did not look frightened. He squared his shoulders like a boxer. He was slight, slim-hipped, athletic-looking. The muscles around his neck tensed and his hands flexed into fists. Then he reached into the pocket of his blazer and pulled out a crumpled piece of paper. He smoothed it open, just enough for her to see what it was. It was Autumn's favourite picture: a line of those same tall, thin, spiky people she drew over and over, something Giacomettian about them. They were all grinning, bearing pineapples on sticks, waving them like banners; in spite of its childishness, the painting was suffused with joy.

Levi tore it in half, and half again, and then screwed up the pieces. He held his hand in the air and opened it. He laughed wildly, loudly. The fragments spiralled into the wind and landed, floating momentarily over the path, before drowning in the mud. Then he smiled at her.

Something inside her snapped. She wanted to kill him. He was so close to her that it only took a shift in her weight, a slight movement forwards and she was right there, her hands on his chest, and then she pushed, as hard as she could. She saw his eyes widen in surprise as he staggered backwards. It might have been okay – he was loose-limbed and agile – but as he started to right himself, his foot slipped in the mud. Too late, Laura reached out a hand towards him. He fell away from her, half twisting, landing hard. And even then, it might not have been too awful, his fall might have been broken by the damp earth, the grassy incline – but his head snapped back and he hit a rock, breaking like a blunt molar from the ground. Laura felt the dull crack in her own jaw. For a moment he lay still, half on his side, his fingers digging into the soil. Behind him, seemingly in slow motion, the six lads opened their mouths and she saw shock and dismay spread across their faces.

When he started to sit up, his head strangely loose on his neck, his cheek was a dark purple. The sharp edge of the stone had split the skin beneath his eye. The gash was bloodless for a second, and then the red welled out of it.

A high-pitched screaming was coming from somewhere. It rang in her ears. Slowly Levi started to rise from the ground. The screams were Autumn's. Laura ran to her child, pulling her towards her.

Oh my God, she thought, *oh my God. What have I done?*

'Mummy,' said Autumn quietly now. 'Mum.'

The anger that had filled her so quickly drained away. Laura seized Autumn's satchel and put it over her own shoulder. She grabbed her child's cold hand and ran, dragging her daughter with her, across the meadow. Behind her there was an ominous silence. She didn't dare look. Her heart was stammering. Would the pack of older boys retaliate?

Suppose they follow us?

At the edge of the wood she glanced back, half expecting to see the gang coming for them.

What if they wait until we are in the wood? No one will hear us.

The two of them slid down the path through the trees.

'Are you okay?' she asked when they reached the allotments, turning to check if anyone was following them.

Autumn only nodded. They walked back home in silence through the rain. Once inside, she ran Autumn a bath and stripped off her wet, muddy clothes. Autumn, her skin red and blotched, shivered and winced as she climbed into the hot water and hugged her knees to her chest.

Downstairs, the front door clicked and Vanessa called out, 'Hello?'

Laura opened the bathroom door fractionally and shouted, 'Autumn's having a bath. Be right with you. Go ahead and have a shower downstairs, there's plenty of hot water.'

She closed the door behind her and leant against it. She didn't feel able to speak to her mother just yet. The tips of her fingers trembled, the muscles in her thighs twitched.

'I'm so sorry about your pictures, Autumn,' she said. 'They were beautiful.'

Autumn said nothing. She gradually uncurled and slid into the water. Laura wanted to take her in her arms and hold her tightly. She thought of those moments when Autumn was a baby, sitting on her knee as she dried her after a bath, kicking Laura's legs with her fat little feet, holding her fingers with chubby hands, delicious rolls of fat around her legs. Those moments, unbearably precious now, as Autumn no longer wanted to be held and cuddled like an infant.

'What's going to happen?' said Autumn in a small voice, surfacing and pushing her hair out of her face.

Laura thought about standing in the rain in front of Levi, rage, like a drug, pumping through her veins. Pushing him with all her might, with all her strength. She shuddered. What had she been thinking? Levi was a *child*. Ten, eleven at the most.

'What I did was wrong,' she said, feeling wretched.

'Will you get into trouble?'

'I'll talk to his parents on Monday and apologize. I'll tell them what he's been doing to you. They'll make him say sorry too.'

Autumn didn't look at her. She poured some shower gel onto her face cloth.

'I meant what I said,' said Laura. 'I shouldn't have pushed him. But I was furious with him. There is nothing I would not do to protect you.'

She felt ill as she remembered facing those overgrown school children. Had they even looked that threatening? She couldn't claim she had acted in self-defence. They'd done nothing to her. Even if she could justify pushing him – those older kids encircling them, Levi's bullying, his abusive tone – she had *made* him fall. She thought of the bruised gash on the boy's beautiful face.

'Will you take me out of school?' asked Autumn.

'Let's talk about it later.'

Autumn looked away and then said quietly, 'I'd like to get washed by myself now.'

Laura tried to hide her hurt expression. She left Autumn on her own. Downstairs in the kitchen, she opened a bottle of red wine. As she was pouring herself a glass, her mother walked in and frowned. Laura held up the bottle to see if Vanessa wanted one too.

'It's a little early for that, isn't it?' Vanessa was in her late fifties and looked fantastic for her age. She had olive skin, polished by the sun and wind over the years she'd spent in Africa, and high cheekbones. She had the same thick hair as Autumn but now, with her hair wet from the shower and slick against her skull, her face looked sallow and almost gaunt.

The combination of Vanessa's silver bob and her pale-grey eyes gave her a misleadingly ethereal quality. She was slim and toned from decades of running and watching what she ate, and she was dressed immaculately. Apart from when she was working in Namibia, Vanessa stuck to a strict regime of taupe, white and grey in summer and navy and white in winter. Even though she'd just returned from a run and had spent the day working in the spare room and then in a local café, she was wearing navy palazzo pants with a cream jumper and a necklace of sea-coloured glass that matched her eyes.

Laura took a deep gulp of wine and said, 'Autumn is being bullied by a boy at Ashley Grove.'

'I'm sorry to hear that,' said Vanessa.

'He's called Levi. He's in the last year of primary school.'

'Have you spoken to his parents?' asked Vanessa sharply, looking over her shoulder at Laura.

'I don't know who they are. I talked to Autumn's class teacher today. She says she'll have a word with Levi's teacher but she didn't really take it seriously.'

Vanessa sat down at the kitchen table and opened Laura's laptop. She suddenly slapped her hand on the wooden surface. 'I knew that school was no good,' she said.

'It had perfectly good Ofsted grades.'

Vanessa made a series of annoyed groans as the Wi-Fi wavered. 'It's the only school she can go to in the area.'

I could have told her that, Laura thought.

'The other option is to go private,' said Vanessa. 'There are plenty of excellent fee-paying schools in Bristol.'

Laura hesitated. 'It's a bit soon to be thinking of taking Autumn out of the school,' she said flatly.

She hated arguing with her mother and she hated the thought of Autumn being teased by this boy, but it seemed an extreme reaction. On the other hand, she knew her mother had always wanted her to have Autumn privately educated. She thought about when she'd spoken to Mrs Sibson – how she hadn't managed to make her listen. She needed to speak to her again, or go to the head or the boy's parents.

'You and Damian went to the best school we could afford,' said Vanessa.

Because it meant you could travel and continue to work, thought Laura. You don't get twenty-four-hour childcare at a comprehensive.

Vanessa and Julian, her father, were both social anthropologists at University College London. They studied the Himba tribe who live in the Namib Desert. Among other things, they noted the Himba's kinship structure – their relationships to one another, who held the power and made the decisions, how they allocated their time, who did which chores, how many children they had, who the children were genetically related to, compared to who raised them, and how many goats they kept. Vanessa also collected data on the local animals; in the early days she'd followed a baboon troop that lived in the same area as the tribe. Now she had a team of PhD students who kept tabs on the primates and others who studied the rest of the desert fauna and flora.

The study had been expanding for almost thirty years and had become famous in academic and political circles. There had even been a BBC documentary about it. The Namibian government, which had relatively recently gained independence, was interested because of the politically sensitive nature of the treatment of indigenous peoples, and international environmental groups had become involved since the Baron-Cohens' data indicated how the desert ecosystem worked and how humans could live and survive within its harsh strictures without upsetting its fragile water balance.

But while their parents had spent long hours in the desert and been building their academic empire, Laura and her brother, Damian, had been shuttled backwards and forwards between a boarding school in Primrose Hill and an international school in Namibia's capital, Windhoek.

'Matt was privately educated too,' continued Vanessa. 'Surely you don't object on ethical grounds?'

'How Matt was educated has nothing to do with it,' said Laura, thinking that actually, yes, she did, and the fact that her mother didn't know that showed how little she really knew her. Laura, who was not particularly interested in politics, thought that all children should have access to a decent education no matter what their parents earned. But she could also admit to herself that, in this case, she was less moved by some high-minded socialist principle, and more by her dislike of the schools she'd attended. Her view of education was tarnished by the bitter knowledge that she had been of less importance than her mother's career. It didn't make her feel any better knowing that her mother had done her best, moving them to Namibia because it meant that at least she could see her children every two or three weeks when she and Julian returned to Windhoek for supplies.

'Your child's welfare and education is the chief consideration,' said Vanessa.

'I'm a gardener! I'm trying to launch my own company with Jacob, the guy I met at college, and I'm paying pretty steep tuition fees for my degree! Do you have any idea how much private schools cost these days? How many gardeners do you know who can afford to privately educate their kids?'

Vanessa gave her a steely look. Laura knew what she really wanted to say was that she should get a proper job, give up the idea of having her own business and stop wasting money studying horticulture when she had a perfectly good degree in English already. Instead she turned back to the laptop and threw up her hands. 'Completely lost the signal again and now the whole thing has crashed. This contraption is a wreck.'

'I've arranged for someone to have a look at it tonight,' Laura said, trying not to sound defensive.

'Don't you think Matt would pay? Before your machine died, I saw there's a wonderful girls' school nearby,' said Vanessa.

Laura sighed. The last thing she wanted was to feel indebted to Matt in any way. He'd objected to her moving to Bristol – taking Autumn away from him, as he'd put it – and he'd already been more than generous, allowing her to take three-quarters of the profit from selling their house in London. Money that Laura felt acutely she hadn't actually earned.

After Autumn started school when she was five, Laura had planned to return to her job as a researcher on an arts programme with the BBC, but during those few years spent looking after

Autumn, she'd lost her ambition, her confidence, the skills required for that kind of job, plus any flexibility about working hours.

She remembered the first job interview she'd had once Autumn had started nursery. Every time she thought of that interview, she felt a surge of shame. Her prospective boss, the series producer, had sat with her back to Laura after she'd been ushered into her office and continued to work. Several minutes later, she swung around on her chair and said acidly, *What makes you think you can tell a story?*

The series producer had done her best to undermine Laura. She pointed out that, while Laura had been at home looking after Autumn, her peers had all moved up the career ladder and were assistant producers or even producers. As someone who would only be able to work from 9.30 until 3, and not on school holidays, her options were extremely limited. She wouldn't be able to go on film trips or do anything that demanded long hours and a quick turnaround – including the series she had been so rash to apply to work on. The technology had changed too – everyone was shooting and editing themselves, the woman added.

How much experience do you have as a self-shooting producer-director? she'd asked, and Laura, feeling flustered by the thought of even the simplest recording and editing devices, had to admit she had none.

She had come away utterly humiliated. The job had gone to a young, ambitious and childless man.

Without a job, she'd been lonely. Getting an allotment had given her something fulfilling to do and she'd met an odd assortment of people who tended the allotments near hers. It was an elderly man who had leant on his spade, admiring her chaotic profusion of flowers and vegetables, and said, *You should do this for a living*, that had prompted her to sign up for the horticulture degree course in London. When they moved to Bristol she'd transferred to the University of the West of England, where she studied for a day a week; the rest of the time she worked at Bronze Beech. And any spare time she had, of which there was precious little, she spent on the garden-design business she was hoping to launch with Jacob. There was no doubt her mother was as irritated as Matt had been that Laura no longer had what they'd both considered a successful career. It was true she'd made sacrifices in order to be there for Autumn, but that would have to change because now she was the sole parent and breadwinner. She had to make it work: she was all Autumn had.

She looked up and saw her daughter in the doorway. The child's expression cut her to the core. She didn't look angry, only sad, almost resigned; as if she were thinking, *I am on my own.*

She must have heard them talking about private schools. Autumn rushed over to Vanessa and hugged her, but didn't look at her mother. She had dried and brushed her hair and it gleamed as it hung long and loose over her shoulders. She was wearing a burgundy cord pinafore with a pink bird on the bib. It made her look even more child-like than she was.

'Your mum told me about that horrid boy,' said Vanessa. 'You mustn't take any notice. Bullies just want to see they have hurt you. If you don't show how you feel and you laugh off the teasing, he'll soon stop, believe me.'

'I can't,' said Autumn in a small voice. Her face crumpled as if she was going to cry but she managed to stop herself.

'That's my girl, my big, brave girl,' said Vanessa, stroking her hand.

'The boy tore up all of Autumn's paintings on the way home from school,' said Laura.

Vanessa's mouth tightened into a thin line.

Laura didn't add that she'd grabbed hold of Levi and pushed him so hard he'd fallen in the mud and sliced open his cheek. Shame engulfed her. She closed her eyes.

How could I have done it? she thought.

'Mum came and got me. From the boys,' said Autumn.

She said it dully – not, thought Laura, as if she was grateful she'd been rescued.

'You didn't tell me that bit,' said Vanessa, twisting around to look at her.

'I didn't have a chance,' Laura said. 'There was a gang of them, including Levi. Six or seven. They didn't hurt you though, did they?'

Autumn shook her head but she still wouldn't look at her. Laura held her breath. Was Autumn going to tell Vanessa what had really happened? How would Vanessa react if she did? She imagined Vanessa looking at her; she wouldn't have to say a word, only stare at her, her pale-grey eyes bright and hard. Laura felt ashamed at even the thought of Vanessa finding out.

There was a horrible silence. For once she knew that Vanessa was thinking exactly the same thing as her: *what if they had?* What if Laura hadn't got there in time? And if they had so much as touched Autumn, Laura knew that she wouldn't have been able to stop herself. She might have done something even worse.

'I think,' said Vanessa, 'it's time for pizza.'

Autumn forced out a smile, without opening her mouth, and Laura was reminded how sensitive her daughter was about the gap between her front teeth.

Pizza was Autumn's favourite food but Vanessa thought pizza was *terribly bad for one* – all that stodgy white bread and fatty cheese was *a nutritional wasteland* – so Laura knew that her mother must really want to help her granddaughter feel better.

She wondered if Autumn would tell Vanessa the whole story when she wasn't there.

'The computer man is coming round tonight,' Laura reminded her mother.

Vanessa looked at her with annoyance because she was spoiling her plan, and then said decisively, 'Then Autumn and I will go out together. On our own.'

Laura barely heard her. She knew she had crossed a line. What would happen when the boy told his parents? Would they try and track her down? Speak to the school? The worst part of it was that it would reflect badly on Autumn, deflecting attention away from the real issue, away from Levi and his bullying.

'We'll bring you some back,' said Autumn.

Without them the house was unbearably quiet. Laura poured herself another large glass of wine and carried it upstairs to her tiny office. She turned on her laptop and fetched another chair.

She was just about to take a sip of her wine when the doorbell rung. She looked at her watch. Aaron Jablonski was exactly on time.

She ran downstairs and opened the door. 'Come in. It's so kind of you to fit me in at such short notice.'

He stepped in off the street, holding out his hand to her. 'It's no problem, Laura. It's good to see you again.' His grip was firm, warm.

He was taller and leaner than she remembered, filling the space in the narrow hall. She stepped back, flustered. 'My office is this way, up the stairs.'

He shrugged off his coat, damp from the rain, and hung it up before following her, making her pause awkwardly on the stairs; she should have offered to take it from him. When they reached the office, he had to squeeze himself into the space, and as she sat down, she realized how close she was to him.

'It's the Internet,' she said. 'It keeps cutting out and my laptop is always crashing.'

He nodded but didn't look at her or ask for any further explanation. He started to press buttons on the keyboard.

'Can I get you a drink?' She gestured at the wine glass. 'Wine, beer, a soft drink?'

'I know this is going to sound odd,' he said, 'but could I have a glass of red wine and a black coffee?'

'Of course,' said Laura, smiling.

In the kitchen she haphazardly measured out coffee into the cafetière and placed two cups on a tray, another wine glass, the wine bottle and a plate of biscuits. She hadn't eaten since lunchtime and was suddenly ravenous. She ate a biscuit as she waited for the kettle to boil.

The only good thing about today was that the bullying would stop. Faced with an adult who knew what he'd been doing – the boy had practically admitted it – and who'd told him off, any normal child would be too frightened of the consequences to continue.

She carried the tray upstairs but there wasn't even enough space to put it down in her office so she had to set it on the floor. There was something ridiculous – practically abstemious – about making this room into her study when the house was so large. It was almost too small to be called a room, but it had a high window and ceiling and faced out over the garden, which was why Laura had chosen it. There was just enough room for a desk, a chair and a set of shelves.

The house itself had a curious layout. The sitting room opened off the hall, which was where the front door was. On the next floor up there was a largish bathroom desperately in need of renovation and the spare room where Vanessa was sleeping and in between, directly opposite the staircase, the minute room Aaron was now in.

The floor above held Autumn's room and another spare room, and in the attic, nestled into the eaves, was Laura's bedroom. If money became really tight, Laura thought she could rent out one or both rooms – or, now she'd got Autumn into her choice of school, move to a smaller place. But she'd imagined being able to use them as offices for the new business.

The kitchen, dining room and a tiny bathroom were on the

bottom floor, one level below the street and the sitting room. From the kitchen you stepped down to the garden. At some point, she planned to knock through to the small, dark dining room that had become a dumping ground for unsorted papers and piles of clean, unfolded laundry. It was also full of boxes from the house move that Laura hadn't got around to unpacking and pictures that she hadn't hung.

'It's certainly quirky,' said her mother, when she'd arrived at Wolferton Place yesterday.

Laura had frowned. Vanessa meant quirky as a critical comment, not quirky as in: *how quaint and adorably eccentric.* Laura had fallen in love with the spectacular view over the south-east side of Bristol. Sometimes, early in the morning, she watched balloons drifting over the attic window. It was the garden that had really sold it to her though: long and narrow, south-facing with high brick walls and almost nothing in it but a strawberry tree and some shrubs, it held such potential. She imagined it being a showcase, a floral meeting space for new clients.

'It's spooky,' Autumn had said.

They'd been standing in Laura's room at the time and Autumn was holding her grandmother's hand. Autumn didn't like the house and Laura felt trapped, wanting to sympathize with her child yet not wanting to have to explain all the practicalities of buying as big a house as you could afford as an investment; of having to move to a neighbourhood with a good school; of having to be the only adult to make all the decisions from now on.

'Why do you think it's spooky?' asked Vanessa. As a scientist, Vanessa didn't have much patience for opinions about the supernatural.

Autumn shrugged. 'It makes funny sounds – creaks and moans and sighs. And we're all so far away from each other.'

That was certainly true. The house was cold and draughty and needed a lot of work, which Laura could not afford.

To her surprise, her mother had laughed. 'It's an old house, Autumn. Of course the wood will creak. And, apart from me when I'm in the spare room, everyone is an awfully long way away from the loo.'

Laura poured Aaron a coffee and a glass of wine and placed them on the desk. She held up the biscuits but he didn't look at her, so she put them down again.

Aaron's fingers flew across the keyboard. He suddenly stopped and ran his hands through his hair. It was thick and dark, greying at the temples. He took a sip of the coffee and then the wine before turning to her.

'You haven't got a password on your Wi-Fi.'

'No.' She shrugged and eased herself into the chair next to his. Their knees almost touched. 'Who's going to sit outside our house and use our broadband?'

He had dark-blue eyes, almost navy, deeply set with crow's feet around the edges and a fine, straight nose. He looked at her for a moment and shook his head. And then, with a start, she remembered somebody *had* been standing outside their front door at four that morning.

'I'm going to put a password on. Someone could access your computer and hack into your bank accounts. I'll try a few things to get your laptop running more smoothly. If they don't work, I'll have to take it to my office and wipe the hard drive and rebuild it.'

'Oh,' said Laura, thinking she really needed the computer to work – there was the essay she had to do for her course and Matt's Skype call on Saturday.

'I'll do my best to fix it now,' he said.

Laura craned forward to see what he was doing but it made no sense. He typed with great speed as he flicked through screens on the monitor, switching back and forth from computer code to the view that she normally saw. It was disorienting. She knew, of course, that binary was what made her laptop look the way it did, but actually seeing it was like glimpsing another reality; an *Alice Through the Looking Glass* world where appearances were superficial and ultimately treacherous.

Aaron barely spoke other than to ask her for the password to her email and Skype accounts and what she wanted her new password to be on the Wi-Fi.

'Ode to Autumn,' she said, without thinking.

Laura loved her daughter's name. Autumn Wild. It had come to her when she was six months' pregnant, feeling her daughter kick and stir as she walked through a field of barley, the sheaves soft as silk against her calves, the green of their stems turning a dry gold.

Autumn. It had seemed a perfect name for a child who would be born at the tail end of such a glorious season. Every time she said it to herself, Laura pictured vermillion Virginia creeper leaves, the smooth, sweet gleam of conkers cracking through their grenade-like casing, scarlet haws amid the downy tangle of old man's beard. Although now, of course, Autumn's beautiful name had been the first thing her daughter had been bullied about, she thought.

Aaron wrote *oDetOauTumn21* on a piece of paper and passed it to her. 'Safer,' he said. 'Harder for a hacker to crack.'

Aaron had rolled up his shirt sleeves as he worked and Laura noticed how muscular his arms were. She thought about standing opposite Levi, a boy, a child, and how weak she'd felt.

'Do you work out?' she asked.

'Yes,' he said. He didn't seem surprised at her question. 'I do martial arts. I have a black belt in Taekwondo.'

'Oh,' she said. She'd never heard of it.

He typed something and then turned the screen around so she could see. It was a YouTube clip of two men in white robes and trousers trimmed with black, wearing black belts. They bowed before circling one another, wary as tigers. One lashed out with a high kick; the other deflected the blow with ease.

'It's a two-thousand-year-old Korean martial art,' said Aaron. 'It means "the way of the foot and the fist".'

'Oh,' said Laura again.

It looked deadly yet, at the same time, graceful. She could see that Aaron would be good at it; he appeared lithe yet strong and his focus seemed unshakable.

He didn't ask her why she'd asked or if she was interested in trying Taekwondo, and Laura was grateful. He clicked the video off and returned to his examination of her laptop. She should really get fit, she thought. Jacob would smirk when she told him. He'd been telling her to exercise since they'd met when she first moved here. *Easy for him* to say, she thought, since he was an ex-marine and already incredibly athletic. She'd ask his advice when she saw him tomorrow.

Aaron stood up and stretched. 'Mind if I have another glass of wine and a cup of coffee?' he asked.

'Oh, of course.' Laura poured him one of each. 'How are you getting on?'

'Nearly there,' he said. 'Before I leave I'm going to install a remote device that will allow me to operate your laptop from my office. If you have any problems over the weekend or next week, I'll be able to access the hard drive and sort it out for you. If you're still having trouble, I'll have to wipe it and start from scratch, but I think it'll be fine.'

Laura was a little taken aback by his suggestion but Aaron didn't seem perturbed by the intrusiveness of such a program.

'Don't worry,' he said, sitting back down and staring at the laptop. 'Hopefully it'll just be a temporary measure to check you're not getting any glitches when I'm not here. I'll be working this weekend so feel free to call me any time if you need to.'

It had grown dark. The only light in the room was the small desk lamp, which cast a bubble of radiance around them. Laura, warmed and relaxed from the wine, felt slightly less shaky. The threat that Levi posed and the terrible thing that she had done started to diminish a little in her mind. She resolved to talk to Mrs Sibson again and find out who Levi's parents were. She would speak to them and apologize, but she'd make sure they understood how awful Levi's behaviour had been. And she would get fit and become strong. Horrendous as it was, pushing Levi would put an end to his bullying. Bullies were fundamentally cowards and she had stood up to him.

'You're right by the nature reserve, aren't you?' said Aaron, interrupting her thoughts.

'Yes,' she said. 'The allotments are over there' – she waved in their general direction, now a black window into the night with a small, bright-white reflection in the corner from her desk lamp – 'and the reserve is behind them. Why, are you interested in wildlife?'

Aaron shook his head. 'It's the highest peak for miles around. On a clear night I go and sit on the hill.'

She looked at him quizzically. She hadn't thought that someone who was an expert in computer technology would have a romantic side to him.

'It's the best place to see the stars in the city,' he explained.

'Oh. You're into astronomy,' she said, smiling.

'Correct. The pollution from street lights is minimized out there.' Aaron tilted his head to one side. He was staring out of the window, now spotted with drops of rain. 'At this time of year it's easy to spot Jupiter.' His voice was deep, resonant, quiet. She had to concentrate to hear every word. 'I'm hoping to see The Great Red Spot – it's a storm twice as wide as earth that's been raging for three hundred years.' He paused and smiled before saying, 'Did you know Jupiter is made of what was left over after the sun was formed? It's a giant ball of gas with the largest ocean in the solar system – a sea of liquid hydrogen. Can you even begin to imagine what that might look like?' His eyes were shining. There was something beautiful about the cadence of his voice in this single, simple moment.

The front door opened and Vanessa and Autumn came in, accompanied by a blast of chill, fresh air and the sound of rainfall. Laura stood awkwardly and pushed her chair backwards. Autumn was staring up at her from the hall, but as soon as Laura smiled at her, she looked away. Autumn and her grandmother walked up the stairs towards them.

'This is Aaron, Autumn, Vanessa. Autumn is my daughter and Vanessa, my mother. Aaron's fixing my computer,' she said. She could feel her cheeks burning.

Aaron shook hands with them both. 'Fixed,' he said, and then turning to Laura, he added, 'I'd prefer cash.'

'Oh,' said Laura, suddenly embarrassed.

The jolt, from listening to him telling her about Jupiter's sea to asking for money, felt harsh. She realized she hadn't thought about how she would pay him and she didn't have any money in her wallet. Worse – since they were on such a tight budget and she'd never had to account for every pound so stringently before – she wasn't even sure how she'd manage to pay Aaron this month.

'I've got it,' said Vanessa, touching her arm. She delved inside her handbag for her purse and Laura flushed as she realized her mother had noticed her agitation.

Autumn hasn't told her, Laura thought, as she watched Vanessa. *Thank God.*

The child slid past them and disappeared up the stairs, switching on lights as she went. Laura wanted to rush after her, but she felt compelled to stay as her mother handed Aaron some notes. They both walked him down the stairs to the hall.

After he'd put his coat on, Aaron said, 'Actually, I'd prefer to go out the back. I'd like to go home through the nature reserve. It looks as if the rain is beginning to clear up.'

'Of course,' said Laura, and led the way down to the kitchen. She opened the door and said, 'I'll come with you. There's a key code on the gate. You need it to get out.'

'Don't trouble yourself,' said Aaron. 'You'll get cold. And you haven't got any shoes on.'

Laura hesitated and then said, 'It's 2003.'

Aaron said, 'The year Autumn was born? You should change that to something more secure. I'll make sure the gate's closed properly.'

He smiled at her and stepped out into the night. Laura, watching him vanish into the darkness, wondered if he'd call her, if perhaps he might come around and drink red wine and black coffee and talk to her about the planets.

Vanessa raised an eyebrow at her as Laura locked the kitchen door.

'He's into astronomy,' she explained. 'He wants to do a bit of star-gazing on his way home.'

They waited at the window until they heard the gate click shut and then Vanessa said, 'Autumn's very tired, poor dear. Unsurprisingly. As must you be. There's pizza for you. We thought you would be starving by now.'

Laura, a little woozy from the wine, nodded.

'Thanks, Mum,' she said and hugged her. It was the first time she'd called her mother Mum and not Vanessa since she was seven, she suddenly realized. She was glad her mother was here, she thought. If only she could stay until Monday – see Mrs Sibson with her, talk to Levi's parents. Take charge.

'I'll just go and say goodnight to Autumn,' Laura said.

I'll tell her that it's all over now, she thought. *I'll say: Levi won't dare bully you again.*

AUTUMN

Autumn lined her toys up in her bed as she had done every night since they'd moved into the new house: Little Bear; Big Bear; Ruby, a patchwork alligator; Jerome, a black boy doll complete with male genitalia wearing a pink dress; Stephanie, a rabbit with a missing ear; Hum Drum the elephant; and George, a lion with a mane that Autumn had brushed until only a few wisps remained. They looked back at her with their glassine eyes, a small, raggedy army assembled to protect her from all the creaks and moans and groans in this eerie house. They all used to be in her bed but, during the night, her mother would always remove them. This was the compromise: they were still tucked in but at the foot of the bed.

She'd asked her grandmother to read her a bedtime story and her mother had looked pained. Autumn hated it when she hurt her feelings, and then, even worse, her mum tried to pretend she hadn't. But the alternative had been to hurt Granny's feelings and Granny was only here for a little bit. She'd said she was *holding the fort* while her mum was working over the weekend, but she was only holding it for a short time. Really, thought Autumn, she felt guilty about not visiting them sooner. Granny was leaving on Sunday. Autumn counted to herself: two more sleeps, if you included tonight.

She looked around the room. It glowed with an alien blue light that didn't quite diminish the dark or light up the deepest recesses and shadows in her bedroom. It was from a clock her mum had bought her when she was two. It had stars on it and when it was the proper time to get up, it turned yellow and the stars became a sun with a smiley face. It had been supposed to make her stay in bed until morning but it hadn't worked, Mum had said.

Her dad hadn't approved of the clock because he said children shouldn't have lights in their bedroom.

It's bad for your eyes. And aren't you too old for that?

He'd set it to the dimmest possible background light, a weak blue that barely banished any shadows. That was before he moved into his new girlfriend's flat. In their new house Autumn had been frightened to even get out of bed and creep across the creaking floorboards. Once she'd wet the bed in the night because she was too scared to get up. She didn't know which was worse: the fear or the humiliation of weeing in her bed like a baby.

She'd found the instructions for the clock – Dad had kept a file in his office labelled *Autumn*, with boring paperwork about school, report cards, her red medical record book, and what he called *Odds and Ends*. He'd given it to her mum when he went and Autumn had found it in one of the boxes. Her mum hadn't even unpacked it. Autumn read the instructions through carefully first and then sat down with it and the clock in front of her and followed each step, like Dad did. She was pleased when she managed to increase the brightness of the clock and it was now as light as it could be. She'd replaced the instruction manual in the file. She was sure her Mum didn't even remember there was an *Autumn* folder.

She felt funny thinking about her dad. He loved her, she knew that, and she loved him, but it was a kind of sharp love that hurt inside. He didn't really understand her. He wanted her to be *more*. He wished she was bigger, somehow – but not taller or older. The ruts in his forehead grew deeper when he looked at her pictures and, although he always said they were nice, really he wanted her to go and play outside. Actually, she thought, he'd be a lot happier if she was a boy. A proper boy, not one like Caius, from her old class, who was thin and mild-mannered and had blond hair in mad corkscrews and read poetry books.

And now she hardly saw him and she felt bad for even thinking about loving him differently than other kids loved their dads. When they talked every Saturday on Skype it felt tricky. He always asked the same questions about school and friends, and he said the same thing whenever he said goodbye: *Be good for your mother*. Which showed a serious lack of imagination because she always was good for her mum.

She was trying not to think about what had happened today. After the slugs yesterday, and her mum talking to Mrs Sibson this morning, the rain on her way home had been like an extra, final punishment as she ran, shivering and slipping in the mud, clutching her portfolio under one arm. Until, that is, she saw Levi and his boys at the end of the metal bridge. He was smiling, the crooked, wicked smile that he reserved especially for her.

The boys that were with him banged sticks and their hands against the bars. Their voices warped and echoed within the cage and ricocheted across the humming railway lines. They were like the chimpanzees in London Zoo: loud and strong and out of control. She felt as if she had no bones, like a jellyfish, hooked from the sea. She walked slowly towards them, her ears ringing, but they ignored her. All except for Levi, who stood at the end, his hands in his pockets, smiling.

She walked past them and they stopped banging and shouting. The silence was far more frightening. Levi stopped smiling. They closed around her in a circle. One of them pushed her. Another one pulled her hood down. And then one snatched her portfolio. She cried out but they just laughed. They passed it between them and then to Levi. She ran towards him, trying to retrieve it, but he held it above his head and opened the zip, and her paintings cascaded out.

And then her mum had come – too late. They'd already torn

all her pictures up and scattered them in handfuls of bleeding ink into the rain and tossed them across the grass. Her mum had shouted at him and the boys had backed off. She thought of her mum, white and shaking, her face wet with rain, her voice trembling, frightened and angry; and Levi, beautiful, glowing, smiling, his hands clenched into fists at his sides. And his horrid laugh. It had made her shiver.

She clutched Big Bear to her.

And then her mum had pushed him and he'd fallen, and when he looked up his eyes were funny and unfocused and his cheek was bleeding and all bruised. Autumn shuddered. She couldn't bear to think of what might have happened. What if her mum hadn't come and got her? What would happen now?

She'd tried not to dwell on it when she was out with Granny but she was worried. Her mum had looked terrible when they'd left: pale and hurt, as if she wanted some sort of reassurance, as if she wanted Autumn to tell her that it would all be okay. She couldn't do it, she couldn't think of the right words.

'Let's choose a special pizza for Mum,' she'd said, and they'd ordered one with extra toppings, all of Mum's favourite food.

When they'd arrived home, she'd felt sick. She thought they might walk in and find Levi's parents talking to her mum. But she was sitting upstairs, half in her office, half on the landing, with a man. The one who'd come to fix her laptop. He didn't look like a computer repair man. He looked... Autumn struggled to describe him... *charming*, like a prince in a fairy story.

Her mum was clutching a glass of wine and leaning towards him as if he was the most fascinating person she'd met. It had shocked Autumn, this still tableau, lit with a single lamp, burning in the darkness of the house. And he was odd, this man, Aaron. He'd shaken her hand as if she were a grown-up, but he hadn't looked at her. He hadn't *seen* her.

She'd grown agitated and run up the stairs, turning on all the lights. She hoped he would go, this strange man with the blankness inside him, who seemed to have enchanted her mother. Would he become her mum's new boyfriend? Her mum had come up to say goodnight and she'd stroked her hair and told her that Levi would never bother her again.

It was wrong to push him, she'd said, as she'd said several times before, *but I stood up to him. He won't hurt you now.*

She was frightened of Levi, Autumn thought, but she still came to get me, she told him to stop bullying me in front of all those boys. Maybe it will be okay.

She hugged Big Bear more tightly.

SATURDAY 27 OCTOBER

LAURA

'You could try British Military Fitness,' said Jacob.

Laura made a face.

'I'm not kidding,' said Jacob. 'It would get you fit extremely quickly. You could go into the blue group, the easiest one.'

'I'd hate it.'

Laura was barely listening. The first thing she'd thought of when she'd woken that morning had been Levi. The child's face when she'd pushed him. His eyes opening wide with shock, his head rolling back. Thank God she wasn't at home this morning. Would his parents be able to find her address? How could she explain why she'd done something so terrible?

'Don't know until you try,' Jacob continued. 'You never know, big hulking soldiers yelling at you might turn out to be your thing.' He smiled at her expression. 'I'm kidding. We only yell a bit.'

Jacob was small and wiry with tattoos covering both arms; he'd been discharged from the marines two years ago. He and Laura had met just after she'd moved from London in the summer. UWE had held a study day in August for the students on the horticulture course she'd transferred to. Laura had been nervous: she was moving onto a degree that had been running part-time for a couple of years already. The others were friendly but, as Laura had expected, they'd already established friendships. Jacob, like her, was an outsider. He'd also swapped from another college, joining last year when he'd moved to Bristol. Like her, he also seemed a little adrift.

He'd told her about the garden-design business he was starting up and, as he'd described it, she saw immediately how they could be partners, instead of setting up a rival company of her own. With her BBC training and background, she would be better than him at designing publicity material and marketing the company. She also had several years of practical experience from growing plants in her allotment – experience that Jacob was lacking. Over lunch that day, she discovered that he'd spent a few years in Africa as a child too: his father had been a lieutenant in the army in Rhodesia, as Jacob called it, correcting himself quickly, and giving her a lopsided grin, as if in acknowledgement of their expat pasts.

He'd liked the idea of working with her. Neither of them had any money or much time though – Laura had Autumn to take care of and her job at Bronze Beech, and Jacob ran British Military Fitness classes. Today she and Jacob were creating a new garden for their first client, Ruth Jones. Like all the planning for their fledgling business, working on Ruth's garden had to be done sporadically and usually at the weekends.

It was a perfect autumnal morning: it had finally stopped raining and the sky was a brilliant blue. The sun was warm, although the early morning air was still chilly. Vanessa had taken Autumn shopping, to her delight. Laura was pleased: it meant Vanessa and Autumn would be out of the house if Levi's parents came round.

Ruth lived in a beautiful flat in Clifton, the wealthiest part of Bristol, but, as it was their first job, Laura and Jacob were charging less than she knew Barney would if his company redesigned the garden. Laura's ideas seemed to chime with Jacob and Ruth. She couldn't quite call it a design, it was more of a concept: a wind garden inspired by Namibia. She hadn't been able to explain it properly, she recalled with embarrassment, but Jacob and Ruth had grasped what she meant instinctively; Ruth had lived in South Africa as a child too. In any case, Laura thought as she dug in forkfuls of sand, it had to work: this garden would be a showpiece to attract new customers. And it was only through running her own business that she'd have the flexibility – and, eventually, the money – she needed to look after Autumn as a single mother.

They were shaping the part of the garden that Laura thought of as the wind section: a large curved bed they were going to fill with grasses that differed subtly in height and colour. As they grew they would rustle and whisper in the slightest breeze, their leaves stirring like a current passing through the savannah or sand shape-shifting in the desert.

The sand was to leaven the clay soil that trapped water and would kill their grasses, which all stood in little hessian wraps in a pile at one end of the garden, ready for planting. Laura disliked sand: it was beautiful at a distance, but she couldn't abide the gritty feeling of it against her fingers and the memories it conjured, of sand in her eyes, her shoes, every fold of her skin; her utter loneliness as her mother disappeared again, like a mirage into the desert.

Jacob turned over great clods of soil and dug in spadefuls of the stuff as easily as if they weighed next to nothing while she puffed and sweated and managed child-sized forkfuls. It had been easy to tell Jacob that she was unfit without him suspecting an ulterior motive; without having to explain about Autumn and Levi and how weak she'd felt when she'd confronted him, how determined she was to be strong enough to protect her daughter.

Jacob told her about the British Military Fitness classes he led around Bristol: it was physical fitness for civilians, he said, taught by ex-soldiers.

'Push-ups, sit-ups, sprints, that kind of thing,' he added, when she asked him to explain. 'It's not pretty but it is effective. I've got a class timetable in the car. Remind me and I'll give it to you when we leave.'

I will hate it and I'll look stupid, she thought as she hauled over another bag of sand, her back aching with the effort. Laura reminded herself she would be doing it for Autumn's sake. Besides, she hated gyms and at least BMF was outside in the park.

'No one cares what you look like,' said Jacob, as if reading her mind. 'Everyone ends up covered in mud. Besides, the clocks change on Sunday – it'll be dark. You'll hardly be able to see anyone else anyway.'

She wiped her gloved hand across her forehead.

'First one's free,' said Jacob.

'I'll give it a go,' she said reluctantly.

She felt her phone vibrate in her pocket and took one glove off to retrieve it. It was a text from Matt saying that they were setting off on their trek into the Himalayas tomorrow. He would go to an Internet café tonight so he could Skype Autumn.

Would Autumn tell him what she'd done? she wondered. What would he say?

And then she thought of Aaron: the long muscle running down his thigh, his strong fingers balanced delicately on the keyboard, how his eyes had lit up when he'd talked about the planets. She wondered if she would see Aaron again, if he'd contact her to check her laptop was working.

The double doors from the flat opened and Ruth came out, picking her way past the piles of driftwood that Laura and Jacob had salvaged on a walk along Burnham Beach. She was small, in her fifties, with dyed-black hair and tasteful clothes. Today she was wearing a jade jumper and navy trousers with a thin, silk lime-green scarf. Laura had never seen her wear jeans.

'What a beautiful day,' she called out as she approached them.

They both stopped working and Jacob hurried to take the tray she was carrying. She'd brought them mugs of coffee and a fruit loaf, cut into thick slices, glacé cherries glistening like cut gems. They sat on wooden chairs, surrounded by the plastic bags of sand, and let the weak sunshine warm them.

Ruth reminded her a little of Vanessa, Laura thought; she had that same grace and timeless elegance and something indefinable that people who've spent many years in Africa have. Entitlement – the kind of superiority that those from developed nations display in poorer countries. But she was being uncharitable. It was more than an expat mentality, she thought; it was as if they'd witnessed something raw and elemental, and everything in life would be measured against that knowledge and fall short. It created a calm grittiness in a person, Laura concluded. Jacob had it too. Calm was the last thing she felt.

Jacob was tapping her foot with his boot.

'Nice cake,' she mumbled, putting her piece down. She knew she'd end up eating Jacob's too, because he would only take a bite to look polite.

'Ruth was asking us what stage we're at with the garden,' said Jacob, smiling at her.

Laura swallowed and tried to concentrate. She turned to Ruth. In the bright sunlight, the silver threads in her hair sparkled. Laura explained that today they'd finish digging in the sand and they'd plant the grasses tomorrow. There was another bed that had to be created, and the patio area – it was going to have large terracotta pots on it containing giant cacti.

'I've found an acacia that'll survive the frost,' she said, thinking of the ones in Namibia, with their cruel thorns that grew alongside dry river beds. Elephants would travel for miles to feast on their giant orange seed pods.

It wasn't the order that everything should be done in, this piecemeal approach, but it depended on when they had time and money and what they'd learnt and managed to source. Everything was new to both of them.

Laura heard a loud rushing noise, a whoosh of air. She looked up. A red balloon was drifting past through the cloudless blue sky, just above their heads. A jet of flame soared upwards and the balloon glowed like a Chinese lantern.

AUTUMN

The hot chocolate had tiny marshmallows floating in it. Autumn could feel it sliding smooth and sweet down her throat, the froth bursting like milky bath foam against her lips. Granny had bought it for her as well as a biscuit topped with a scary pumpkin in frightening orange. She couldn't quite believe her luck. Granny, of course, was sipping a pale-pink herbal tea and had frowned when she saw the array of cakes encrusted with witches and ghosts in icing as thick as gouache.

She closed her eyes, inhaling the scent of the chocolate. She would remember this moment, this day. Granny had taken her to John Lewis and whisked her around the girls' department, seizing clothes and ordering two assistants about. Now they were in the café with a bulging bag of new outfits tucked under the table. And there was more to come! This afternoon she was going to Tilly's house!

On Friday, when Rebecca had come to pick her up, Tilly had casually swung her glacially blonde hair over one shoulder and said, 'See you on Saturday. Mum says we're going to make cupcakes for you.' The thought that right now, as she sat in John Lewis, Tilly was whipping butter and icing sugar together – for her! – was almost more than she could bear. She imagined Tilly tucking her hair behind her ears, piping the buttercream in fat swirls over the cupcakes, her lips in the little kiss shape she made when she was concentrating, a haze of sweet dust powdering her forearms. Imagining Tilly making cupcakes was exactly what she needed to do to stop thinking about Levi and her mum shoving him and what was going to happen to Mum now.

She opened her eyes. 'Granny?'

'Yes, darling.'

'We have to do a project for Humanities. You have to ask your grandparents some questions.'

'What kind of questions?' Vanessa sipped her tea and then carefully set the thick mug on the table, as if disappointed that she was not drinking out of a cup and saucer with a teapot and extra hot water standing by.

Autumn knew that it wasn't the right time to ask these questions. She was going to ruin her day. She also realized that there never would be a good time. Granny was going to leave soon. She was flying to Africa. Autumn took the notebook and pen that her granny had bought her that morning out of the plastic bag and ran her fingertips over the cover. It showed a princess with long hair that floated in and out of vines and through a jungle of trees sprouting fuschia-pink flowers.

'You know. For History.'

'History? Do you mean because you think I'm old?'

Vanessa's brow wrinkled. She was wearing an odd brooch: a sheet of silver rolled into a scroll, which was thin and sharp at the ends. The princess on Autumn's new notebook might use it as a weapon.

Autumn smoothed down the first page in her pad. 'Where did you grow up?'

'Well, I'm half French – my mother was from Versailles – and so although we lived in London, every summer I'd travel to Paris for a few days with her and visit the Louvre and the Musée d'Orsay, and then we'd spend the rest of the time at my granmère and grandpère's farm in the countryside. Picking cherries for tarts and pressing wild flowers. Swimming in the river and helping to bring in the hay—'

Autumn interrupted. 'And what did you used to do?'

'What did I used to do?'

'When you were working?'

'I'm still working,' said Vanessa indignantly. She sighed as she retrieved the tea bag, looking annoyed because she hadn't been given anything to discard it in; she plopped it on a pile of napkins that slowly grew sodden and turned a dull mauve. 'I'm a social anthropologist. I study animals and people in Namibia.'

As Vanessa described the Himba ladies with red mud in their hair and the baboons, the males with canines as big as a lion's, and the babies, who rode like jockeys on their backs, clinging on with tiny pink fingers, Autumn bent her head lower and lower over her new notebook. She could already feel the dryness in her throat, the catch in her voice, when she'd have to stand up in class and tell everyone what her grandparents did. After the other kids read out their work on grannies who baked them squidgy chocolate chip cookies and grandads who took them to Disney matinées and bought them too much popcorn and Coke in those giant buckets, she could imagine how the others would look at her when she talked about Grandmother Vanessa who strode through the desert with her binoculars, counting kudu.

She turned over the page and wrote: *My Granny makes me hot chocolate from real chocolate. She melts it first and mixes it with hot milk. She learnt how to do it when she lived in France when she was a little girl and drank hot chocolate and ate croissants for breakfast every day.*

'Look, Mum! Look what Granny bought me!' Autumn rushed downstairs to the kitchen with her bags and tipped her new clothes and colouring pencils out onto the table.

Her mum was heating soup for lunch, still wearing her muddy work clothes.

'What a gorgeous colour,' she said as Autumn held up her red coat, but her face had a funny expression.

Was it because she hadn't bought any clothes for her, apart from her school uniform, which, technically, her dad had paid for? Autumn faltered; she hadn't meant to make her mum feel bad.

'Can I put this skirt on now to go to Tilly's house?'

'That's so pretty. Yes, of course, but come and have some lunch first.'

'I hate soup,' said Autumn, snatching up her purchases. 'You know I hate it,' she shouted as she left the kitchen. Sometimes it was hard feeling sorry for other people.

'I'm afraid I gave her rather too large a snack before we left John Lewis,' Autumn heard her granny saying as she dashed up the stairs.

She was too excited to eat any lunch, although Granny, who was much stricter than her mum, insisted she sit at the table and *Have half a piece of toast, at least.*

It seemed to take ages for her mum to have a shower and get changed and then, as they were finally in the car and driving, she suddenly pulled over.

'Wait! This isn't Tilly's house.'

'I thought I should get something to take. Rebecca said not to, but we can't turn up empty-handed. You can stay in the car if you like.'

Autumn shook her head and followed her mum into the corner shop. Why couldn't she be like other mums, she thought, hopping from one foot to the other as her mum looked at the baked goods, stacked on wooden shelves, all wrapped in plastic packaging. Other mums *made* things to bring to their friends' houses, or else they bought cakes from nice delis or Waitrose. They didn't forget about it until the last minute and then buy some rubbish from Best One. She filled her cheeks with air and blew out. Chloe's mum wouldn't have minded, but somehow Autumn suspected that Rebecca would.

Her mum hovered for ages and then chose a Bakewell tart covered in thick fondant icing and plopped it on Autumn's knee when they got back in the car. She looked down at the cake, the icing already sticking to the wrapping.

'Mum?'

'Yes?' Her mum didn't take her eyes off the road.

'Have you told Granny?'

Her mum seemed to go still even though she was driving.

'Not yet.'

She didn't say anything else. They reached the edge of Clifton.

'You haven't told her, have you?' Her mum glanced at her in the mirror.

Autumn didn't know if her Mum really meant, *Don't tell Granny.* She wasn't sure what the right answer was. She *hadn't* told her, but she wanted to ask Granny what would happen now. Would the police come and take her mum away? Her mum had done something wrong. Really wrong. But maybe Granny would be cross with her. And with Autumn for putting her mum into such a tricky situation. She looked out of the window as the car slowed down and turned into a wide, curved street.

Her mum sighed. 'I will tell her. Later,' she said. 'Please don't worry about it, Autumn. The main thing is that Levi won't bully you again.'

'We're here!' shouted Autumn, spotting the house number. She'd memorized Tilly's address. She jumped out of the car and ran up the short garden path, but then, at the front door, she handed her mum the Bakewell tart and slipped behind her.

Rebecca answered the door. She was wearing white wide-legged trousers, silver shoes like a ballet dancer's and a soft grey tunic. Autumn couldn't help noticing that although her Mum had changed out of her army trousers, she was wearing old jeans and a baggy top. She didn't look as – pretty wasn't the right word because Rebecca wasn't really pretty – as *elegant* as Tilly's mum.

'Come in, come in,' Rebecca called, kissing both of them and ushering them down a hall with lots of tiny framed pictures of elephants and ladies in saris and across a giant rug of a splotchy Union Jack.

The kitchen was ginormous. Autumn walked over to the windows. There was a dizzying drop down to the river. On the opposite wall was a huge picture of nothing but massive polka dots.

'I know you said not to bring anything...' her mum was saying, holding out the Bakewell tart.

'Oh thank you, darling. Just put it over there,' said Rebecca, pointing to a kind of bar next to a big fridge and a large silver bin.

The table was already laid for afternoon tea with rose-print crockery and a proper cake stand piled high with cupcakes decorated with fat swirls of vanilla buttercream and rice paper flowers.

'The girls helped me make them,' said Rebecca, seeing Autumn looking at the tower of cakes. Rebecca then went back into the hall and shouted up the stairs, 'Girls? Tilly, Poppy!'

Her mum helped her take her coat off and told her to take her shoes off too. It was only when her mum had gone to put them in the hall that Autumn remembered she had a hole in her tights. You could see her big toe poking out. She tried to pull her tights down, past her foot, but it didn't really work: they slid up and you could see her toe again.

The two girls appeared silently, both flicking their long, blonde hair over their shoulders, and said mechanically, 'Hello, Laura, hello, Autumn,' before slipping onto a caramel-coloured bench running down one side of the table.

Autumn hesitated and stood on one foot, tucking the one with the hole in behind her calf.

Rebecca noticed. 'You go next to the girls, and we'll sit this side,' she said, gently steering Autumn towards them. 'David's working today,' she added. 'Filming a shoot at Codsteaks, you know, the studio near the train station?'

Her mum shook her head.

'They make things for movies, like the pirate ship in the last Aardman film,' said Poppy.

Poppy was eleven, although she seemed a lot older.

Her mum looked over at her as if she was expecting her to say something and when she didn't, she said to Poppy, 'Autumn's dad is at the foot of the Himalayas. He's setting off into the mountains tomorrow for his film trip.'

'Really?' said Poppy. 'Like, Everest?'

'Well, near, but not that high,' said her mum, sounding as if she didn't really know. 'He's filming a Buddhist tribe and they probably won't live at that elevation. Autumn's going to chat to him on Skype today before he sets off.'

Autumn took a tiny bite of the cupcake. The icing was so sweet and soft, almost melting in her mouth. The three of them ate silently and drank their pink lemonade as their mothers talked. Autumn observed Tilly through a gap in her hair. She wondered if Tilly really did want her there. Perhaps she was wishing Rebecca hadn't invited them.

'Your cupcakes are delicious,' she said.

Tilly smiled.

As soon as they had finished eating and had wiped their hands and mouths on the rose-patterned paper napkins, Rebecca told the girls to show Autumn their bedrooms and to *be nice*. The two sisters ran off at once and Autumn followed more slowly, feeling her mother's gaze like a weight on her back. When she reached the corner of the stairs, she ran too, catching up with Tilly and Poppy.

'She's *my* friend,' announced Tilly, 'so we need to go in my bedroom.'

Autumn felt relieved. So Tilly *did* want her there. They climbed another set of stairs.

'My room is that one,' said Poppy airily, indicating one of the white doors.

Tilly's had her name spelt out in letters covered in flowery fabric. Her room was large, with a thick, cream carpet. Her bed was really high and underneath it she had a little desk. The walls were painted a dusky pink and there were proper paintings hanging on them, signed by the artist. All her toys and books were stacked in white cube shelves – so many of them! – but, best of all, she had a giant dolls' house, almost as tall as her, painted pink to match the bedroom walls, with a car parked in front and a set of swings and a slide.

Autumn thought of her own bedroom. It was cold. Air seeped through the cracks in the floorboards. You could hear the wind rattling the panes of glass in their frames. They didn't have triple-glazing like in their old house in London, which, technically, was a new house. You could hear the heating chugging on and sluggishly turning off. Her mum had said they could decorate her room, but there hadn't been time yet. She'd wanted blue paint, so it would feel as if she was surrounded by a cloudless sky, but now she wasn't sure. Her mum didn't know how to hang up pictures but she said she'd figure it out. In the meantime, she'd bought a poster of an Olympic gymnast. Autumn hated it. The girl was poised and beautiful; she was wearing a sparkly leotard. Autumn knew she'd never be like that.

There was even a wooden Wendy house in her bedroom that was supposed to go in the garden, and boxes of her things were still stacked in one corner of her room. Her mum kept saying she'd help her unpack them but she didn't want to. Then it would feel like she'd really moved in, like they were definitely here to stay. But the Wendy house made her feel safe: a house within a house.

'Wow,' breathed Autumn, and Tilly smiled again.

'Look,' she said, and took her hand and led her over to the dolls' house. 'It's even got stables and horses. Shall we get the girls ready to go riding?' She opened the front of the dolls' house and brought out two Barbies. 'We need to put their jodhpurs on first.' She passed one of the dolls to Autumn and said, 'Why doesn't your dad live with you?'

Autumn froze, clutching the Barbie to her chest.

Poppy rolled her eyes and sighed. 'It's so common, Tilly. Lots of mums and dads get divorced. Mum says it happens all the time if you work in the media.'

Tilly nodded her head sagely and handed Autumn a horse-riding outfit. 'In our class Jason and Olive and Kate's mum and dad don't live with each other.' She frowned. 'I don't think they work in the media though.'

Autumn let out her breath and started to ease one plastic leg into the beige tube of the jodhpurs.

Poppy said she was too old to play with the dolls and started fiddling around with Tilly's iPod and speakers. Autumn saw them both notice the hole in her tights and glance at each other but Tilly didn't say anything mean. Poppy fetched lip gloss, a brush and a hair band. She carefully painted the gloss on Autumn's lips. It smelt of strawberries and was gooey. She took Autumn's bobbles out and undid her plaits, then brushed her hair and put the hair band in place.

'There,' she said, as if Autumn was one of them.

Perhaps Tilly would be her friend at school now, thought Autumn, looking at her reflection in the mirror, the two blonde sisters peeping over her shoulder.

'It's so pretty,' she said. The hair band was white with a red rose.

'It suits you,' said Poppy.

'You should keep it,' said Tilly. 'I've got lots of them.'

Autumn touched the flower. 'Really?'

'Yeah, sure.'

She looked from Poppy to Tilly. They were both smiling at her. Perhaps it was going to be okay living here after all. She smiled back at them.

LAURA

As soon as they reached Wolferton Place, Laura rushed inside and checked the answerphone. There were no messages. Vanessa was in the kitchen. She wondered if she could tell whether any irate parents had visited while her mother had been here on her own this afternoon simply by the way she was chopping vegetables. She went downstairs and Autumn followed.

'Hello, darling,' Vanessa said, smiling at her, and then, looking over at Autumn, she asked, 'Did you have a nice time with Tilly?'

Autumn nodded. 'She's got the biggest dolls' house you've ever seen. With thoroughbred horses and stables. And *all* of Beyoncé's songs on her iPod.'

Surely Vanessa wouldn't look this casual and relaxed if Levi's parents had come round? Laura thought. She opened her laptop and switched it on. It booted up swiftly and she started to do an Internet search for schools in the area. When they'd moved here, Autumn's school had been the only one in their catchment with a spare place, but there was a slight chance that the situation could have changed – someone might have moved or even been expelled since September. But as she suspected, there were still no vacancies. She was about to close Google when an email pinged into her inbox. It was from Aaron. Vanessa was absorbed in cooking dinner and Autumn was sitting opposite her at the kitchen table, drawing and talking excitedly about Tilly, so she rose quietly and went upstairs to her office.

Hi Laura

Is your laptop and the Internet working properly? I'm on call over the weekend if you need me but I trust the problem is sorted now.

I had a fine view of Jupiter last night before the sky clouded over and the rain kicked in.

Best,

Aaron

She quickly pressed Reply and started typing.

Dear Aaron,

Thank you so much for fixing my laptop, it's working!

Glad you could see Jupiter! I wouldn't know how to tell any of the stars – or planets for that matter – apart.

Thanks again for your help...

With best wishes,

Laura

She pressed Send and waited for a moment. She wondered if he was there, at his laptop too, and if he would reply straight away. She hoped he might suggest meeting up. He could show her Jupiter, or...

She jumped when her laptop started ringing. It was Matt on Skype.

She pressed Connect and felt the strangeness of seeing his grainy image in a brightly lit Internet café, a poster in Sanskrit and a faded photo of Everest on the wall behind him. He was looking well, healthy, lightly tanned. She wondered whether Autumn would tell him what she'd done to Levi.

'Hi!' she said. 'You're early. How's it going?'

'Brilliantly so far,' Matt said. 'The athletes have met their Buddhist families and there's tension already. It's not exactly luxurious – one of them is staying in what's basically a cow shed. She's not happy!'

Laura nodded. At least she didn't have to listen to his endless tales about filming any more. 'I'll call Autumn...' She turned and saw she was already standing in the doorway.

'Is it Daddy?' She sounded excited.

Laura moved so Autumn could sit in her chair, and she perched on the edge of the stairs to give her daughter the illusion of privacy.

'I went to Tilly's house today. She's thinking about being my best friend. We had cupcakes. Tilly and her sister made them.'

She could hear Matt's voice, echoey with distance. 'I'm glad you're making friends. How's school?'

'Can I go to a new school? Granny says there's a really good private one just up the road.'

Laura sighed. This was not what she wanted Autumn to bring up with Matt.

'Why would you want to do that? You're at a great school, Autumn. It takes a little while to settle in, that's all.'

'But I really, really hate it. I don't want to go there any more.'

'Give it a chance, Autumn. Besides, I can't afford to send you to a private school. They're expensive, you know.'

He didn't even mention her, Laura thought – as if it was blindingly obvious that she wouldn't be able to afford the school fees.

'Granny could. Why don't you ask her to pay?'

Matt laughed.

'Okay, Daddy needs to go soon. Can you say goodbye and then go downstairs and help Granny with the dinner? I'll be down in a few minutes,' said Laura.

Reluctantly, Autumn pushed herself upright and slouched away.

'She's being bullied,' said Laura as she sat back down in front of the laptop.

An email flashed up in the corner of the screen. The heading read, *Jupiter*. It could only be from Aaron.

'I spoke to Mrs Sibson yesterday – her class teacher. She said she'd speak to the boy's teacher and let me know what he said. But I didn't feel she was taking it as seriously as I'd have liked. And then we had a bit of scare in the evening. Autumn didn't turn up so I went to find her – she was in that nature reserve with Levi and a gang of boys. They'd ripped up all her pictures...'

She hesitated, not knowing how much to tell Matt. She felt the prickling sensation of a blush beginning to spread across her cheeks and throat. After all, it wasn't his problem to deal with Autumn on a day-to-day basis – and if she told him what she'd done he'd be shocked and think she couldn't look after Autumn properly. Oh God, she thought, *she'd* been so focused on thinking about Levi's parents, she hadn't considered the alternative. Any rational person would call the police, wouldn't they?

Matt was looking behind him and nodding at someone. He turned back to her. 'Damn kids. I'm sure it'll blow over. She needs to learn to stand up for herself. Look, I don't want Autumn to walk through that bloody nature reserve you like so much – not now that it's getting dark in the evenings.'

'No, no, of course not, I don't think she should either. Not on her own—'

Matt interrupted. 'I've got to go. The rest of the crew are here waiting for me.' His image broke up into pixels. '... down the mountain in a week for supplies so I can talk to Autumn over Skype again then,' he was saying when the flesh-coloured squares reassembled themselves as his face. 'I'll be back in a fortnight from now and then I want Autumn to come and stay for the weekend. Okay?'

Laura nodded. 'Of course. But you need to pick her up. She can't travel on the train by herself. And I'm not bringing her.'

He nodded curtly. They'd had this argument several times before. Matt wanted Laura to drive Autumn to London so she could stay with him at the weekend and she'd refused.

'I've got to go.' He was already speaking to someone else as he pressed a button on his keyboard and severed the connection.

That evening Vanessa poured them both a large glass of wine. It was a Sancerre, Vanessa's favourite white; she'd gone to the nearest off-licence to buy a couple of bottles that afternoon. Autumn was finally in bed. She'd made Vanessa read her an entire chapter of *The Amber Spyglass* before letting her leave.

Laura swept out the minuscule fireplace in the sitting room and started methodically laying a fire.

The first one in the new house, she thought as she carefully created a wigwam of kindling over tightly rolled balls of newspaper. Should she tell her mother what had happened about Levi? If she was going to say anything, this would be the perfect opportunity – Autumn was in bed, they were drinking a bottle of wine, she would soon have a fire going. After all, she might not have another chance. Vanessa was leaving tomorrow afternoon, and the following morning she was flying to Namibia to spend several weeks with the Himba. Laura wouldn't even be able to phone her.

Vanessa took a sip of her wine and said, 'Do you remember learning how to do that in Namibia?'

'Lighting a fire? No,' said Laura.

'You were always so self-sufficient as a child.'

Laura looked at her mother in astonishment. It wasn't how she thought of herself at all. When she and Matt lived together he'd gradually taken over doing everything practical: from pumping up their bike tyres, putting up shelves, hanging pictures to organizing their household finances. He'd never disguised his annoyance at her practical ineptitude or her disorganization. It was true, though, she realized. Once she had been self-sufficient, and she could be – she had to be – like that again.

'Nkemabin taught you to light fires when you were only four,' said Vanessa, chuckling. 'I was horrified. But you were both so careful.'

Laura had a sudden image of herself as a child crouching on her haunches in the blazing heat of the afternoon, training a piece of wind-worn glass – the thick, round bottom from a Coke bottle – onto a scrap of dried welwitschia, the fibres glowing with bright sparks.

Nkemabin had clapped and laughed and shouted, 'Quick, quick!'

He'd wanted her to feed the sparks with scraps of paperbark, shaved from the trunks of the trees, but she'd been too slow and the fibre curled into dark twists of ash and the fire died. Nkemabin, who smelt of woodsmoke because he didn't live in the farmhouse with her parents, but in a mud hut nearby.

'He looked after you since you were a tiny baby,' said Vanessa.

Laura struck a match and lit the newspaper. She waited for the kindling to catch light. Nkemabin had always been there, every time she'd returned to Namibia, but she hadn't realized that her mother had entrusted her to him at such a young age.

'You were about nine months old,' said Vanessa, taking another sip of wine. 'It was our first field trip since you'd been born and I thought I wouldn't actually be able to collect any data at all. Damian was only two and a half and very boisterous and just into everything. I had visions of him picking up scorpions or trying to play with a puff adder. But I simply couldn't imagine leaving you at all. You were so pale, I thought you'd burn without me there to smother you in sun cream every half an hour and make sure you stayed in the shade. I don't think I'd left you for more than an hour up until that point and even then, only with your father.'

Laura looked at her mother in astonishment. She hadn't thought Vanessa would have any felt any kind of guilt or longing to be with her as a baby because she'd always seemed so ambitious and focused on her career. She remembered how sharply her mother had spoken to her yesterday when she'd told her about Autumn being bullied, how disappointed she'd seemed that Laura hadn't already found out who Levi's parents were and gone to speak to them. She closed her eyes, imagining how much worse it would be once Vanessa knew what she'd done to the boy. She could picture her anger and disapproval when she realized exactly how badly Laura had handled the situation.

Her mother continued with her story. 'But Nkemabin persuaded me to leave both of you. I didn't know whether to trust him or not. He'd been so good with Damian the year before, but then Damian had been older than you were and he was also a robust little boy. I was so desperate to get back out and see the baboons and track the other wildlife, and I also thought that your father wouldn't get any decent interviews with the Himba women – and I really didn't want to spend the entire field trip looking after both of you while your father got to spend all day in the desert – so, in the end, I agreed.'

This was more like her mother, Laura thought. The kindling had caught alight and she put a couple of logs on the fire. If she told her mother now, Vanessa would talk about it for the rest of the evening, turning over Laura's actions and debating the consequences. The dissection would last until she caught the train home tomorrow afternoon. Her mother would say that the police were sure to be here on Sunday, since they hadn't been round today. Perhaps, thought Laura, the boy's father might track her down and pay her a visit himself. That would be so much worse. Maybe she should ring the police and get it over with? She looked across at her mother. Should she risk it? Vanessa was the only person whose advice she could ask right now. And she had promised Autumn that she would tell her grandmother.

'But after only an hour I was so wracked with guilt and convinced that something dreadful would happen to you, that I doubled back towards the farm house.' Vanessa slipped off her shoes and tucked her feet beneath her on the sofa. 'When I reached the dry riverbed, I hid behind one of the acacia trees and trained my binoculars on the house. At first, I couldn't see anything and I thought, well, either you were inside with Nkemabin, or... well, you can imagine the kind of scenarios that ran through my mind.'

Laura moved over to the armchair and picked up her glass. She took a sip. It was a heady blend of peach and elderflowers. No wonder her mother loved it. It was such a treat to drink expensive wine: since she'd moved to Bristol she'd taken to buying whatever was on offer from Lidl, and only opening a bottle at the weekend. She rested the cool glass against her forehead, trying to make up her mind what she should do.

'Just as I was about to run as fast as I could towards the farmhouse,' Vanessa continued, 'I saw you. Nkemabin had made a play area for you in the courtyard. It was shaded by a bougainvillea and Nkemabin had also strung up sheets to create a little den. Damian was crouched at his feet, completely absorbed in building a sandcastle and decorating it with sticks and pebbles. You were sitting on Nkemabin's lap and you were both staring at each other in mutual adoration. And then you started to laugh, that gorgeous, chuckling belly laugh that babies make. And I knew you would be all right.'

It had been years since she'd thought of Nkemabin. She wondered how he'd felt: a poor Namibian caring for two white children while their parents wandered around the desert looking at animals. What had happened to him after they'd grown up? She felt ashamed she'd never asked. She took a long draught of wine and her eyes filled with tears. She hadn't realized that she had mattered to her mother so much. Maybe her mother wouldn't judge her as harshly as she expected.

'I can't describe how relieved I felt,' said Vanessa with a half laugh. 'But I guess you may not be able to imagine my feelings.'

'What do you mean?' asked Laura, putting her wine glass down.

'I mean, you looked after Autumn yourself. You didn't put your career first. You never left your child in a potentially dangerous situation because you couldn't bear not to work.'

Laura rose and stacked another log on the fire, turning her back on her mother so that she could collect herself. In that moment, her tearfulness turned to anger. How little her mother knew her, how little she seemed to understand her. She *was* trying to work! Couldn't she see that she was juggling a job, looking after Autumn, retraining and launching a business all at the same time? Worse, how could she possibly tell Vanessa that she *had* placed her child in a dangerous situation – one that was entirely her own fault? How could she admit that, in front of Autumn, she had pushed a boy so hard he'd fallen and cut his cheek open?

SUNDAY 28 OCTOBER

LAURA

Laura rose earlier than usual to attend her free British Military Fitness session. It was the last thing she wanted to do – she was reluctant to leave Vanessa and Autumn on their own in case the police turned up. She could imagine Autumn's face, how frightened she would be, thinking the officers were about to take her away; how Vanessa would bluster at them since she was not normally in a position of knowing less than anyone she confronted. Plus it was cold, dark and wet. But she had to go. She had to get fit, just in case. What if the boy's father came round? What if Levi attacked Autumn? She was sure he wouldn't be so bold – but if he had a few kids on his side, who knew how he'd behave.

As she dressed, shivering, she remembered that the clocks changed today and tomorrow it would be dusk when Autumn came home. Autumn had gymnastics after school so, on Monday at least, Laura could walk her to the class and avoid an argument about whether she was allowed to go home on her own.

The weather was relentlessly miserable: on the exposed grassy area of The Downs, the drizzle knifed in at a sharp angle. Laura pulled on a blue bib with a number nine on the front. Jacob was taking the more advanced groups, the reds and the greens.

'You'll be in safe hands with Jeff,' he said, smiling at her and winking at another man, who, like Jacob, was dressed in army fatigues and boots. Jeff was lean with a bald head, sharp features and a slightly wild look in his eyes.

'Right,' he barked. 'Blues. Follow me.'

They jogged in a line around the edge of The Downs, following Jeff as he ran through the middle of puddles and the centre of slicks of churned earth. It was, as Jacob had said, full of press-ups, sit-ups and sprints, and in the wet grass and rain and mud, it certainly was not pretty. Halfway through the session, Laura thought she was going to throw up. She did more star jumps than she would have believed humanely possible. She was introduced to torturous combinations of exercises, such as burpees, where, from a press-up position, she had to jump her feet to her hands and then leap in the air. Her legs ached and she struggled to breathe. Jeff patrolled round them, shouting by way of encouragement.

The class was horribly competitive: in pairs or on their own they had to race through their shuttles and sit-ups to finish first. It reminded her of a party Autumn had gone to when she was about three. It had been in a park and the birthday girl's mother had organized a race from one end of a mini football pitch to the other. The children had obediently lined up and the mum had shouted, *Get set, ready, steady, go!*

All the children had pelted to the far end. All, that is, apart from Autumn, who'd looked at Laura with a worried expression and said, *But why?*

Why indeed? thought Laura grimly, as she lay on the ground crunching her abdominals and felt water seep through her tracksuit.

Not pretty but it is effective, Jacob had said.

She pictured Aaron. Did he think she was attractive? She'd inherited her father's features rather than her mother's, his broad face, his wide, snub nose and his grey-green eyes. She usually wore her strawberry-blonde hair in a messy bun pinned with a large, flat silver clip that Lucy had given her. When she was in her twenties, she'd worn it down and it had been smooth and fallen in soft waves. She'd used nut oils and plaited it at night as the Himba women had shown her. She'd always worn make-up then too, which had made her already youthful skin glow with a dewy finish – none of the things she had time for now. At least it couldn't hurt to be stronger.

She gritted her teeth and finished her sit-ups.

Laura held Autumn's hand as they stood in the ticket hall at Bristol Temple Meads station. Vanessa was bobbing from side to side in front of them, scanning the screens to check when her train was leaving. From the entrance she could see a tiny patch of blue sky; the rest was covered by dark-grey clouds. A chill draught whipped around their ankles and pigeons with deformed feet hobbled and flapped between the stone pillars and exploded into the cavernous roof space. The two of them were jostled by passengers attempting to reach the ticket barriers.

Vanessa turned back to them and said, 'There's no point in you two waiting here. You'll catch a chill. I'll go on through.' She snapped open her handbag and took out her ticket.

Autumn held out her arms to be hugged. She was wearing the pale-pink mittens her great-grandmother had knitted just before she died. Vanessa, as far as Laura knew, had never touched a knitting needle in her life. Autumn looked as if she might cry.

'I don't want you to go,' she said.

Vanessa embraced her tightly. 'My darling. I don't want to either. But I'll see you very soon. Be a big, brave girl.'

'I'll miss you, Granny.'

'I'll miss you too.'

Laura realized she'd miss her mother as well. She'd be lonely without adult company. She wished Vanessa could stay to lend her moral support, to come with her to see Levi's parents. She'd been too worried about her mother's reaction to tell her what had really happened, but now she thought Vanessa wouldn't be angry with her. Autumn was precious to her too; she'd have understood. Perhaps, she thought, she could tell her mother what had happened right now. There might still be time.

Her mother stroked Autumn's cheek and then hugged Laura. She could smell her mother's perfume, a bright, fresh, floral scent. Laura couldn't remember when Vanessa hadn't worn it. The perfume immediately transported her back to being a child in Namibia. She had a good sense of smell and she'd been able to detect the faint odour left by animals that had just passed, as if it was an invisible thread draped between the paperbark trees – the hot, monkey scent of baboons, an earthy aroma of warm hay when a kudu had picked its way through the stones, the sweet spice of a civet. And her mother – when she wasn't following the animals she studied, as then she wouldn't even wear deodorant – left a living green seam in the air, as if, just out of sight, the desert had burst into bloom.

Her recollection reminded her that her mother had praised her once – a rare occurrence – for her ability to track animals through the desert using smell and the minute signs they left of their passing, but had then swiftly followed up the compliment by saying she'd always thought Laura would become a biologist like her and use her skills to study animals. *Such a waste*, she'd concluded, and Laura was left to feel, yet again, that even her talents, such as they were, disappointed her mother.

She drew away from Vanessa and watched her thread her way through the crowded concourse and onto the platform, her silver hair gleaming in the grey light. Autumn slipped one mittened hand in hers and she started to walk out of the station, tugging the child with her.

MONDAY 29 OCTOBER

AUTUMN

'But, Mum! It's actually lighter right now!'

'Well, yes. But your dad said he doesn't want you walking through the nature reserve on your own. And neither do I.'

'In the dark! He meant when it was dark!' Autumn stopped, wondering whether her mum would figure out she'd been eavesdropping on their Skype conversation.

Her mum sighed. 'Okay, okay. I'll be there this afternoon to take you to gymnastics. And don't worry about Levi. I'll make an appointment to speak to your head teacher today.'

She bent to kiss her on the cheek.

'What!' Autumn pulled away. 'No way, Mum. Why do you think Levi tore up my pictures? It was because *you* complained to Mrs Sibson about him and then she spoke to Mr Bradley. *And* she talked to all the dinner ladies! What do you think he's going to do if you see Mr George?'

'Autumn, we have to...'

'I won't speak to you ever again if you do,' said Autumn, stepping out of the back door into the garden and slamming the door behind her.

It had been so sunny on Saturday but today it was grey and cold with a sharp edge to the wind. Autumn did up the buttons on her new coat and jumped into the lane. Her mum had promised to tell Granny what had happened, but she couldn't have. Autumn was sure Granny would have talked about it on Sunday but she didn't, not even when she was about to catch the train home. All she'd said was, *Be a big, brave girl.* And that meant she couldn't ask Granny what would happen to her mum. Not now, not ever, because soon she'd be in Africa.

She pulled her woolly hat out of her pocket and jammed it on her head. She still felt angry at her mum for breaking her promise. What would Levi do to her now? Her mum was convinced he'd leave her alone but Autumn didn't believe her. He'd have a bruise on his face. How would he explain that? And how would he live up to losing his cool in front of his mates? She knew the answer: by taking it out on her. She felt a cold dread at the prospect of another day at school.

Monday mornings always started with Exciting Writing, which Autumn liked, as long as Mrs Sibson didn't ask her to read out what she'd written. She rushed over to her drawer in the classroom to get her special pen. The case was black with a red, velvety interior and opened and shut with a satisfying click. The pen was thin and gold and wrote in black ink, which Autumn thought was sophisticated. Her mum had given it to her when they left London for Bristol in the summer.

A present, she'd said, but it wasn't Autumn's birthday.

She didn't know why her mum had given her the pen, but she thought it had something to do with leaving her friends and her school and the house she'd always lived in. And maybe leaving Dad too. Although, technically, he left first.

It was empty. She felt as if her stomach was falling, the sick feeling you get when a lift goes down too fast. She stood in front of her open drawer, holding the case, and shut her eyes in disbelief. She could feel her throat beginning to swell as if she was about to cry. Her mum would be sad if she knew she'd lost it. It looked expensive and she knew her mum didn't have much money any more.

But she'd been so careful with the pen. She'd always remembered to replace it in its case. She thought back to Friday. She'd put it in the drawer, she was certain of it. Although she shouldn't have left it over the weekend at school. Slowly, she put the case back and closed the drawer. It had to be Levi who'd taken it. It was his way of punishing her for what her Mum had done to him.

After lunch, just before all the other children were about to come in, she went to speak to Mrs Sibson. The teacher was bustling around the classroom, tidying up and straightening desks and chairs.

'What is it, Autumn? It's not the end of break yet.'

Autumn closed her eyes, took a deep breath and then opened them. It was hard to make the words come out.

'I think someone has stolen my pen,' she whispered. 'I think... I think it might have been Levi.'

'What pen?' asked Mrs Sibson, turning away to wipe the blackboard clean. 'The gold-coloured one?'

'Yes,' Autumn mumbled.

'I told you before, it's too valuable to have in school. Do you think you might have lost it?'

Autumn wanted to leave. She wished she hadn't said anything to Mrs Sibson. She could feel her cheeks glowing red and hot.

The teacher sighed and turned to face her. She set the board rubber down on the edge of her desk with a small, sharp bang.

Autumn flinched.

'Why on earth would you think Levi took it? Year 6 pupils don't come into this classroom.'

She strode across the room and yanked open Autumn's drawer. She took out the small faux-leather case and opened it.

'The pen's here, Autumn. You must have misplaced it,' she said. 'I suggest you keep it at home from now on. I know how important it is to you.'

Mrs Sibson snapped the case shut and held it out to her. Autumn hesitated and then reached out her hand. She opened the case slowly, as if it were a magic trick and the pen would vanish once more. It was there. Like a solid gold talisman, smooth and shiny and perfect. She touched it with one fingertip. When she looked up, Mrs Sibson was still staring at her.

'It's very serious to accuse another child of stealing. You do know that, don't you?'

Autumn nodded and felt the flush burn into her ears and crackle along the roots of her hair.

Mrs Sibson's face softened, as if she regretted speaking abruptly to her. She was about to say something else, perhaps something kinder, but the bell rang and children started to barge into the classroom.

That afternoon break a group of older boys gathered around her, pushing and jostling. They leant in towards her, singing, 'Liar, liar, liar', but softly so the teacher, who was in the far corner of the playground, wouldn't hear. She didn't know where to look, what to do. She stared at her feet. The toes of her navy-blue shoes were scuffed beige from wear. Catching sight of the yard out of the corner of her eyes, she realized that she was alone. All her friends, who'd been sitting on the tree log with her, had disappeared. Melted away.

The chanting. It was to do with the accusation she'd made about Levi.

But how did he know? Had he been watching her through the classroom window?

She became abnormally aware of every part of her body, from her bony knees stretching her tights threadbare, the collar of her polo neck shirt itching against her skin, her hands splayed flat on the log, with their spade-shaped nails mottled red with cold. She couldn't move. She felt if she did she'd draw even more attention to herself. Pressing her hands into the hard wood helped her stop thinking she might cry. She wished and wished that time would speed up, that the bell would ring for the end of break, for rain, for hail, for snow, so she wouldn't have to play outside.

Levi was standing a few metres away now, arms folded, leaning on the climbing frame. He looked as if he were not part of the mob he had created. He looked pleased with himself. There was a crust of dried blood under his eye and his cheek was a dull purple, the colour of a plum. When the bell finally rang, the other boys wandered off. She felt trapped, like one of those butterflies pinioned through the abdomen in museum cases. Levi, with his hands in his pockets, sauntered over.

He leant in close to her and said softly, 'It feels good, doesn't it? Nice clean line. Cool in your hand.'

She remained outside until the playground was empty.

How does he know how my pen writes if he didn't take it?

She thought about the Skype call with her Dad on Saturday. She'd been looking forward to seeing him so much and then he'd laughed and said, *You're at a great school, Autumn,* and she'd felt like she was drowning because he wasn't listening and her mum was making it all worse and no one would take her out of this place.

Slowly and stiffly, she stood up and walked inside.

LAURA

It was so hard to hear with the wind whistling past her mobile. Laura was attempting to retrieve the tools one-handed from the back of the Land Rover and ignore Ted's frown as she called the school. The line had either been engaged or it had gone straight to answerphone when she'd tried phoning as she was walking to work. Just as she was about to hang up again, the secretary picked up.

'Ashley Grove Junior School. May I help you?'

'Yes, hello, can you hear me okay?' Laura put down the shears she was tugging out of the boot and opened the back door to create a wind shield. 'It's Laura Baron-Cohen, Autumn Wild's mum. I'd like to arrange an appointment with the head teacher, please.'

'Can I ask what it's regarding?' said the secretary.

Laura wanted to say, 'No', flatly and loudly. Instead she said, 'I want to talk to him about how Autumn is settling in. I've already spoken to her class teacher and she suggested I make an appointment.'

It was only a small fudging of the truth, she thought. Mrs Sibson hadn't phoned to tell her if she'd actually spoken to Levi's class teacher or not. And, in spite of what she'd said, Autumn couldn't know for sure either. She was certain the teacher wouldn't give her Levi's parents' number if she asked for it. What she couldn't understand was why the police or the boy's father, or even his mother, hadn't been round to see her, so it was better to speak to the head first, before anyone reported her. She would explain about the bullying and make sure something was done about it. She felt guilty, thinking of how upset Autumn had been this morning when she'd told her she was going to try and see the head. Would it make the situation worse? She had no idea, but she had to make sure the boy never had a chance to hurt her daughter again.

'Mr George doesn't have any availability today. The earliest he could see you would be tomorrow at 2.30. Is that any good to you?'

She saw Levi's face as she'd laid her hands on his chest, before shoving him viciously; how he'd fallen away from her, almost in slow motion.

'Yes,' she said quickly.

'I hope you're not going to make a habit of this,' Barney said, squinting at his watch.

It was just before three. It *was* a little early to leave work, but she wanted to pack away her tools and make sure she wasn't late to pick Autumn up. She certainly wasn't going to let her daughter walk anywhere on her own in the late afternoon now that it was starting to grow dark, no matter what Autumn said.

'No, of course, not. I'm really sorry, Barney. Just having a few problems with Autumn. I'm going to have to leave early tomorrow too – about two. Appointment with the headmaster. Hopefully it'll all be resolved then.' She smiled at him. She couldn't afford to lose this job. 'I'll see you tomorrow.'

Barney merely grunted and Ted smirked at her. She hovered for a moment and then set off through the nature reserve to reach the school. Partly because it was so overcast, it already felt like dusk. Laura stumbled as she struggled to see the path. The wind scattered a few bedraggled leaves from the branches above her head and splattered her with icy rain drops. She'd felt unsettled all day: she'd kept thinking about Autumn and hoping that she was okay.

Levi would have to be brazen to continue bullying her, but she couldn't be sure. She wondered if she'd see Levi in the playground and if he'd say anything to her. His class teacher was bound to ask about the bruise on his face... Would he tell Mr Bradley what had happened? She quickened her pace.

She hurried across the road to school, looking at her watch. Right on time. There was a small huddle of mothers in the playground: Rebecca, tall and statuesque in the middle, with Amy, Rani and Lily on either side. She was listening intently to a man who was standing in front of her. Laura walked towards the group, but changed direction when she saw Autumn coming out of the entrance. Autumn was pale and she looked upset. She glanced at the man and ran over to Laura.

'How was your day, sweetheart?' asked Laura, her words catching in her throat.

Before Autumn could answer, Rebecca's head snapped up and she looked straight at Laura. Laura half-smiled and waved and then dropped her arm in confusion. Rebecca's mouth was set in a hard line. She gathered Tilly and Poppy towards her and turned away. Laura felt as if a smooth stone were slowly turning in her chest. Rebecca must have found out. The other mothers, the women she was starting to think of as her friends, looked over and their expressions were a mixture of anger and shock.

'It's him,' said Autumn, but so quietly Laura could barely hear her.

'Who, love?' she asked.

The man swung around to face her. It was Aaron. He looked agitated, running one hand through his hair.

'Hi,' said Laura, startled to see him again so soon. She thought about his last email, the one where he'd described how to spot Jupiter. She hadn't replied yet – she was still thinking about what to say without sounding too flirtatious or needy.

'You! It's her. She's the one who did it!'

Rage had turned him into a different person, his eyes wide, his features rigid, as he flailed his arms stiffly, pointing at her. Laura instinctively pulled Autumn towards her. Aaron strode in her direction.

'How dare you? I even spent the evening fixing your fucking laptop, barely a couple of hours after you assaulted my son.'

'What?' said Laura. 'You must be—'

'My son. Levi.'

'Oh,' said Laura, and her face started to burn.

'Oh, you remember now. How could you? He's a child.'

'Levi? But I...'

She started shivering. Aaron raised his arm and she thought he might be about to hit her. She stepped away from him, pulling her daughter with her. Autumn stumbled and almost fell. Laura helped her up and looked back to see Aaron dragging Levi towards them.

'She knocked him to the ground! He hit his head on a rock!' he announced loudly.

The circle of parents watching had grown larger. Laura swallowed painfully and felt her scalp tighten as the blush spread to the roots of her hair.

'You're sure it was this woman?' said Aaron, turning Levi towards her and pointing at her.

'Yes, it was her,' said Levi, looking at her expressionlessly and folding his arms across his chest.

The group of parents were all staring at her. Even as ashamed and uncomfortable as she was, Laura thought there was something different about Levi. It was his voice, she realized. He sounded like a nice, middle-class boy. The urban gangsta accent had gone.

'He cut his cheek open!' said Aaron.

Laura forced herself to look properly at Levi. It was bad, but not quite as horrendous as she'd thought. His cheek, just below his left eye, was puffy and bruised, and there was a scab of dried blood, where the stone had sliced his flesh open. Thank God it was small enough not to need stitches.

'He could have lost his eye,' said one woman.

'He wasn't staying with me this weekend so I didn't find out about it until now. But by God, if I'd known earlier...' said Aaron.

Rebecca looked directly at her. She had an arm around each of her girls. 'Is it true?' she asked. 'Did you do this?'

'He was bullying Autumn,' said Laura. 'He tore up her paintings!'

Rebecca didn't reply. She turned and walked away quickly, hustling Tilly and Poppy in front of her. Levi calmly put his hands in his pockets and regarded her coldly.

'There's been some misunderstanding...' said Laura desperately.

'You're right there,' said Aaron. He jabbed his finger at her. 'I'm considering whether to report you to the police. In the meantime, I suggest you stay away from my son.'

He put his arm around Levi's shoulders and led him away. A few parents muttered and shook their heads. Autumn suddenly burst into tears.

'It's okay, it's okay,' whispered Laura, hugging her and wiping away her tears.

When her daughter had stopped crying, she took her satchel and her hand and they walked through the empty playground out of the school.

'I want to go home,' said Autumn.

Laura hesitated and then shook her head. 'Let's go to gymnastics, sweetheart. It'll take your mind off what happened. If we go home, we'll both keep thinking about it.'

It was dark as they turned past Ashley Grove and cut through the side streets to reach the School of Gymnastics, which was in a former church on Gloucester Road.

'At least we know who Levi's dad is,' said Laura shakily, her heart rate beginning to slow.

'He was in our house,' said Autumn.

'How did it go today? Did Levi say anything to you?'

Autumn stared straight ahead and said nothing.

'Autumn, love, I asked you a question.'

'No, he didn't.'

'There you go. I told you he'd leave you alone from now on,' she said.

So that was why the police hadn't called. Aaron didn't know until today, until just now. *But why didn't his mother tell anyone?* she wondered. *And what will happen if Aaron does report me to the police?*

Laura pushed open the heavy door into the old church and was hit by the smell of chalk dust and stale air. Autumn went to change and Laura sat on a bench at one end of the church hall facing the array of beams, rings, a vaulting horse, a trampoline and mats. She felt like crying when she remembered Aaron's face, twisted with hatred, the mass of parents backed up behind him with their horrified expressions. Rebecca would never let Autumn go round for a play date again. She could try phoning Aaron later when he had calmed down, she thought; she felt ill as she imagined his response.

She had a lump in her throat as she watched Autumn. Her daughter had been doing gymnastics since she was a tiny child and although she wasn't particularly agile and she was often clumsy, years of practice and her own determination had lent her grace and strength. She'd been nervous about starting a new class; in London Autumn had gone to the same School of Gymnastics with the same coaches since she was two.

Autumn was waiting for her turn on the beam and a couple of children had already pushed in front of her. It reminded Laura of those early days when she was even more crippled by shyness than she was now. One time the teacher had held out a box of bean bags for each child to take one. Autumn had stood, rooted to the spot, as her classmates ran over and grabbed them. The teacher didn't notice Autumn waiting and when the others had all returned to their places and started throwing the bean bags around, she'd put the box away. It tore her heart to see her child standing there, unable to ask for assistance for something as simple as a bean bag.

One more child pushed in front of Autumn and then it was finally her turn. She was supposed to take a couple of steps along the narrow beam, toes pointed, and then do a handstand, sideways on, before cartwheeling around and standing upright again.

She's so pale, thought Laura. Autumn had dark-purple shadows under her eyes. *She can't be getting enough sleep.*

Autumn looked down at the beam.

'Look up, keep looking straight ahead,' shouted her coach, Tess.

Autumn stumbled and righted herself.

You can do this, Laura silently encouraged her.

She'd been so proud the first time she watched Autumn do a handstand on the beam, a feat unimaginable to her. Autumn took a step. It didn't look right, thought Laura – Autumn had gone too far along the beam. She was moving jerkily, stiffly.

Laura stood up, her heart starting to flutter.

Autumn bent and twisted, placing both hands on the beam, her legs rising. There wasn't enough space left for Autumn to land on the beam.

Laura started to walk towards her.

It felt as if it were happening in slow motion. Autumn's hand slipped and now Laura was sprinting across the hall as Autumn's elbow gave way. Tess held out her arms to catch her but she was too far away, her reactions too slow. From the corner of her eye, Laura saw the other instructor running across the hall towards Autumn as the child spun in the air.

Laura leapt onto the crash mat.

Autumn's foot missed the beam and she started to fall.

Instinctively, Laura held out her arms.

Autumn fell, cracking one arm against the beam, her leg catching Laura's shoulder. She tumbled backwards, clinging to her daughter. The air was knocked out of her lungs as she landed with a loud thwack on the mat. For a moment there was silence. She lay motionless, Autumn a heavy, hot weight on top of her. She was aware of her daughter's heart-beat, sparrow-like, her own breath ragged in her throat, Autumn's hair tickling her neck, the feel of her daughter's ribs beneath her hands, the smooth sheen of her leotard against her skin.

The two instructors bent over her and then Jack, the older teacher who'd once been a professional gymnast and was now thick-set and solid, was lifting Autumn up and smiling and saying, 'Mrs Wild, you should be an athlete. I've never seen anyone run as fast in this gym.'

Laura sat up, propping herself into sitting position with her arms behind her. Autumn looked dazed and then burst into tears.

'Come on, duck, let's have another go,' said Tess.

'I don't think she's ready,' said Laura, looking at her aghast.

'My arm hurts,' said Autumn, rubbing it.

'Let's have a little look,' said Jack. He held her arm between both of his hands and turned it between his meaty palms, bent it at the elbow and then gave her a little pat on the shoulder. 'Just bruised.'

'The best thing is to get back on as soon as possible. Otherwise she'll be too nervous the next time,' said Tess, smiling at her.

Laura looked at her furiously. *You didn't catch my child. And you were right there.*

Autumn shook her head. Laura stood up. She could feel a tremor in her limbs. She put out her hand and took Autumn's. There was silence as they walked across the hall. In the changing room, Autumn started crying again.

'I'm no good at anything,' she wailed. 'I'm so clumsy.'

'Oh, love, you're not clumsy. You're brilliant – you're a wonderful gymnast. You're just upset about what happened today with Aaron.'

Snot and tears were running down Autumn's face. She shook her head. 'It's all my fault.'

'What's your fault?' asked Laura, wiping her cheeks.

'It's my fault that man shouted at you.'

'Of course it wasn't your fault. I was the one who pushed his son. Listen, we'll get it all straightened out tomorrow,' said Laura, trying to sound upbeat. 'I'll speak to Aaron and apologize and hopefully Levi will say sorry to you too.'

She'd brought a warm tracksuit with her and now she crouched at Autumn's feet and helped her put it on over the top of her tights and leotard. She stuffed Autumn's school uniform into the bag and took out a cereal bar and a carton of apple juice, thinking Autumn would need a sugar boost to give her enough energy to make it home.

She pierced the carton with the straw and handed the juice to her daughter. She cupped her face in her hands before Autumn could take a sip and said, 'Just remember, I caught you. I will always be there for you. No matter what.'

Autumn shrugged out of her grip and stuck the straw in her mouth without looking at her mother.

TUESDAY 30 OCTOBER

AUTUMN

She could imagine it. Down below the nature reserve where the ranks of red-brick houses were, there used to be watercress beds and a stream meandering through the middle. Women in long dresses, tucked into their petticoats, bent to pick the cress to sell at the market on Corn Street, or even as far away as Covent Garden.

Mrs Sibson spoilt it. People always did. It was History and they were doing 'Where We Live', which was all about Bristol. Autumn didn't know much about Bristol and, at first, she thought it would be dull. They'd done The Great Fire of London two years ago at her old school and The Great Plague last year. She didn't think there would be anything Great that had happened in Bristol.

'Please, Mrs Sibson, can we talk about the black men that were sold on Blackboy Hill? That's why it's called Blackboy Hill,' said Jason loudly to the class.

Mrs Sibson frowned. 'That's not why it's called Blackboy Hill. We will be learning about slavery but not until spring term.'

Autumn felt confused. Why were black children sold on a hill? She didn't really know what slavery meant either, only that it was something old and shameful. Mrs Sibson unrolled a large map and asked for volunteers to help her stick it on to the wall. It was like an ancient drawing done in sepia-coloured ink. Autumn was so focused on the key – the pictures down the side that stood for real things on the map – the way the artist had drawn a sprig of watercress, like a miniature cabbage balanced on a wiggling root, that she didn't hear the start of the next bit.

All the houses had collapsed, Mrs Sibson was saying, waving her hand to show an entire hillside of terraces. Subsidence, Mrs Sibson said, and something about floods. Autumn didn't know what subsidence was either. It sounded biblical.

'That is why this area is now devoted to allotments. No one dared build on this hillside again.'

Autumn thought of all those houses. Rows and rows of them. Where the railway workers had lived. Their families. She thought of piles of rubble and rooms, suddenly opened to the sky so that people could look in as if they were giant dolls' houses and see raggedy wallpaper and broken sofas and baby cots. She thought of the children, children the same age as her, who suddenly had no home. And now, where they used to live, where perhaps they had wandered around with no food in their tummies, rubbing their eyes and looking for their mums, there were sheds and sprouting broccoli and dead dahlias and alien squash.

Mrs Sibson asked her – had to ask her twice, in fact – to go and fetch the card. They were going to make model houses, like all the ones that had tumbled into the earth whose roofs and red bricks had rolled down the hill and buried the watercress. The card was thin and white and in a thick pile in one of the art drawers. The drawers were in a long unit underneath the window and were covered in carved pumpkins and plastic spiders and cotton-wool webs.

Autumn didn't know whether to try and lift all the card out at once or just a few sheets at a time and, if she did that, she didn't know where to put the card to gather it all together before she gave it to Mrs Sibson, because she didn't want to ruin her autumnal display. She started to feel panicky. It was the sick feeling from thinking about the houses collapsing on babies, combined with knowing how clumsy she was. She was sure if she picked up the card in a pile, it would slide, nice and smoothly and quite catastrophically, out of her hands and fan across the floor, and Mrs Sibson would tut and wish she hadn't trusted her to do a grown-up task and the other children would laugh.

Her hands were growing damp and sticky. She had a few sheets of card in them and she was looking out of the window in a kind of anxious trance. The classroom faced across the playground. A woman burst out of the main entrance and started running across the yard, mud falling off her boots, her fleecy jacket open, her hair tumbling out of her bun. She swallowed. It was her mum.

What was she doing in school this early? Autumn wondered. It wasn't home time yet. And then she knew. She felt as if something had curdled in her stomach. She glanced, involuntarily, towards Levi's classroom, although all she could see was the big map of Montpelier on the wall separating her from him. But his class also had windows that looked out onto the playground. Maybe he wouldn't notice. Maybe no one would notice. She straightened up and looked away.

Tilly stood on tiptoes. 'Isn't that your mum, Autumn?' she said loudly.

Everyone got up to have a look.

'What's she doing here?'

'Sit down, please!' said Mrs Sibson.

Her mum tore through the gate and it clanged loudly as it slammed shut behind her. Someone sniggered. There were bits of red earth in a line across the playground, like the crumbs scattered by Hansel and Gretel through the wood. The drawer full of card slid from beneath her hands and landed upside down on the floor.

LAURA

Laura worked until the last possible moment before hobbling to the Land Rover to put her tools away. The work was physically hard and her back was stiff and sore. She looked down at herself: she was muddy and wet, not quite how she wished to present herself to the headmaster.

Ted rested on his spade and said, 'Leaving already?'

'I've got an appointment at my daughter's school. I told Barney about it yesterday.' She glanced over at him and saw from his annoyed grimace that he'd forgotten.

''S not like you can make up the time, is it?' said Ted.

She'd thought he was a laid-back hippie when she'd first met him, but Ted was like a chippie cabbie with a mean streak.

'You know I can't pay you for this last hour, don't you?' said Barney.

Laura, turning away from Barney, picked up her spade, her cheeks burning.

'Of course,' she said, shoving the spade in the boot and shutting the door. 'I'll put Autumn in an after-school club so I can make up the hours.' Even as she said it, she could see the impossibility of it: it would be torture for the child if she had to stay at school any longer. And now that the other mothers had found out what she'd done to Levi, they wouldn't want to help her out.

As she walked to the school, she rehearsed how she would speak to the head. This time she would sound calm but authoritative.

She would state her case politely but firmly. At the very least Levi should be suspended from Ashley Grove. She would say nothing about what she had done to him, she thought. After all, she knew who Levi's father was now and she had his phone number. No doubt he'd be in touch.

Laura kept her coat on to hide as much of her wet trousers as possible, but although she'd tried to wipe the soil off her boots at the door, she was acutely aware of each muddy print she left as she squeaked down the linoleum-lined corridor towards Mr George's office. She took a deep breath and knocked on the door.

'Come,' said Mr George.

She pushed the door open and walked in.

'Ah,' he said, looking up and taking off his glasses, 'Mrs Baron-Cohen. How are you?' He stood up and shook her hand and then indicated a chair in front of his desk. Dileep George was originally of Indian origin and had a sallow complexion. He was in his fifties, grey around the temples and balding on top.

Laura sat down and wrapped her coat around her.

'The school secretary tells me you're here to talk about Autumn, how she's settling in.'

'Yes,' said Laura. 'I've already spoken to Mrs Sibson.'

He glanced down at some notes on his desk. 'We're delighted with how she's doing. She's a natural artist and gymnast. She's a quiet child. Hard-working. She appears to be fitting in with the other children in her class.' He was parroting Mrs Sibson – he must have asked her for a progress report, she thought. She noticed him looking at her trousers, her boots, coated in red clay. 'Do you have any particular concerns?'

'Yes. That's what I wanted to see you about. A child in the year above has been bullying her. Autumn's class teacher doesn't appear to be taking it seriously.'

'You mean Levi?'

'Yes,' she said, surprised. Perhaps Mrs Sibson or Mr Bradley had already spoken to the head – maybe they'd witnessed him bullying Autumn.

He rubbed the bridge of his nose and said, 'Mrs Sibson is taking the matter extremely seriously, I assure you. She's spoken to both me and to the boy's teacher. She has filed a report of the conversation you had with her, as well as Autumn's, exactly as we are instructed to do by the council when any allegation of bullying is made.'

'She spoke to Autumn about it too? Without me?'

'Apparently Autumn made a false accusation about Levi – she said he'd stolen her pen, although the pen was actually in her drawer and had not been moved.'

'Oh. She didn't tell me. I can't imagine Autumn lying about something like that. There must have been some reason why she thought—'

'In any case, aside from whether your daughter is making up these allegations regarding Levi, the more serious issue is your behaviour.'

'*My* behaviour?'

'Aaron Jablonski came to see me this morning. I thought that perhaps you were here to discuss your attack on his son. I think you're extremely lucky. Mr Jablonski is a reasonable man. I've managed to persuade him not to press charges.'

'What?' said Laura. She felt her throat start to constrict. She had a vivid image of Aaron shouting at her in the playground surrounded by other parents. 'Surely you don't...'

'Mr Jablonski does our IT here on a voluntary basis,' continued Mr George, putting his glasses back on. 'I've always found him to be trustworthy and diligent. If he does go to the police, I think you'll find yourself facing a serious charge.'

'Mr George, I'm not here to discuss that... that incident,' said Laura, her voice trembling. 'Levi has been bullying my daughter. He should be suspended.'

'Your daughter made another accusation against Levi – that he put slugs in her drawer. We've spoken to both Levi and his teacher. Mr Bradley says it's not possible for Levi to have done it – the classrooms are locked when the children are not in them with their teacher. Levi denies it too. But moving on to your attack on Levi – I'm afraid we do need to discuss the incident, as you refer to it. Levi told his father that six children say they saw you knock him to the ground, where he hit his head on a stone. Seven if you include Levi himself. I haven't spoken to Autumn but presumably that would make it eight. Eight witnesses.'

Eight children had seen her push a child. She swallowed and closed her eyes. She could feel sweat break out on her palms, the start of a blush flame across her cheeks. How should she try and explain this to Mr George?

In an accent that spoke of Eton and Oxbridge, he said, 'Mrs Baron-Cohen, if you thought Levi had been bullying Autumn, then you should have followed the correct procedure for dealing with it by making an appointment with Autumn's teacher, which you did not. I gather you spoke to her before her class was about to start and she said she felt harried and did not have the time to explore the matter fully with you. You have come to see me now – but only *after* you confronted the child in question yourself and then physically assaulted him.'

Laura sat back in the chair. She was shivering. 'Physical assault is a bit strong for what actually happened. I didn't *knock* him down.'

'But you did push him over? He did hit his head on a stone and cut his face?'

'What I did was inexcusable. I am incredibly sorry. I lost my temper. I can understand Mr Jablonski's anger and why he hasn't accepted my apology. But I spoke to Mrs Sibson about Levi's behaviour. It's not just slugs and a missing pen. It's more than that. It's name-calling. Intimidation.'

It was so hard to explain how devastating the bullying was. Citing *name-calling* seemed trivial compared to the impact the bullying was having on her daughter. Mr George made a steeple with his fingertips and looked at her over the top of his glasses. She was transported back to being a child of ten at her boarding school in London.

'Hence you thought you'd simply handle the situation yourself?'

She held up her hands. 'You still haven't dealt with Levi! You need to investigate his behaviour. He ought to be disciplined, even suspended if that's what it takes to stop him.'

'Let me be clear: I am not going to discipline a child in this school on the unsubstantiated account of a parent. Particularly one who has behaved as you have done. We will monitor Levi's behaviour closely. As you know, we do not tolerate any bullying in this school. I am, however, considering whether to ask you to remove Autumn. Your daughter has, so far, behaved in an exemplary manner, but at Ashley Grove Junior any misdemeanour towards any of our pupils or staff is taken extremely seriously. The only reason, absolutely the only reason I persuaded Mr Jablonski to try and resolve the situation with you rather than take the matter to the police is for the sake of our school's reputation. But if he does report you, I will support him every step of the way.'

Laura stared at him in stunned silence.

'In my experience, Mrs Baron-Cohen, physical aggression does not manifest itself in isolation. I would recommend that you see a counsellor and take a course of lessons in anger-management. I will also speak to Mrs Sibson to see whether we ought to refer your daughter to Social Services for her own protection.'

'That is outrageous!' She was on her feet. 'If you don't start taking my claims seriously and investigating Levi's behaviour, then I shall speak to the council about you and report you to Ofsted.'

Before Mr George could reply, Laura strode out of his office, slamming the door behind her. She tore down the corridor and burst out of the school. By the time she reached the playground she was running, only slowing down as she neared the edge. How could the head trust Aaron instead of her? Mr George didn't seem to believe that Levi was bullying Autumn. The thought that he could even consider she might be abusing her daughter turned her anger to shame. What if he did call Social Services?

Outside the school gates, she stopped. She looked at her watch. Matt was still at the Buddhist village and she wouldn't be able to reach him. Not that she wanted to talk to him about it. Vanessa and Julian were somewhere over the Atlantic, en route to Namibia. That only left her brother Damian. She'd Skype him this evening in case he was in the research station and not following his lemur troop. There was no point in going home, even though she was too early to pick Autumn up. She waited, sitting on the low stone wall surrounding the playground, growing increasingly cold.

Rani was one of the first mums to reach Ashley Grove, striding towards the school in her fuchsia coat. Rebecca, Amy and Lily, as well as a few other mothers Laura didn't know, gathered around her. Laura hesitated and then walked over to them.

'Hi,' she said uncertainly when she reached the group.

The women fell silent. A couple of the mothers glanced at her and then looked away.

A woman with a hard face and deep lines across her forehead said, 'You should be ashamed of yourself.'

'Is disgusting what you did,' agreed a girl, barely in her twenties, her bleached-blonde hair scraped into a pony tail.

Laura looked at Rebecca, hoping she would say something to defend her. Rebecca was facing towards the school, resolutely ignoring her. She swung around sharply as if she could feel Laura's gaze.

'I can't even begin to describe how shocked I am, we all are,' she said. 'I don't want to discuss it now. It's hardly appropriate with children around. And it's nowhere near as important, but I wanted to make you aware, in case you are not, that you've been sending Trojan viruses to all of us.'

'What?' said Laura.

She didn't even know what a Trojan was apart from a mythical horse in a Greek legend.

'I advise all of you to check your emails and delete any that have come from Laura, regardless of what they say or what the header is,' said Rebecca, her voice carrying loudly and clearly across the playground.

'But I haven't even emailed any of you – I haven't emailed anyone at all for the past few days,' said Laura.

Rani looked at her and Laura automatically smiled back. After Rebecca, Rani was the person she most liked to talk to at the school gates. She was a voluptuous British Sri Lankan with skin the colour of polished bronze. She had a large nose with a bulbous tip, wide lips and her wavy hair was cut in a thick, glossy bob. She had a wickedly sarcastic sense of humour and, of all the mothers Laura knew in Bristol, Rani had always seemed to be the person having the most fun. Rani did not return her smile.

'I opened one of your emails and stupidly clicked on the attachment, thinking you were sending me a document,' said Rani. 'It wiped several of my files and some programs. I've called Aaron to see if he can fix my laptop but I'm going to send you the bill.'

Laura stared at her, aghast. At that moment, the doors opened and children began to pour into the playground.

Amy started to speak. Laura cringed, expecting her to describe a computer malfunction or make some damning pronouncement about how Aaron should go to the police. Or add that she was going to send Laura the bill for her IT repair work too. Amy was Autumn's friend Molly's mother and Laura had always found her cold and distant. She looked like a doll, small and fragile, with a strangely expressionless face and flawless, apricot-coloured skin. Amy had a thin, reedy voice, which was all but drowned by the shouts of the children rushing towards them. Laura just caught the tail end of her sentence.

'... hear Laura's side of it.'

Autumn slipped her cold hand inside Laura's and gave a quick tug before breaking away. Laura followed her out of the playground, feeling stunned. She had no idea how to put a stop to a malicious virus, if that was what a Trojan was.

'How was your day?' she asked Autumn, who was walking so fast she was almost running.

Autumn did not reply.

'Sweetheart, I asked you a question.'

'I don't want to talk about it.'

'Did something happen? Did Levi say anything to you?' She felt a surge of panic rise within her. When Autumn remained silent, she said, 'Come on, Autumn, please speak to me. If you don't tell me, I'm only going to imagine the worst.'

Autumn stopped and swung around to face her. She was furious. 'You promised not to talk to the headmaster. And you did. I saw you – and so did everyone in my class.'

'I know you asked me not to speak to Mr George, but I had to. How else can we stop Levi from bullying you? I told him to take Levi out of the school.'

'You mean expel him?' said Autumn, looking hopeful.

'More like suspended,' said Laura uncertainly.

'So will he be suspended, Mum?'

Laura sighed. 'No, love. I'm afraid he won't be.'

Autumn looked crestfallen and then, to Laura's consternation, resigned, as if she had known all along that Laura would not be able to protect her.

'Because you pushed him,' she said. 'That's all anyone will think about.'

They walked the rest of the way home in silence. Laura was wondering what to do now. Mrs Sibson clearly didn't believe them, particularly since Autumn's pen had not actually been stolen. Levi must be angry: presumably his class teacher would have given him a grilling about the cut on his face. Dileep George believed Aaron's account – that Levi was innocent of any wrongdoing – and Laura hadn't managed to explain herself convincingly.

Had she tried hard enough, she wondered? She'd left his office so abruptly and no doubt he considered her Ofsted threat vacuous. She should have stayed and argued. But what else could she have said? What she'd done was so wrong, so shocking, it would have made no difference to Mr George's reaction.

What if Aaron did go to the police? She wondered what the charge would be. There was no one to turn to, no one who could stop what was happening to her and Autumn. Rebecca wasn't talking to her. She should call Rebecca when they reached the house and try and explain herself. There must be something she could say to convince her – but the thought of trying to persuade Rebecca not to hate her made her wilt inside.

Rani was about to invoice her for destroying the hard drive on her computer. The other parents at the school appeared equally angry and would continue to be enraged if they received the virus from her. At least she only had Rebecca, Amy, Rani and Lily's email addresses, she thought with relief. And then she remembered with a jolt that Rebecca ran the Parents and Teachers' Association at Ashley Grove and had created an email group for it. She'd recently put Laura on the mailing list. Which meant, thought Laura, that the virus could have been sent to everyone on the PTA, including all the teachers, the reception staff and the governors of the school.

She was so lost in thought that at first she didn't notice Autumn had stopped. They'd reached Wolferton Place and were almost opposite their house. She turned and held out her hand to Autumn to cross the road with her. Autumn was staring silently at the house. Laura swung around to see what she was looking at. Everything appeared normal: there was their chipped blue front door, the bins on the pavement, which she should have pulled back to the house wall, a large terracotta pot she'd planted with a fig tree and lavender around the base of the trunk. No one had broken in or smashed a window, no one was waiting on the doorstep for them.

And then she saw it.

AUTUMN

She didn't understand it at first. It was almost like a sculpture, not a recognizable object. It was a child's bicycle, leaning up against the bins outside their house. No other children lived on their street and so the bike looked even more out of place than it might have on another road. Why was it there? There was something wrong with it, it was crooked, like a maimed creature. And then she understood. It was her bike.

She'd got it for her eighth birthday. Autumn loved her bike: it was metallic pink with a fat white seat and had a shopping basket hung between the handlebars decorated with red and orange artificial flowers.

She'd gone for a cycle ride on Sunday and her Mum had said the bike was too muddy to bring in. She'd left it in the garden and her mum had said she'd hose it down and put it in the dining room, but she must have forgotten. How had it got here, to their front door on Wolferton Place?

Someone had slashed the chunky tyres. The bubblegum-pink frame had been spray-painted scarlet red. The basket was bent, a broken tangle of wire like a smashed lobster pot. The final touch was the flowers: the garish fabric petals were scattered across the pavement like the ones at her great-gran's funeral.

'Oh no, your bike!' Her mum spotted it and ran over towards the mangled frame. 'It's been vandalized. Someone must have got into our back garden.'

She remembered the summer before last, the summer she turned eight and they were all in the park – all the mothers and their children. Once a month they met up, the mums who'd been pregnant at the same time; usually someone was missing but that day everyone was there. It was Maya's birthday and they were having a picnic. She and Cleo had cycled there. Her happiness had fizzed along her limbs like sherbet; she'd dropped her new bike in the grass and started to turn cartwheels, the sun and the sky and the trees all spinning, green and blue and gold. And when she'd stopped and stood still, out of breath and dizzy, all the mums had clapped and looked at her like they loved her every bit as much as her own mum did.

She felt the hot trickle of tears on her cheeks.

'Oh, love, I'm so sorry. I should have brought it in. I thought... I was sure no one could break into our garden.'

Autumn wiped her tears away quickly. She didn't want her mum to make a fuss and start dabbing at her face with a tissue in the middle of the street. She thought about riding the bike on Hampstead Heath, that same summer, on her actual birthday, the wind in her hair, sticking her feet out and screaming with laughter. She hadn't considered happiness then, or thought about the fizz in her fingertips. She'd just been happy.

'I'm sure we can fix it, Autumn,' said her mum, opening the front door. She dragged the damaged bike over the threshold.

They both looked at it, a crimson riot of mangled metal and broken spokes.

No one could fix that, thought Autumn. She stepped over the bike and went straight upstairs to her room without even taking her coat off. It was her mum's fault. If she hadn't gone to see Mr George, Levi wouldn't have gotten into their garden and trashed her bike – and then left it on the front door step like some kind of signal. It was a message. Autumn understood that. Her mum wanted to help but she just made everything worse.

She couldn't face her homework. Instead, she decided to write a letter to her real best friend, Cleo. She couldn't remember writing a letter before. Usually she made thank-you cards and wrote inside them or sent an email. She chose yellow paper because that was Cleo's favourite colour and she drew squirrels in the margins because they were Cleo's favourite animal. She kept having to start again. She wasn't very good at drawing squirrels. And the letter kept going wrong, as if the words on the page deliberately turned into different words than the ones she meant.

It was an invitation to Cleo to come and stay and it was supposed to be full of descriptions of nice things, of her new school and her new house to make Cleo want to visit. But every time she started telling Cleo something that had happened, she'd remember the other bit, the bit that wasn't so nice.

When her mum told her it was time for dinner, she threw all the butter-coloured sheets of messed-up squirrels in the bin. Later that evening, after her mother kissed her goodnight, Autumn retrieved her toys and tucked them in with her. They were much too far away at the other end of the bed; she couldn't even reach them with her toes. She pressed her hand against her forehead. She'd had a headache since the night before.

She tried not to think about her bike. Instead, she remembered going to gymnastics. She hated it there. Her old gym class in London had been in a brand-new sports centre. It was a proper gymnasium with a sprung floor and beautiful shiny hoops and a vaulting horse made of soft suede and gleaming wood. This one was in an old church. There were statues – white marble saints boxed into Perspex coffins that stared at you, or rolled their eyes towards heaven, palms pressed piously in prayer, and grotesque stone gargoyles leered down where the joints in the roof arced into a pointed dome.

She remembered the horrid feeling of falling, the dread that had engulfed her. It was going to hurt, she felt sure of it. And then, as she was twisting and spinning, she'd seen her mum, running towards her, arms outstretched. Her mum hadn't *caught* her exactly, she'd broken her fall, and they'd both landed on the mat, winded. As they lay there, a jumble of limbs and beating hearts, all she'd noticed had been the stone arches high overhead making a pattern like a pointed lily, the dull glitter of one of the stained-glass windows, a stone saint's ghostly white face. That was when the throbbing in her arm started and she realized she'd banged it on the beam. Jack had appeared and he'd smiled and helped her up and she'd felt mortified. All the other girls would be thinking how clumsy she was.

If her granny had been there she'd have agreed with Tess and made her climb back on the beam. Her mum had been more sympathetic but now Autumn knew that she never would be able to *get back on the horse*; she'd never walk along that narrow thread with pointed toes and lift and spin effortlessly in the air again.

LAURA

As soon as Autumn was in bed, she called the number for the local police to report the vandalism of Autumn's bike. She'd checked the garden, but there were no signs of a break-in, and she'd taken pictures. The call-taker she spoke to didn't seem to be that interested.

'Bikes go missing or get vandalized all the time, love,' he said. 'We don't have the resource to go chasing after the culprits. And if you leave one right outside your house, it's asking for trouble. Let me take some details though, and I'll make a note of it on our system.'

She hung up, angry he wasn't going to send a police officer round, and turned to her laptop. She'd try Damian first, she thought. Her older brother by two years, he'd always been benignly protective of her.

Laura opened Skype but there was something odd about her account. Instead of showing pictures of Vanessa, Julian, Damian, and Matt in the Contacts section, her address list was empty. She opened up the 'Find Contact' box and typed in Damian's name and pressed enter. An error message appeared. Laura frowned. She was useless with computers, with any kind of technology. She tried a few more times with the same result. She put in Damian's name but the familiar error message appeared. She turned off the laptop and then switched it back on again, intending to try again. This time, when her laptop started, she couldn't find Skype on her computer at all. Normally it was on the desktop but now it wasn't even under the list of programs.

Surely it wasn't a coincidence? The email virus and then Skype malfunctioning in such an odd way? She thought of Aaron and how he had set up a program that would allow him remote access to her computer. She shivered. She felt like smashing her laptop.

She called her best friend, Lucy. She was the perfect combination of optimism and sympathy. Laura imagined her as she listened to the phone ringing: Lucy was petite with long, blonde hair in tight curls. They'd met on Laura's first job in TV, when Lucy was starting out too, as a production assistant. Perpetually on the hunt for the perfect man and childless, Laura had bursts of envy when she heard the latest details about Lucy's life – cocktails in Soho, in London and New York, long, lazy Sunday pub lunches, coffee and the papers in bed on a Saturday morning after a late night out on Friday – but she knew Lucy well enough to know that she was probably jealous of Laura too. It was hard being in your mid-thirties and single, and because she'd recently been diagnosed with polycystic ovarian syndrome, Lucy might never be able to have a baby.

Lucy's voice was warm and chirpy. It brought tears to Laura's eyes. She was tempted to call her again, just to listen to the message. She resisted the impulse and put the phone down firmly.

WEDNESDAY 31 OCTOBER

LAURA

There'd been a cold snap overnight and each blade of grass was rimed with frost. The orange-red fruit of the strawberry tree shone amid the glossy evergreen leaves, silver-tipped in the wan light. Laura held her mug of tea tightly to her chest. The radiators made choking sounds; they probably needed to be bled.

She looked at the clock. It was growing late. Autumn, silent and pale, had picked at a piece of toast and stirred some Rice Krispies around the bowl without actually eating anything. She'd gone to brush her teeth but she was taking longer than she needed to.

'Autumn,' she called. 'We need to leave now.'

Laura struggled to achieve the right tone. She didn't want to sound cross. She walked upstairs to the hall and put her trainers and fleece on. She was about to shout again when Autumn appeared, though not from the bathroom as she'd expected. She came running down the stairs and paused near the bottom.

Laura gaped at her. Autumn looked at her defiantly, then jumped down the last two and grabbed her coat.

Laura swallowed back her instinct to shout, *You can't go out looking like that.*

Instead she said softly, 'Why have you done that?'

Autumn shrugged. 'All the girls do.'

She bent to put on her boots. She'd taken her hair out of her plaits and was wearing an Alice band. She must also have rummaged about in her room and found Laura's old make-up case. She looked like a drag queen, with large spots of pink on her cheeks and a slash of lipstick and purple eyeshadow smudged over her eyelids. It might have been comic but the effect, with her pallor, the dark circles under her eyes and her perfect child's skin, was horrific.

'No,' said Laura. It came out much louder and firmer than necessary. 'They don't. Not to school. Go upstairs and take it off.'

Autumn stood up and looked out of the window for a moment, one boot on, the other lying like something eviscerated on the floor. She burst into tears. Laura hugged her tightly. Her daughter felt scrawny and hard; she was unresponsive to her touch.

'Everyone says I'm ugly,' she sobbed.

'You're beautiful,' said Laura. 'Who says you're ugly?'

'Levi. And then the other boys and some of the girls say I am too.'

'Well, they're wrong,' said Laura. 'You're perfect.' She crouched down. 'Hard as it is, you have to learn to ignore Levi. He's trying to hurt you. You mustn't let him.'

So the bullying hadn't stopped, she thought grimly.

She took Autumn's hand and led her upstairs to the bathroom, where she found a half-empty bottle of make-up remover and some cotton wool and gently started to sponge the garish colour off her daughter's face. She remembered this had once been a nightly ritual for her too, before Autumn was born, when she'd made herself up to look artfully fresh, as if she were not wearing make-up at all.

'Your skin is so pretty,' she murmured, as the make-up came off, revealing Autumn's smooth, unblemished cheek. She kissed her and Autumn, almost reluctantly, hugged her back. It was a hug lacking in strength or feeling, thought Laura, dropping the soiled cotton wool in the bin and watching her daughter slowly descend the stairs.

Autumn pulled her boots on and turned to let herself out the back of the house.

'It's Wednesday.'

'Oh.' Autumn stopped and waited for her at the front door.

'Had you forgotten?' said Laura, putting out a hand to stroke her hair. That wasn't like her. Autumn jerked away. Laura always dropped Autumn off at school by car on a Wednesday as that was the day she went to university for her horticulture course.

'Are you feeling okay?' asked Laura, as she pulled out of Wolferton Place. Autumn looked peaky and was staring glumly out of the window. She didn't reply. It was such a short journey to school by car; even so, Laura felt relieved that it was almost over. She had no idea how to try and cheer Autumn up, or make her feel better about herself; she found her passive-aggressiveness hard to deal with and she was at a loss to know how to stop Levi.

Just as they reached the school, Autumn sat up straight and said, 'Did you speak to Tilly's mum about the sleepover?'

'It's not until Friday, Autumn.'

Autumn slumped back against the seat. Laura pulled over and Autumn opened the door while the car was still moving.

'Autumn!' shouted Laura.

Her daughter grabbed her satchel and jumped out without looking at her.

'Bye. I love you,' called Laura, but Autumn had already slammed the door.

She watched her for a moment; her daughter was walking along the pavement as if she were about a hundred instead of nine. Laura doubted that Autumn would be welcome in Tilly's house, but she hadn't talked to Rebecca about it. She couldn't bear the thought of Autumn's disappointment. This was the first time she'd been invited to have a sleepover at any of the other girl's houses since she'd joined this new school and she was desperate for Tilly to be her friend.

A car hooted behind her and she held up her hand in apology before easing back into the stream of traffic. She'd have to speak to Rebecca tonight after school and tell her that whatever Rebecca believed she'd done, it was nothing to do with Autumn and her friendship with Tilly.

Her classes started at ten, so there was usually just enough time after parking at the Frenchay campus to grab a coffee. It was disgusting stuff though. She was standing in the corridor, sanitized graffiti on the walls like lobotomized impressions of street-wise students, her rucksack full of text books slung over one shoulder, the coffee burning her fingers through the thin plastic cup, thinking about Autumn wearily trudging the last few metres to school this morning, when Jacob walked in.

'Hey, how are things? What did you think of Sunday's class?' He gave her a wolfish grin.

'I'm still stiff,' she said, managing a smile. 'I could barely walk. Climbing all those stairs in our house is torture.'

Jacob laughed. 'Are you going to give it another go?'

'Sure,' said Laura. She didn't know how she'd manage to attend another class without Vanessa or, indeed, anyone else, to look after Autumn, but she was determined to try. 'I hated it, Jacob, I want you to know that. But I'm going to get fit if it kills me.'

He laughed again and patted her on the shoulder. 'Well, if you come to another session, I'll buy you a coffee afterwards.'

'And chocolate cake. It'll be the only thing that'll keep me going,' she said.

'You ready to go in?' he asked, glancing at her full cup of coffee.

'I don't know why I bother,' she said, smiling at him, 'it's the worst coffee I've ever had.'

Laura always had to leave her classes early to reach school on time and usually she left as late as she possibly could but, today, she left even earlier than normal. When she arrived at Ashley Grove, Rebecca was already there, surrounded by a small knot of women. She steeled herself to speak to her. As she walked over, Rani and Lily hugged Rebecca. Poppy had her arm around Tilly's shoulder, as if she was comforting her. Amy, holding a baby in her arms and clutching the hand of a small boy, straining away from her like a dog on a short leash, was standing with her daughter, Molly, to one side of the group. She and Molly looked up at her as Laura approached, their small, heart-shaped faces pale. Rebecca swung around, looking furious.

'I was prepared to put your behaviour to one side for Autumn's sake, but this is the limit,' she spat out. 'Autumn is no longer welcome in my house.'

Laura opened her mouth to speak but Mrs Sibson came bustling out. She was frowning, her expression pained.

'Could you please come inside for a moment?' she said to Laura.

'What's happened?' asked Laura, walking past the hostile group of women.

'I kept Autumn behind so I could talk to her. I'm concerned about her. She copied Tilly's work today.'

'What?' said Laura, raising her voice. 'That's ridiculous! Autumn would never do that.'

'It would be easier if we could discuss this inside,' said Mrs Sibson, looking annoyed at Laura's reaction.

Laura felt chastened. She never normally shouted. It was the stress, she thought, as she followed the teacher into the classroom. There were plastic spiders hanging from the ceiling and three pumpkins lined up in the window, tiny candles guttering through the holes cut in their skin, all sharp teeth and ghoulish grins. Autumn was sitting in the far corner, bent over a piece of paper, her hair resting on the desk. When she saw Laura she burst into loud, noisy sobs.

'I didn't copy her work. I didn't do it,' she wailed.

Laura rushed over to her, tripping over small desks and chairs.

'I know you wouldn't do that, love.' She hugged her and sat down on one of the tiny chairs. 'What happened?'

'We all had to write a story about autumn, what happens in autumn and what we like best. We did it on the computer and saved them in a folder. Then today when Mrs Sibson printed them all out...' She was having trouble speaking through her tears, gulping and choking on snot and saliva. 'Mine was the same as Tilly's, but Tilly had written hers earlier – she used the computer before me. So everyone said I'd copied hers.'

She put her head on the desk.

'What did you say you liked best about autumn?' asked Laura gently.

Autumn didn't look up and spoke very quietly through her hair. 'I said I liked the smell of bonfires and making gingerbread with raisins and dressing up on Halloween with my best friend, Cleo. Tilly said she liked toffee apples and spiky sweet chestnuts and red leaves. They were different, Mum. I don't like *all* the same things as Tilly.'

Laura put her hand on Autumn's. The child withdrew hers. Laura looked up at Mrs Sibson.

'I think you've jumped to conclusions far too rapidly. Isn't it obvious she didn't copy Tilly?'

'Tilly's story was cut and pasted into the document that was labelled as Autumn's work. Autumn had changed a couple of things – she'd added that she liked the smell of bonfire smoke and eating gingerbread. All the rest of it was identical to Tilly's.'

'Did you copy Tilly's work?' Laura asked Autumn.

'No!'

'Someone must have done it deliberately to get Autumn into trouble,' said Laura, standing up and facing Mrs Sibson.

'No one else has access to this classroom apart from these children and the other teachers,' said Mrs Sibson.

She looked resigned, as if dealing with Autumn and her mother was one more chore she had to endure before she could leave and go home. Laura suspected that this brave new world of tablets and iPads did not interest Mrs Sibson in the slightest; she was the kind of woman who wanted children to copy lines neatly from the blackboard and paint pictures with poster paints, and she was grimly slogging her way through digitized photos and touchscreen drawings for her final few years until retirement.

'It was probably Levi.'

Mrs Sibson sighed again, as if her evening with a meal for one and a glass of wine on a tray was now utterly ruined. 'You seem to have a real problem with Levi. And Aaron. By the way, we received a virus from you. Aaron managed to pick it up and contain it before it did too much damage. But that's not what I wanted to discuss,' she went on quickly before Laura could interrupt. 'I think we should have a proper discussion about Autumn. She's clearly unhappy and displaying some odd behaviour. I know Dileep, Mr George, is planning on speaking to Social Services about your attitude.'

'My attitude? Social Services? Are you out of your mind?'

'Mrs Baron-Cohen, our PE teacher says Autumn's arm is severely bruised.'

'And you think *I* did it? Come on, Autumn. Get your coat. My daughter is not spending another minute here,' said Laura, sweeping up Autumn's satchel and grabbing the child's arm.

Autumn whimpered and flinched.

'Oh, sorry, love.' She'd seized her sore one.

'I think you should know,' said Mrs Sibson quietly, as Laura reached the classroom door, feeling even more ashamed than before, 'Aaron changed his mind and he did file a report with the police...'

'What?' She spun back towards Mrs Sibson.

'He told us that today they started interviewing the boys who saw you hit Levi.'

Laura slammed the door behind her, a childish act that made her feel better momentarily and then mortified. The teacher hadn't spoken to her out of anger or malice; she'd actually been attempting to be sympathetic, Laura realized.

'Tilly's not going to let me go round for a sleepover, is she?' said Autumn as they walked across the deserted playground, their breath freezing in small clouds around them.

Laura inhaled deeply and tried to focus on Autumn's concerns and ignore her skipping heart-beat and jagged adrenaline surge.

She said carefully, 'If she didn't believe you, she's not worth having as a friend, Autumn. It takes time to build new friendships but, I promise you, by the end of the year, girls will be falling over themselves to invite you to their houses. You've still got all your friends from London and you're making friends here. What about Molly? I bet she didn't think you'd copied Tilly's work.'

She looked down at her daughter to see how she was taking the disappointment and her pep talk. Autumn's face was set in a cold, hurt expression. Laura wanted was to shake Rebecca for breaking her daughter's heart.

AUTUMN

Her mum became all sparkly like tinsel at that point. She was trying to make it up to her, Autumn could tell. She felt bad about the sleepover but not *that* bad. If she'd felt *that* bad she'd have done something about it – gone round to speak to Tilly's mum, or something. Instead of making everything worse with everything she tried to do.

Let's go and buy a pizza, she said in her new bright and shiny voice, *and watch a movie on TV. It'll be fun!*

Autumn could practically see the exclamation marks hovering in the air. Her mum fished the car keys out of her handbag and they drove straight to the supermarket without even going back to the house. Autumn trailed listlessly behind her. She hated being in school uniform out of school. Everyone stared. And it wasn't proper pizza and not a proper treat if it came out of the freezer from a shop and not from a pizza place. Even if it was a school night. Tilly had pizza at Napolita every Friday with her mum and dad and Poppy. If her Mum hadn't ruined it, Autumn would have been eating proper pizza in a proper restaurant with her new best friend and all the other most popular girls in her class on Friday too.

Her mum picked up two pizzas, which Autumn supposed was a bit of a treat because normally they only bought one and shared it. Her mum put a chocolate Swiss roll and some mango juice and a bottle of sparkling wine and a bag of cheap sweets in the basket too. Autumn guessed the mango juice was for her but she didn't even like it. It had been her favourite drink when she was, like, eight, but not now, not now that she was *nine*. And the sweets were distressingly rubbish if anyone were to come round tonight for Trick or Treat.

After a few minutes, Autumn realized that they were still wandering around the shop instead of going to pay.

'What about this one?' her mum said.

'It's a mobile,' said Autumn listlessly.

'Yes. I think you should have one.'

'We're not allowed them in school,' said Autumn, feeling a little more interested.

She'd asked and asked for a mobile all last year and her mum had said no, she wasn't old enough. And the one she was holding was pink.

'I don't care,' said her mum. 'You're more important than their rules. You can turn it to silent. If there's a problem, call me.'

Autumn nodded and her mum tossed it into the basket in a kind of carefree manner. They went to the self-service tills and Autumn was looking at the display of chocolates, wishing her mum had bought a Mars bar or a Snickers instead of a horrible Swiss roll, when it happened. The red light started beeping on the top of the flagpole-like thing and her mum looked uncomfortable and Autumn didn't know where to look. People were staring. A black girl with her hair in millions of plaits and two-inch plastic leopard-print nails sauntered over.

'Your card's been rejected.'

'Yes. I was wondering if you can try it again. There's nothing wrong with it. There's money in the account.'

The girl gave her mum a sidelong glance like she'd heard that one before. She tried the card two more times. Autumn looked at her feet. There was a queue of people building up, shuffling impatiently. The woman behind them sucked her teeth and rolled her eyes. Her mum had gone bright red.

'Not going through,' said the girl, handing it back. 'You got another one?'

Her mum looked through her wallet and took out a credit card. She handed it over triumphantly, like she'd won the egg and spoon race on sports day.

Thank God, it's worked! thought Autumn, trying to roll her eyes like the lady in the queue and not look mortally embarrassed.

And after that everything just got worse. Her mum put the pizzas in the oven and poured herself a glass of wine and told Autumn to go to their Netflix account on the TV and look for a movie she wanted to watch, any movie, so long as it had a U rating.

She quickly chose *Pirates! An Adventure with Scientists,* because that was the film Tilly's dad had been involved with and she'd felt stupid when Tilly had mentioned it.

I mean, who would have thought Hugh Grant could act like that! Poppy had said and Autumn had no idea what she was talking about. She'd thought it was a kind of cartoon.

Autumn tried to download the film but nothing happened. The password had been rejected, the message on the TV said. Autumn knew the password off by heart although she was only allowed to download films her mum approved of. It was very easy. It was AutumnWild. She tried it several times. Then she tried it using all lower case and then all upper-case letters and then a mixture of the two. Her mum tried it too and the pizzas burnt.

Amazon said it would reset the password if they clicked on the link it would email her mum. But, of course, her mum no longer had an email account.

While her mum was trying to *salvage the pizzas,* Autumn put in the DVD she'd been watching every night. Her mum sighed when she came in and saw it, but she didn't say anything. It was *Deadly 60.* It was all about animals that could be a bit tricky if you tried to catch one, or so Uncle Damian had said when he'd given it to her. She liked the one about Madagascar the best because that was where he worked, looking after his lemur troop. The programmes reminded her of him, and her dad and Granny and Grandad. They were all intrepid people who liked to go off into the wilderness and look at animals.

She had no desire to search for, find or touch any large snakes or scorpions or spiders or sharks. But there was something comforting about the repetition, watching it over and over and over again. You knew what was going to happen. There were no surprises. And even though all those animals bit, squeezed, stung, spat or poisoned, they did it because they were hungry or frightened. They didn't do it because they thought you were stupid and ugly and they wanted to hurt and humiliate you.

THURSDAY 1 NOVEMBER

AUTUMN

At twenty-five past eight that morning Autumn let herself out of the kitchen door. The garden was filled with mist that rolled away from her in fat coils. She breathed out and her breath hung in front of her, like a dragon's. Her mum hadn't wanted her to walk to school by herself. What would Granny say? She would have wanted her to go on her own, she concluded. She was fearless. Autumn wished that she herself was.

Her granny always said, *Get back on the horse.*

She didn't mean a real one. She meant, if you fell or were frightened by something, then you needed to pick yourself up and do it again straight away to conquer your fear. Besides, thought Autumn, it wouldn't be so bad. She lifted her satchel over her head, so the strap was across her body, and opened the garden door. She almost never saw anyone walking to school this way. She didn't know where Levi lived, but it wasn't near Wolferton Place or she'd have seen him before. He'd followed her on Friday deliberately to tear up her paintings and then he'd gone back up Briar Lane towards Ashley Road.

Sometimes people were out walking their dogs. When they saw her, they almost always grabbed hold of their dog and said, *Don't mind him, he's friendly.*

Mum said not to talk to strangers, but she always said hello and stroked the dog's head when people did that. She heard the chink of a stone behind her and wondered if someone was out with their dog now. She looked over her shoulder but she couldn't see anything through the mist. She opened the swinging gate from the lane outside their house into the allotments and let herself in. The gate shut with a metallic clink.

Most of the vegetables in the allotments had died back but one, tended by a Jamaican man, was full of squash. They lay among the dying leaves, rimmed with frost, huge, orange and alien, half hidden by the mist. They reminded her of the fairy stories she'd read as a young child, of white horses and gold carriages that turned into mice and pumpkins on the stroke of midnight. Earlier in the season the Jamaican man had grown a crop of custard whites – *cucurbits*, her mum had said – which looked like creamy spaceships. Behind her the gate closed softly, as if whoever had come through had held it so that it wouldn't bang.

Autumn left the allotments and entered the wood leading to the nature reserve. It was cold and she wrapped her scarf more tightly around herself. The mist was entwined around the trunks of the trees and she walked in her own capsule of grey space. The snap of a twig startled her. She stopped and looked around. She half expected a dog to burst through the fog towards her. Sometimes she saw a Siberian husky here, like a white wolf with blue eyes; a canine changeling.

If it was a dog walker, she thought she'd have heard the sound of the dog's lead or its collar, the animal panting as it trotted up the hill. But there was silence. A couple of magpies chattered in the branches and, in the distance, she could hear the traffic on the road outside school.

Two for joy...

She turned to start walking again and then she heard it. The definite sound of footfalls, the soft rustle of frozen leaves.

Especially strange men, her mum had said in one of her frequent warnings about talking to people she didn't know.

Autumn started to walk more quickly. Her breath came in short gasps, a private fog floating around her head. At the top, as if it were a magic line, she could see where the mist ended and the nature reserve, rising above it, glowed green, dull as an uncut gem, through the stark, bare branches. She couldn't be certain, but it sounded as if the person behind her was walking faster too.

She was wheezing as she burst out of the wood and into the meadow. She half ran along the path and then stopped. Behind her the wood was wreathed in fog, the path a dark tunnel descending into its depths. She could see a shape emerging through the mist, moving steadily and swiftly towards her. There was no friendly rattle of a lead or the scrabble of a dog's paws on the stones. It was someone who was on their own. She looked around. There was no one else here. The magpies arrowed across the sky and a wren broke out into a loud, chittering alarm call. In the distance, a siren blared. Should she run? Walk calmly on? Wait to see who it was?

He was wearing something black – a coat, a hat. She half expected the man to emerge from the wood and smile.

Sorry to have startled you.

But what if he were not a friendly man? What if he was one of those men her mum warned her about? Could she run fast enough to get away from him? She only had a half-formed sense of what could happen if a man caught her.

He'll hurt me.

But she didn't know how or why, which made the possibility of what might happen so much worse.

She was backing away now, half turning, ready to run, her heart pounding in her chest, when he stepped free of the mist. She couldn't move. For a moment he simply stood at the edge of the wood and stared at her. Then he started to walk quickly towards her, not taking his eyes off her.

It was Levi.

Autumn began to run. She felt an icy terror flood through her body. He must have been waiting for her in the lane. He'd followed her all the way here. To this open, empty place.

He knows where I live.

She could hear Levi gaining on her, jogging through the mud, the frosted surface splintering beneath his trainers; the splash as he cracked through the ice on a puddle. She was running around the edge of the meadow, sliding on wet stone. It was a slight incline and she wasn't a fast runner. He was so much taller than she was, with longer legs, and he was built like an athlete. It would only be seconds before he would be able to reach out and grab hold of her.

And what then? What would he do to her?

She could hear his breath now, steady and even. Her own was loud and harsh; she was struggling to force more oxygen into her lungs. She felt as if she was running in slow motion, like you do in a dream when you run and run and can't go any faster.

And the monster always runs faster.

Levi was right behind her. He was matching his steps with hers. He was barely running at all.

She rounded the corner of the meadow. There, in the distance, was the end of the nature reserve and the bridge over to Briar Lane. If only she could reach the lane, there would be people, there were houses. She imagined running up one of the back gardens and hammering on the door. A dog suddenly bounded across the grass towards her. Brown and white, some kind of mongrel, sniffing at the rabbit holes, its tongue lolling out. She couldn't breathe. If there was a dog, there was bound to be an adult nearby. She slowed to a walk and behind her she could hear Levi slowing too.

Her neck prickled. She looked into a half-melted puddle and saw his reflection in the earth-brown water. He was barely inches away from her, so close he could touch her. Someone whistled and she looked over to the peak of the nature reserve where the sound had come from. The dog's head jerked up and it raced away, over the brow of the hill. They were alone again.

When was he going to do it? How would he do it?

She gulped in air and walked faster, as quickly as she could without breaking into a run. They crossed the bridge together, his shadow falling over hers. There was fresh graffiti today: vermillion, purple and gold, the chunky, indecipherable calligraphy of the street. His footsteps echoed hollowly, the sound bouncing around the cage they were in, suspended above the railway line. The light, splintered by the metal bars over her head, hurt her eyes.

It seemed to take a year of her life to reach the lane, the gravel and grit crunching beneath her shoes; an identical crunch came from directly behind her. She saw a small group of children further ahead, satchels and rucksacks slung over their shoulders, wearing black and navy, the Ashley Grove school uniform. She hurried towards them. She didn't recognize them; they looked as if they were in the year above. She slowed.

Was it a trick?

If Levi's gang were waiting at the exit to the main road she'd be trapped between them and him. She looked at the back gardens, no longer the welcoming place of safe refuge she'd imagined, but forbidding with high walls and heavy iron gates. She could be caught in one of them, pounding on the door, the owner at work. No one would be able to see her. No one could hear her.

She looked back at the group. There were two girls and they were smaller than she'd thought. They were pupils from the other class in her year, she thought with relief. She bent her head and walked steadily towards them. In the corner of her eye she could see Levi's arm swinging. He was still there. The other children reached the end of Briar Lane and spread out across the pavement. One of them pressed the button for the pedestrian crossing. Autumn looked up at the lights. They were green. She was behind the other children now, but still in the lane. In spite of the cars going past, Levi was so close she could feel her neck prickling.

The lights turned red and the green man lit up. Autumn leapt forward and, as she reached the pavement, she turned to see what Levi was going to do.

He was motionless, watching her. He held up one arm. Between his thumb and forefinger he held a scrap of paper. It was washed a cerulean blue. It was part of a painting: a single segment of a harebell. He opened his hand and the paper drifted upwards and away in the wind.

LAURA

That evening she felt jittery with nerves. She thought about the pile of laundry that needed to be done, the mountain of clothes that were clean and dry but hadn't been folded and put away, the radiators that needed to be bled, the online shop she had to arrange, the essay that was due in for her course, the To Do list for the garden-design company, which included applying for a start-up grant and finishing off their business plan.

She opened her laptop, determined to make Skype work before the weekend so that she could contact Vanessa when she returned to Windhoek and Autumn could speak to Matt when he descended the mountain to the nearest village. She couldn't find the program on her hard drive and when she tried to download it, she kept receiving error messages. She didn't want to risk opening her email account, so she clicked on Facebook instead.

As she browsed through status updates, she saw that one of the mothers from her NCT group had posted a link to an article in *The Washington Post*. The word *Bully* was in the headline. *It's just a coincidence*, she thought, but she had an oily feeling in her stomach as she selected the website and opened up the article. It was about a man who had hired a teenager to beat up his daughter's bully. The teenager ended up being badly assaulted by the bully. Even so, the bully's parents successfully sued the girl's father.

Laura shut down the article before she could read further. She paced around the landing outside her office. Autumn had ignored her this morning. She'd gone to bed early too, without being prompted. She'd turned her face away when Laura had tried to kiss her. Laura had heard her footsteps though, as her daughter paced in her bedroom during the night. She thought about the previous morning, the dreadful sight of Autumn as caked in make-up as a child beauty queen, followed by her sobs because she believed she was ugly.

Laura sat down and clicked on her folder of pictures. Since Autumn had been born, she'd mainly only taken pictures of her daughter – there were hardly any of her. She would make a montage, she thought, of all the best photos of Autumn, to show her that she was beautiful.

She opened up Photoshop and created a blank document to cut and paste the photos into and then she returned to her files to choose the pictures. She'd always meant to put them in order but they were jumbled together, photos of Autumn as a baby alongside the latest ones of her aged nine. She hadn't taken any since they'd moved to Bristol, she noticed.

She chose one that made her smile: Autumn dressed up as a pumpkin for Halloween. She was wearing an orange costume with a green frill around her neck and she had orange face-paint on. She was laughing so hard she had her eyes shut. Cleo had her arm around her shoulder and was wearing a black lace curtain over the top of a pair of dungarees and a pointy hat. She must have been about six, she recalled. Autumn had wanted to make ghoulish buns: they'd divided the cake mixture up and baked lime-green, blue and Fanta-orange-coloured cupcakes topped with sickly sweet swirls of buttercream and stuck plastic spiders in the icing. Autumn had laughed and shuddered at the same time and wouldn't eat a single one. Laura copied the photo and clicked Paste on the document. Nothing happened. She tried again.

She returned to the original photo and tried to copy it, but as she highlighted it, it disappeared. She felt the same anxiety she had when she'd tried to restore Skype. She was so dreadful at anything technical.

This should be simple, she thought, hating her ineptitude.

She opened another picture. It was of Autumn on her seventh birthday. She was smiling straight at Laura; her large, grey eyes glowed in the light from the candles on her cake. She could see the cute gap in her teeth that Autumn hated. The cake had raspberries and white chocolate chips in it, Laura remembered, just as Autumn had requested. The raspberries had been frozen ones and their dampness had made the cake sag in the middle.

The picture disappeared. Laura blinked. She clicked back on the folder of photos. It was no longer there. She scrolled up and down searching for the picture. How could it have vanished like that? As she was looking, other photos started to disappear, slowly at first and then more rapidly. Spaces appeared between the photos and the white screen predominated as the number of pictures diminished. Not all the pictures were being wiped, she realized. To her horror, she saw that it was only the ones with Autumn in.

There was one of her and Matt at Autumn's eighth birthday party – probably the last one taken of the two of them together. They looked frazzled; they were both clutching half-empty glasses of fizzy wine and looking away from each other. She hadn't noticed that before – that they were staring in opposite directions. She did a quick calculation – yes, he must have already been having an affair with Leah then. She didn't want to dwell on that now – she'd only get angry, she thought. She looked back at the picture folder and found it was almost empty. Even the ones of her. She started pressing buttons, to try and close the folder and shut down the computer, as if that would help, and when the laptop didn't respond, she jabbed randomly at the keys.

As the last photo of Autumn winked and disappeared – one of her aged two wearing a dinosaur mask with felt teeth and a pink princess dress – a window appeared in the middle of her screen and grew until it filled the monitor. It flickered into life. She wasn't sure what she was looking at until the camera started to zoom back.

It was a nipple, pink and protruding, the breast hard and full and stiff with veins like a cow's udder. A naked woman with lifeless blonde hair, her lips sticky with red lip gloss, her legs spread wide apart, her vulva waxed smooth. She stretched her labia open, crinkled and fleshy as an amorphous sea creature. Laura put her hand over her mouth. Now the woman was on all fours, her giant breasts bouncing painfully, moaning flatly as a man with chiselled abs, nude apart from a dark-grey tie around his neck, penetrated her from behind.

Laura pressed the ALT and Delete keys and the Off button. She pulled out the socket at the back. It didn't make any difference. The woman continued to moan. She sucked one finger. The man grunted and thrust and there was a rhythmic sticky slap as his thighs hit her bottom. He started to take his tie off. For a horrible moment Laura wondered what he was going to do with it. And then the screen went black.

Laura pressed the On switch. She put the plug back in again. Nothing. The laptop was completely lifeless. Before she could talk herself out of it, she phoned the local police. The voice at the other end was young, bored.

'Hello, this is Natalie. How may I help you?'

'The hard drive on my laptop has just been wiped,' she said shakily. 'I know who did it. An IT repair man…'

'If you've got a computer virus, you need to seek help from an IT company. It's a civil matter, not police business,' said the woman.

'It wasn't a virus. It was deliberate. He's an IT consultant. Aaron Jablonski. He fixed my computer last week and installed a kind of remote device so he could access my laptop and that's how he's done it. It was full of porn. And then everything just vanished. Completely. I can't even turn it on. There's nothing left.'

She thought of all those photos, nine years of her daughter's life, eradicated in a few seconds, and made a strangulated sob.

'Have you spoken to your IT consultant?' asked Natalie more kindly.

'He's sent a Trojan to everyone in my email account. It's malicious.' She was beginning to sound hysterical. 'Of course I can't speak to him about it.'

'And have you got a back-up of all your files?' The woman's voice had a soft Bristolian burr.

'No. Only of a few documents.'

Laura closed her eyes and silently swore at herself, at her stupidity.

How could I have been so careless?

The list of what had been lost was growing in her mind: not just the photos, but all her notes about the horticulture course, her designs and the research she'd done as preparation for Ruth's garden, and for her own. Music; playlists from happier times; her dissertation on Emily Dickinson that she'd been so proud of; the poetry she'd attempted to write.

'I'm sorry, love,' said Natalie, 'but we don't have the resource to deal with this kind of thing. I suggest you take it to a decent IT specialist, see if anything can be salvaged.'

'Thank you,' she said, wiping her eyes, and was annoyed at herself for muttering platitudes when she didn't feel the slightest bit grateful.

It was as she put the phone down that it suddenly hit her. Aaron had installed a program to give him access to her machine. But it was worse than that. He'd set the password to her Internet, which meant he knew it too – *Ode to Autumn*, she'd said, and Aaron had changed it himself! With a sinking feeling she realized that it would not be long before the Internet would no longer be accessible through her phone or the TV.

She'd told him her password! It was the same password for Skype as well as for her email, which is why he'd been able to hack into them. It was obvious to anyone who knew her what it might be: AutumnWild. How terribly unoriginal. And what was so dreadful was that it was the same password. For everything. She rested her head in her hands. Skype. Email. Facebook. Netflix. Amazon. Her bank account. *Her bank account.*

'Oh sweet Jesus,' she said out loud.

How very, very stupid of her. No bloody wonder Aaron had caused so much damage so swiftly. No wonder she hadn't been able to use her debit card.

She blew her nose and tried Lucy's mobile number again. It went straight to voicemail. Could she be away on a shoot? Her mind felt foggy, as if retrieving the tiniest fragment of information would require the expertise of an archaeologist. This time she left a message, trying to sound less despondent and desperate than she actually felt.

AUTUMN

She saw Levi standing behind her, holding a fragment of her painting between his thumb and forefinger. She felt goose bumps on her skin as she waited for him to reach out and touch her.

She wiped away her tears and climbed out of bed. She hadn't been able to sleep last night either. Sometimes in the evening when she was doing her homework or painting, or at bedtime, she borrowed her Mum's iPod. She liked listening to folk songs, but her favourites were her mum's *Classic Chill Out* albums or Mozart. Everyone in her old class was into that kind of music too. Cleo's favourite composer was someone called Bark. But when she'd come to Bristol, Olive had laughed at her. She said no one in Ashley Grove listened to *that old stuff*. They all liked Rihanna and Beyoncé. And now Autumn felt funny playing Mozart. It had been better when Granny was there, knowing she was just below her and her mum was in the room above. Granny liked Mozart too.

She wrapped her quilt around her. She felt alone and frightened. The house seemed to stir and creak. As if it were sighing. As if it were breathing. Standing there in the middle of her bedroom in the night, in the dark, that was when she became aware of it. A noise she'd been hearing for the past few minutes but hadn't consciously been listening to. She stopped in the middle of her bedroom. Her clock lit the room with an unearthly blue glow but still there were strange-shaped shadows in the corner of the room, pools of darkness where something could be hiding.

The sound came again. It was a squeaking, grating noise. It didn't seem to be from inside the house. She listened. It was like a gate, a giant gate rhythmically creaking open and closed. It couldn't be their garden door. It was too far away and her bedroom didn't face in that direction: it looked out onto the street.

And then she knew what it was. Her heart started to flutter erratically. It felt like a moth beating itself to death against a glass pane. She walked slowly over to the window and parted the curtains.

The house was built into the hill, with the kitchen a floor below the street. Opposite them, above the level of Wolferton Place, shored up by a high stone wall, was a small park. It might once have been part of the garden of a great house: in the corner nearest to her was a magnificent Scots pine and a Douglas fir, which dropped needles and elongated, twisted cones onto the pavement below. Her bedroom, two floors above the road, looked directly into this park.

There was a small slide for toddlers and two baby swings. There was a much larger slide with a bouldering wall set into a wooden tower and walkway and a metal fireman's pole. In between were a couple of plastic animals for little children that rocked on springs – a horse and a chicken. There was an odd roundabout – there were only three spaces and you had to stand up on it.

Once she'd seen a boy who only held on with his hands, spinning around, his body stretched out horizontally, as if he were flying. She would never dare do that. Now it moved slowly, as if in passing someone had given it a push. The horse was also rocking, back and forth; obscured by the shadows from the giant trees and half lit by a streetlight, the outsized head cast grotesque shadows on the ground.

The circling roundabout and the rocking horse made no sound. No one was riding them and gradually they started to slow down. The noise she'd heard was coming from the darkness behind the toddler toys: it was the swing for older kids, the unoiled metal hoops grating against one another.

There was someone sitting on it. He had his feet on the ground to push the swing backwards and forwards. As he swung towards her, his face was lit by the orange glow of the streetlight. He was looking directly at her.

It was Levi.

FRIDAY 2 NOVEMBER

LAURA

Half past three and she had still not reached the school. She took deep breaths to try and calm herself. She reminded herself she was only a few minutes away. It would be okay.

Laura had been working at a new garden in Frenchay. Barney hadn't let her leave on time and now she was late and the traffic was awful. Normally it was bad at this time of day as people were picking their kids up from school, but today was worse than usual. She was stuck on a particularly busy and narrow part of Frenchay Road. The traffic was at a standstill.

Her mobile, lying on the passenger seat, vibrated and she saw there was a text from Lucy. She snatched up the phone and read it quickly, before the cars could start moving again.

Hi hun, I'm in Canada, filming. Be back in a fortnight. Tagging on a few days in Toronto. Hope u ok. L xxx

Of course, she remembered now. Lucy was making a documentary about dancers, some kind of reality show hybridized with *The X-Factor*. It was part-funded by the Canadian Film Board and so they had to include some contestants from Vancouver. She'd forgotten that Lucy was taking a few days off afterwards. How like Lucy to remind her so kindly and so subtly.

Laura dropped the phone back on the seat and wiped her clammy hands on her jeans. She gripped the steering wheel.

What on earth is going on?

The cars in front of her started to inch slowly forward and then move onto the opposite side of the road. A silver Audi was stationary in the middle of her lane and cars travelling in both directions were trying to navigate around it. The car hadn't been hit. And then she saw a small group of people on the sliver of pavement next to the Audi. A man – maybe the driver – was bending over a woman who was lying on the pavement and giving her mouth to mouth. The accident must only just have happened, she thought, because there were no police and the ambulance hadn't arrived.

As Laura approached, she saw the woman more clearly. She was young, wearing a short denim skirt and no tights. Her smooth legs were askew, splayed out from each other at an odd angle. Her hands, lying so still on her lap, had short fingernails painted bright blue. She couldn't see any blood. Laura shuddered. She wondered if she should stop, but there were other people there, standing around, watching the man giving the woman the kiss of life. Surely one of them would have called the emergency services? In any case, she was late to fetch Autumn, she couldn't pull over. It was exactly accidents like this that reinforced her belief cars were hazardous, she thought, trying not to dwell on the girl who'd been hit. It was why she'd been so relieved when she'd discovered that Autumn didn't need to walk along the road to school if they cut through the nature reserve. Along a path that she now considered dangerous.

Laura pulled into a side street a few blocks away from the school but couldn't find a space until she was half-way up the street. Leaping out of the car, she started running towards Ashley Grove.

She noticed a small black child across the street. The girl was two or three; her arm was stretched up as far as it would go so she could hold her father's hand. She was wearing an imitation-leather jacket; beneath the hem was an explosion of pink ruffles.

Laura thought of the photo of Autumn in her princess outfit and felt tears prick her eyes. She turned resolutely away from the little girl who was smiling at her and jogged along the gritted pavement to Ashley Grove.

That morning Autumn had been white and the purple shadows beneath her eyes had deepened.

'How are you feeling, love? Are you ill?' Laura had asked.

Autumn had shaken her head and said nothing. She'd eaten two mouthfuls of cereal and then pushed the bowl away. The only thing she'd said to Laura had been that she had a headache, but she'd refused the Calpol Laura had tried to give her. Laura had driven her to school since she had to travel to Frenchay afterwards, and had again felt that horrid sense of relief at having to spend less time than normal with Autumn before escaping to work. Plus it meant that she hadn't had to face any of the other parents. She'd simply pulled over on the double yellow lines, blocking the traffic behind her, and Autumn had clambered out.

'I love you,' Laura had called.

Autumn had slammed the car door and trudged off, her stance as bent and resigned as if she were heading down a mine.

Now Laura scanned the yard for Autumn. There were still a few children coming out of the school and others milling around near the play area with its sawn-off tree trunks like stumps of teeth, the chipped red and yellow climbing frame and kidney-shaped sandpit. As Laura walked towards the entrance, a few of the parents looked over at her and frowned before turning away. At least Rebecca and her clique weren't there, she thought.

There was no sign of Autumn. Laura put her hands in her pockets and her head down and tried to avoid the stares. At the school doors she stopped and looked carefully around the playground again in case she'd somehow missed seeing her daughter. Autumn was definitely not there. The trickle of children filtering out of the school had stopped and the last parents and their offspring drifted out of the gates and down the road. It had started to grow dark and the street lamps flickered into life. A halo of mist swirled around each orange light.

She grasped the cold metal handle of the door and swung it open. Mrs Sibson was bustling down the corridor towards her, her long mustard cord skirt swishing over her boots, her heavy garnet and white necklace swinging in time with her steps. She frowned when she saw Laura.

'I can't find Autumn,' she said. 'I was a little late but she wasn't in the playground when I arrived.'

Mrs Sibson's frown deepened, making the rash across her chin grow redder.

'We finished on time. I saw her go out of the classroom.'

'But you didn't see her leave the school? Could she still be here?' Laura's voice was tight with apprehension.

Mrs Sibson shook her head. 'No. I looked out of the classroom window just after school ended and I saw her in the playground waiting for you. Actually, Mrs Baron-Cohen, I'm still concerned about Autumn. She looks unwell.'

Laura drew herself to her full height. 'I've repeatedly told you that she's being bullied. What do you expect? Did you see her leave the school grounds?'

Mrs Sibson ignored her outburst and shook her head. She said quietly, 'No, I'm sorry, I didn't. I assumed you'd be there to meet her. Could she have gone home with one of the other girls?'

'No,' said Laura. She didn't want to say that none of the other mothers would speak to her, let alone take Autumn home with their daughters. 'I'll go back in case she's gone to the house on her own instead of waiting for me.'

'That's not like her. She's quite a cautious child.'

Laura was taken aback. She'd assumed from Mrs Sibson's manner that she didn't have the slightest understanding of her daughter beyond her academic abilities.

'Over the last couple of days she's wanted to walk by herself,' Laura said. She started to hurry down the corridor, desperate to find Autumn. Over her shoulder she added, 'I agreed she could go to school on her own if I picked her up at the end of the day.'

Mrs Sibson followed her out and called after her, 'I'll ring you at home in ten minutes.'

'Thanks,' shouted Laura, running across the playground. For once she was glad she was wearing beaten-up trainers instead of the stylish footwear Rebecca wore.

She jogged back to the car and then drove slowly home, ignoring the traffic building up. The white van directly behind her was so close she could barely see its bonnet through her mirrors. She scanned the pavements as she drove, hoping to glimpse Autumn wearing her new bright red coat, hurrying down the street.

Laura turned into Wolferton Place; Autumn might be waiting outside the house. But the street was deserted, the doorstep empty. She parked the car and opened the front door. She was shouting, 'Autumn!' even as she stumbled inside, dead leaves and pine needles from the fir in the park opposite blowing in with her.

The house was dark and silent. Autumn didn't know that Laura had hidden a spare key in the back garden under a stone by the strawberry tree but, even so, Laura ran downstairs to the kitchen and then up to the top of the house, shouting her daughter's name, flinging open every door. She stood in her bedroom, out of breath, and saw herself reflected in the dark window set into the sloping ceiling, her hair spilling out of its bun, her eyes wide. The phone started to ring.

She ran back downstairs and snatched up the receiver in her office. It was Mrs Sibson.

'I was about to call,' she said. 'Autumn isn't here and I didn't see her on my way home. I'm going to walk through the nature reserve, in case she went home that way instead.'

'And no one has rung to say Autumn's at their house?'

'No,' said Laura.

'I've alerted Mr George that she's missing. Now I've spoken to you, I'll call the police. I'll make some phone calls to her friends' mothers and then call you back. I'll ring on your mobile, shall I?'

'Yes,' said Laura, checking it was still in her coat pocket.

She ran back down the stairs, snatching up the keys from the table by the front door and then continued to the kitchen and let herself into the garden. It was dusk and she had to struggle to see the numbers on the key pad next to the garden door. She stepped into the lane, shut it and locked it behind her. It was cold and since she'd driven to and from Frenchay, she wasn't wearing a scarf, hat or gloves and her boots were still in the car. The damp mist had resolved into a light drizzle.

She pushed open the metal gate into the allotments and started to jog along the path towards the wood. The beautiful, blowsy pink dahlias had dissolved into a dark, wilted tangle of dead stems. In one of the allotments she noticed a curious little apple tree. It was small with cascading branches, like a willow, and still festooned with fruit. They were hard and perfectly spherical, with dull matt skin in a peculiarly even and poisonous-looking red.

A feeble orange light was flickering in the allotments, low down near the ground. Laura looked hopefully towards it. It was a huge pumpkin, its flesh brick-red, its mouth cut into a crude gash, candle-flame dancing through slits for eyes. There was no sign of Autumn. Laura slipped on the wet stones as she entered the wood. She had a horrid sense of déjà vu. She stopped running, as she was out of breath, and walked as fast as she could up the steep path. It was ridiculous of her to think she'd be fitter after only one session of British Military Fitness.

A white dog, like a wolf, but with startling blue eyes, made her jump. It blocked her path and stared at her, like a creature from a fairy tale who might help or hinder her passage. Its owner appeared, a sullen-faced woman dressed all in black, jangling keys from a carabiner, and dragged the animal out of her way.

Laura paused at the edge of the wood and looked across the meadow. The image she had of Autumn, running home in her red coat, her satchel swinging, couldn't possibly be right. It was almost half past four. Even if Autumn had waited a few minutes for her and then set off by herself and had walked slowly, she would have reached the house long ago. Above her the clouds were dark grey and seagulls circled endlessly on the thermals.

Like vultures, she thought.

A crow cawed loudly overhead and flapped languidly across the path, alighting on the grass in front of her.

Laura's mobile rang, startling her. She answered it, walking swiftly along the path now.

'It's Ellen. Ellen Sibson. Have you found her?'

'Not yet. I've just reached the nature reserve.'

'I've called the parents of all the girls she's friends with in her class and no one took her back home. Molly said that she saw her waiting for you in the playground.'

Laura broke into a jog again.

'I'm going to wait here for the police. They'll call you on your mobile. Please phone me as soon as you see her, won't you?'

'I suggest you ring Aaron and find out where Levi is,' snapped Laura. 'None of you took his bullying seriously. If anything has happened to Autumn, I'll hold the school responsible.'

She hung up and slipped the phone back in her pocket.

She rounded the bend in the path and reached the bridge over the railway. There was no one there. The clouds and the growing darkness had created a strange pattern of blackness on the concrete as what little light was left filtered through the metal bars overhead. Her footsteps echoed hollowly. In the middle she stopped. Suspended over the railway tracks, the wind sang through the wire cage, humming and keening. Laura forced herself to stand on tiptoes, pressing her forehead against the cold metal bars, peering down between them. It was hard to make anything out apart from the tar-black sleepers and the pewter gleam of the tracks. As far as she could tell it didn't look as if anyone was lying down there. She checked the other side and then walked to the end of Briar Lane.

The untarmacked road was pitted with potholes and jagged with exposed grit and stone. It was lit by the sodium glare of the street lamps. After the nature reserve, the lights and the noise from the road were almost overwhelming. A man and his dog were walking towards the school. There was no one else around. Laura turned and ran back towards Narroways, her feet drumming against the concrete, the shadows and the vertical bars making her eyes strobe.

Her phone rang again.

'Any sign?' asked Mrs Sibson without introducing herself.

Laura shook her head without speaking. She started to walk through the damp, tussocky grass towards the hill, the highest peak in the reserve, stumbling in the dark. One star had risen in the east.

Not a star, she thought bitterly – *Jupiter*. She only knew it was a planet because of Aaron.

As if she'd spoken, Mrs Sibson said, 'Mr George called Aaron. Levi's with him. He went to his dad's flat in Filton, straight from school, and was there by a quarter to four. I don't think Levi could have had anything to do with this. With whatever has happened to Autumn.'

Laura hung up on her again. Why hadn't she brought a torch? In her haste to leave the house she hadn't thought about it. Her phone glowed weakly in her hand and she held it out in front of her, using the light from the screen to see where she was going. Her mobile gave out a ghostly light but it didn't reveal much of the meadow. She pressed the home button again, to keep the phone bright, and it gave a bleat. She looked fleetingly at the screen in case it was a text, in case by some miracle it was one of the parents saying Autumn was safely with them. There was an image of a battery, a sliver of red at one end, and a message, warning her that only ten per cent of charge was remaining.

Oh God, she thought. She'd need to preserve the battery so that she could speak to the police. She switched her mobile off and put it back in her pocket. She started to run up the hill. She fell and braced herself with her hands, her palms damp with mud and clover leaves.

At the top, she hauled air into her lungs and turned in a slow circle, surveying the nature reserve spread below her. The place was deserted. The moon was starting to rise; it was on the cusp of being full, but low in the sky and behind the dense barrage of clouds, its stone-cold glow barely illuminated the meadow. She couldn't bear to think of what might have happened to Autumn. If she'd simply fallen, would she even see her in the growing darkness? Would a small body lying in the leaves or the shrubs, the tangle of briar at the edge of the wood, or here, in the open grass, be visible in the twilight?

She switched on her phone. The ominous red line within the waning battery had grown thinner. There was a message – it was from a police officer who was with Mrs Sibson, asking her to ring him back urgently. She started to key the number into her phone. There was the sound of metal warping, an electric hum and then a loud shriek. It was a train, roaring down the track, heading into the city centre. She could hardly breathe. What if Autumn was down there and she hadn't seen her? The train was brightly lit and almost empty. There were two people in one carriage, facing forward, their expressions vacant. Perhaps they were heading home after working out of town or maybe they were on their way from the suburbs into the city to begin a night shift: a nurse, a cleaner, a refuse collector; the unseen, unsung people who toiled to keep the city operating.

Laura looked down at the cliff, its raw, wet jagged clay and sandstone skin like something flayed. The light from the train fractured against its surface. She couldn't see a small child lying broken on its slope. The brake lamps at the back and the afterglow of its empty carriages made the train seem like an old-fashioned Roman candle, blazing into the night through the narrow chasm gouged into the rock.

In the tail end of those lights, Laura saw something, a half-familiar shape.

It was on the flat part of the meadow, by the edge of the wood. In the dying of the light, she'd seen a flare of red, too bright to be natural. She ran down the slope, leaping over the uneven grass. In the darkness, the cold air against her face, it felt less as if she were running and more like falling, falling towards some terrible, nameless deed.

She turned on her phone and held it out in front of her as she reached the bottom of the hill. A small, dark object lay by a stunted hawthorn – Autumn's satchel. In the eerie light from her mobile, below a dogwood, the thorny stems laden with clusters of hips, she could see what looked like a child in a red coat lying on the ground. But the red had leaked and spread across the grass in an enchanted circle. Every blade was coated with it. Autumn's hair was slicked back and damp with maroon darkness; a frighteningly vivid patch of skin shone white against the brilliant red that covered her face.

The phone in her hand chirped and died. Laura was left standing in the pitch dark in front of the body of her child.

She knelt down in the wet, blood-soaked grass and turned Autumn's face towards her. The child was cold. She felt for a pulse in her neck but there was no tell-tale flutter beneath her fingertips.

She bent close to her daughter's mouth. Her breath came faint against her cheek.

Thank God. She's alive!

She ran her hands over the small face, wiping away the red stuff. Laura felt the child's lashes tremble against her palms. Autumn suddenly opened her eyes. They gleamed, black and blank.

'Oh, my darling. What happened? Where are you hurt?'

Autumn's lips moved. She struggled to speak. She tried to sit up. Laura helped her, wondering if she was doing the right thing. Should she put her in the recovery position? What if she'd broken any bones? Now that the sun had set, and overshadowed as they were by the wood, she couldn't tell where the blood was coming from. Autumn was lying just a few metres from the path through the trees. She'd missed her, Laura realized, in her haste, because as she'd come out of the wood, she'd hurried straight on, glancing around, but not directly behind her.

Autumn sat up, and then held out her hand. Laura helped the child to her feet. She picked her up and Autumn clung to her, wrapping her legs around her waist and her arms about her neck. She rested her head in the crook of Laura's neck and she could feel the wetness, sticky against her own skin, pooling below her collar bone. She carried her child carefully through the wood and into the allotments.

It was only when she reached the end of the allotments, and had to balance Autumn on one hip and hold her with one aching arm, so she could open the gate, that she realized Autumn smelt strange. It was the metal, cold beneath her palm, that made her think of it. Clinging to the child was the odour of the outdoors – damp mud and decaying leaves – but there was another smell too. It was fresh, almost like plastic. There was no nausea-inducing iron tang. Autumn did not smell of blood.

She staggered into the house with her daughter and saw them both reflected in the hall mirror. They were like trauma victims, their faces white, the pupils of their eyes dilated, covered in red, some of it wet, other patches dried and flaking, twigs and dead grass sticking to them. She eased Autumn to the floor. Autumn still had not spoken.

'I'm going to call an ambulance,' Laura said. 'We need to get you to Accident and Emergency.'

'No,' whispered Autumn. 'It's paint, Mum.'

'Paint?'

'Red paint. I'm okay.' Her voice was wooden. 'I want a bath.'

Tenderly, Laura helped her remove her clothes, which were all soaked. Autumn was shivering as she stepped out of her trousers, and then pulled her vest over her head. Her daughter's body was smooth, pale, perfect. Laura could not see a single cut or fresh bruise on her – only the large one on her arm from gymnastics, now the dull brown of a rotten apple. She wrapped Autumn in a towel and ran a bath.

As the child slid under the surface, the water turned scarlet, clouds of it spiralling upwards, a red mist that obscured her body. Laura put her hand over her mouth. Autumn surfaced and wiped her hair out of her eyes. She smeared the remaining red across her face as she did so.

'What happened?' asked Laura for what felt like the tenth time.

'You weren't there to pick me up. You're always late,' she said, sounding as sullen as a teenager. 'I walked home. When I got to the bridge going into Narroways—'

'You should have waited! I told you not to walk home by yourself at night through the nature reserve!'

Autumn gave her a warning look. Laura regretted her anger instantly. She wished that she'd apologized instead, for not being there when she had so wanted to be early. Autumn picked up her sponge and pumped some shower gel onto it.

'A boy followed me. He started pushing me. Then he threw paint over me. He hit me with something. And then I don't remember anything until you came.'

'Where did he hit you?'

'Here. Maybe it was the paint. It was in a big bottle.'

Laura felt the back of Autumn's head. She parted her hair. Her daughter's scalp was skull-white. There was a slight bump but she couldn't see a cut and there was no blood.

'A boy?'

'Yes. A big boy. I don't know him. He's not from our school.'

Laura watched as Autumn washed away the paint. She seemed by some miracle to be okay and, apart from the bump on her head, she had no other injuries. And the paint, thank goodness, was water-based.

'We still need to get you to the hospital to check your head. And make a statement to the police.'

'No,' said Autumn.

'So it definitely wasn't Levi?'

Autumn shrugged and didn't look at Laura. 'I never saw him before.'

Could it have been a random attack, Laura wondered?

Out loud she said, 'Maybe Levi asked a friend of his to throw the paint at you. I'm going to ring the police,' she added, getting to her feet.

'No,' said Autumn again.

'I have to, love. Mrs Sibson called them. They'll be looking for you.'

Well, I won't speak to them. It's your fault. If you hadn't pushed Levi over, he wouldn't be doing this to me.'

The words, so full of bitter resentment, sounded unspeakably harsh coming from such a young girl. Laura turned away from her daughter so she wouldn't see her tears, or her anger, a cocktail of relief, guilt and anxiety. Autumn was suddenly growing up, lashing out as a way of asserting her independence – and yet, lying in the bath, she looked utterly child-like, naked, vulnerable, defenceless. Laura resented every bruise that had ever marked that precious skin. She wished there was some way she could protect Autumn for ever.

'I'll make you a sandwich to eat on the way to the hospital,' she said.

AUTUMN

At break Levi had strolled over and sat down next to her. Molly and Olive immediately leapt off the bench and ran to the other side of the playground. Autumn started to follow them, but Levi put out one hand and grabbed the back of her jumper, pulling her down. He was so close she could smell the Chinese he'd had the night before, mixed with the chemical-fresh smell of his laundry powder.

'Look at this face,' he said, gesturing with his other hand, and glancing at his posse of boys, all hanging off the climbing frame opposite her. 'Not even a mother could love it.'

The boys sniggered and she felt herself go rigid. He cupped her chin in one hand and shook her head so hard that her cheeks wobbled.

He laughed. 'Check it out – she's a little fatty.' He leant towards her, his knuckles hard against her spine, and whispered, 'Never mind. You'll get used to being ugly.'

As she waited for her mum at the end of the day, she was terrified Levi would come and taunt her again. Her mum had said she had to wait for her, she wasn't allowed to walk home after school on her own. And then she hadn't been there. She was always late. It wasn't fair. She was supposed to be worried about her. She was supposed to protect her.

She was so relieved to see Levi run off as soon as the school gates opened – and so cross with her mum for making her stand there on her own, looking stupid, that she decided to walk home on her own. She wanted to make her mother worry about her to teach her not to be so late. She wanted to punish her. But in her relief and her rage, she didn't realize she was being followed until she was in the nature reserve and she couldn't turn back.

He waited until she'd reached the other side of the bridge and the dog walkers and the other school children had vanished. She felt something wet against her hair – like rain but it was too big for a single rain drop. She put her hand to her head and when she looked at her fingers, they were covered in red.

She screamed and he started laughing and that was when she knew. She ran across the meadow and he caught up with her easily, throwing crimson liquid that splashed across her and the grass; a violent red that blossomed and slashed her tights, her skirt, her new coat. He was a big boy, maybe fourteen, with an adult's body and a child's face and a curiously vacant expression that frightened her almost as much as one of Levi's smiles. She thought he might be one of the kids who'd torn up her paintings.

And then he hurled the bottle at her. She saw it arc through the air and she looked up and it poured down over her face, cold, vermillion, cruelly vivid against the deep-grey sky, and she fell forward, blinded, a red film over her eyes, and then the bottle hit her on the back of the head and she dropped to her knees.

'That's for Levi,' he shouted.

In that split second she knew there was no point telling her mum that Levi was really responsible. Her mum would only make everything worse. Like she always did.

She fell onto all fours, unable to see, tears and snot and paint dripping down her face. She knew it was paint straight away from the smell. There was something oddly comforting about it; it reminded her of the studio where they'd had art classes with Mr Wu at her old school. But she couldn't stop feeling as if she really had been hurt – it was the colour, bright as blood, the visceral shock of it.

She wasn't quite sure how it happened, how it was that she ended up lying under the dogwood, the thorns arching over her, the grass high and wet and slick with the red stuff all about her. She thought of the fairy story her mum used to tell her about a child who fell asleep in the green, green grass under a rowan tree and then the little people came and stole him away. For seven long years. She wasn't sure what time it was, how long she had lain there, the paint chill and drying on her skin, the dew seeping into her clothes. When they let him go, no one he loved was alive. And after a while, it felt as if she and the changeling-child in the fairy story were one, that an absence had opened up in her heart – for if she returned, after seven long years, no one would know who she was.

LAURA

She had that bilious feeling you get when you stand too close to the edge and you don't want to look down at the drop below you. She was sitting in the car and she couldn't see where the cliff ended. She leant as close to the steering wheel as she could. *It must be just a metre or two away*, she thought. The grass was deceptive, long and lush. It could be hiding the cliff edge. She felt dizzy just thinking about it.

Perhaps it had been an old quarry. Now, many metres below, was a lake, artificially circular, bound by sheer-sided cliffs. The water was deep and cold and jade-green, hinting at unimagined depths. She thought of what might be at the bottom: the sharp wires of broken shopping trolleys, burnt-out cars, glutinous strands of weeds that would wrap themselves around your ankles and hold you fast as your last breath was sucked from your lungs.

As she leant forwards, the car started to roll. She snatched at the handbrake but it was slack in her palm and didn't stop the vehicle. She stamped on the brake and her foot went flat to the floor without hindering the progress of the car, which was now beginning to speed up. The bonnet eased out into space. She pressed the catch on her seat belt and yanked open the door. As she was falling sideways out of the car, the damp grass rushing up to meet her, she remembered.

Autumn is in the car.

She was sitting in the back in a pink baby seat, fastened in securely. She was two years old. She was wearing her favourite cardigan, the one with the lilac flowers on it, and she was watching her mother.

I've saved myself and left my daughter in the car.

She pushed herself upright and in slow motion held out her hand as if she could arrest the path of the car. It lurched over the edge and for a sickening couple of seconds was suspended in mid-air. Laura scrambled to her feet and rushed to the cliff edge. The car slid, nose first, into the lake and disappeared. Autumn was strapped in. She wasn't old enough to undo the buckle of her car seat. The door was open, which meant it would fill with water and sink immediately. Laura started to scream.

She sat up, drenched in cold sweat, the dream clinging to her still.

How could I? How could I have left her in the car?

She wiped her damp forehead and then shivered. She looked at her watch. It was a little after midnight. She rose and wrapped her dressing gown around her and then went to check on Autumn.

They were both so tired. After she'd called Mrs Sibson, and the police officer who'd left her a message, she'd made Autumn a sandwich and a flask of tea for herself and then driven to A&E. It had taken over three hours for a doctor to look at Autumn's head. By that time the bump had gone down and she claimed not to have a headache. They were allowed home – the doctor had told Laura to keep an eye on Autumn and make sure she had plenty of fluids. Someone – Autumn said she wouldn't recognize him again – had poured red paint on her. What would the police have said or done if she'd told them the details? There was nothing substantial to say. There were no witnesses and there was nothing to link the event back to Levi, although Laura was sure he was at the bottom of it. Autumn must have been frightened, terrified even, Laura thought miserably, but she hadn't been badly hurt.

And then she remembered the article she'd read in *The Washington Post* about the parents who'd hired a teenager to attack their child's bully. It was Aaron. It had to be. He must have hired the boy to terrorize her daughter and make it look as if Levi were not involved. If she complained about Levi now, when he'd clearly been at home with his father throughout this evening, she'd seem malicious, vengeful even.

She pushed open Autumn's bedroom door and looked in. The room was lit with a cold, blue light. It was coming from the clock in the corner, the one she'd bought her daughter when she was a toddler. It had a smiling star in the centre and seven stars around the sides, representing how many hours there were until morning. Autumn must have turned up the brightness, she realized.

She might not have had the courage to go to the police and the headmaster was unlikely to support her if she went back to talk to him – particularly if Autumn said that the boy who'd thrown paint over her had not been Levi – but she had to do something. She had to do whatever it took to stop him.

Autumn's bed was empty, the duvet pushed back, obscuring the row of toys at the end of the bed. She felt as if a shard of ice had been lodged in her chest. Perhaps her daughter was in the bathroom, she thought. She listened for a moment but couldn't hear anything. She was about to go downstairs and check when she saw her. Autumn had wrapped herself in the curtain and was standing staring through the window. Her legs were like thin, white sticks beneath the bunched-up fabric. She was looking at the park opposite. Through the gap in the curtains, Laura could see the steel bright shadows cast by the empty swings.

One of them was still moving.

SATURDAY 3 NOVEMBER

LAURA

Laura and Autumn left early the next morning. She was frightened about what the police would do. She wondered how long it would take to complete the witness statements from the children who had seen her push Levi. Hiding in Ruth's garden was not going to prevent the inevitable from happening. But it would stop her from thinking about it. Just for a short while.

I just want one last morning uninterrupted by a police investigation, the threat of Social Services, Aaron and his nastiness.

The engine coughed and spluttered. It was freezing, the pavements glassine with black ice.

Come on, car, don't die on me.

The engine made a noise like a patient with tuberculosis, a dying wheeze.

Autumn was most definitely not pleased about being woken up so early and bundled into warm clothes to sit in a garden in Clifton when it was minus two degrees outside, but it would distract her too from what had happened yesterday evening. Laura sat up and sucked in a deep breath of arctic air. She would get through this. She'd texted Jacob to say they were leaving earlier than planned but to come later, at the arranged time, if he wanted. No point getting him up at the crack of dawn too. She blew on her gloved hands and turned the key in the ignition once more. If only she could have bought a new car instead of making do with this rattling heap of junk. The engine gave an asthmatic gasp and burst into life.

Thank God.

They drove in silence over to Clifton. The city was shrouded in a chill mist, the sun like a blood-red yolk on the edge of the jagged skyline. *Thank goodness we finished planting the grasses last week before the frost*, she thought.

Today they could concentrate on fitting part of the decking. A cool white, wintry light glazed the buildings on the highest hill: Will's memorial, the unsightly chimney from the hospital, the modernist cathedral in Clifton. The jumble of styles and eras lent the city the semblance of a medieval Roman town. Laura drove the long way round, up past the Clifton Suspension Bridge, strung like an a engineer's dream over a river sinking into the mud. Leigh Woods was on the far side, the trees dark, bereft of leaves, clawing at the sky.

It was too early to call on Ruth so she parked around the back. She had the key to the padlock on the garden door. To her surprise, it wasn't locked. She pushed it open and it sagged on its hinges, falling forwards. She held the handle and manoeuvred it enough to allow the two of them to squeeze through.

Laura jumped. Ruth was standing in the middle of the garden. She was wearing a blue flannel dressing gown and a pair of men's pyjamas. She had wellington boots on her feet. Her face was raw, her eyes pink-rimmed and her hair was standing on end.

'Ruth!' said Laura, reaching for Autumn, an automatic reflex at even the smallest hint of trouble.

The ground beneath her feet felt unstable, uneven. She glanced down. She was standing on sand. And then she saw the rest of the garden. The bags of sand they'd bought to mix in with the clay had been poured out over the garden. The driftwood salvaged from Burnham Beach was blackened and shattered. The baby grasses had been pulled up, trampled, hacked down. The exotic acacia with its royal-purple leaves had been sawed in two. The wood for the decking was gouged and splintered. On every single surface, the walls, the floor, Ruth's house, her bench, one word was spray-painted over and over again in bright red.

Bitch.

There was a screech and a groan, followed by a crack as the garden door swung completely off its hinges and crashed to the ground, just missing Laura and Autumn.

'Sorry about that,' said Jacob as he walked in. 'I didn't realize it was... Christ, what's happened here?' He paused and looked around.

Bitch, bitch, bitch.

The colour of the red made her feel nauseous, a visceral reminder of finding Autumn the night before.

'I'm so sorry, Ruth,' said Laura. 'What a terrible thing to wake up to. Did you hear anything in the night?'

Ruth shook her head, as if she didn't trust herself to speak.

Jacob picked up a bit of driftwood and sniffed at it. He nudged a can of spray-paint with his toe.

'Do you think this is anything to do with Levi and his dad?' Autumn asked.

'This has something to do with you?' snapped Ruth.

'I... I... well, I don't know.'

Ruth's expression hardened.

'It could be a man I know. He's waging some kind of hate campaign against me. Autumn's bike was wrecked – we found it in front of our house the other day, the tyres slashed, spray-paint all over the frame. The same colour as this.'

'I'd like you to leave,' said Ruth, pulling her dressing gown more tightly around herself. 'I appreciate all the work you've done but I can't take the risk. I hope you understand.'

'Have you phoned the police?' asked Jacob.

She looked at him sharply. 'Both of you. Please don't come here again.'

'But…' said Laura.

Ruth turned and went back inside, her boots crunching on the sand.

They went to a greasy spoon just outside Clifton Village and once Jacob had ordered, he winked at Autumn and disappeared outside. The only reason Laura knew that Jacob was upset was because he smoked two cigarettes, one after the other, rolling the second one as he smoked the first.

Laura was still reeling from the destruction of the garden. She closed her eyes and massaged her temples. The word *Bitch* shone in scarlet in her mind.

'I said I didn't want anything to eat,' said Autumn as the waiter put a plate of scrambled eggs, beans and toast in front of her.

Laura ignored her. Autumn had been looking peaky for a few days now, and when she'd bathed her to remove the red paint last night, she was convinced that the child had lost weight, which she could ill afford. A small, nasty part of her wanted to force Autumn to eat the scrambled eggs precisely because she didn't want to. She waved at Jacob to tell him his breakfast had arrived and he stubbed out his roll-up and came inside, breathing out one last cloud of cigarette smoke.

'We should at least go back and clear up,' said Laura, taking a sip of her cappuccino.

Jacob shrugged. 'She made it pretty clear she doesn't want us around.' He rubbed his shaven head with one hand and stretched his legs out under the table. He had a sharp nose and chin and large brown eyes with thick black eyelashes; the eyes of a spaniel in the face of a weasel. Or a thug. 'Do you want to tell me what this is about?' He glanced from one to the other of them.

Autumn looked away.

'A boy in the year above Autumn has been bullying her. He's called Levi. It's become…' she searched for the words, 'like a revenge attack. His father – Aaron – is an IT consultant and he repaired my laptop. Since then – I mean, since I reported his son's bullying to the school – he's hacked into it and destroyed the hard drive. I've lost everything: my photos, my music, my college work, my poetry.'

Jacob whistled.

'Before he wiped the laptop, Aaron had access to all my records, including the brochure and website we were making with the photos of Ruth's garden – and her address,' said Laura.

Jacob turned to Autumn. 'Do you think the boy could have done it? I mean, he's only ten, right? Seems a bit drastic for a ten-year-old.'

'He's twelve,' said Autumn.

'What? He can't be. Eleven at the most,' said Laura.

Autumn shook her head. 'His mum took him to live with her family in Barbados for a year and when he came back, the school made him repeat a year.'

That explained it, thought Laura, why he was so tall and so knowing, somehow, compared to the other school children. She wondered what else Autumn knew about Levi that she hadn't shared with her.

'Still,' said Jacob, 'he'd have to be one pretty angry twelve-year-old.'

'You provoked him,' said Autumn, crossing her arms and sitting back in her chair.

Jacob paused, one fork full of bacon and egg halfway to his mouth, looking at Laura to see how she would react.

'Please don't be rude,' said Laura. 'I'm trying to help.'

Autumn rolled her eyes. 'And every time you try to "help"' – she made an exaggerated quotation mark gesture in the air – 'it gets worse.'

'Where did she get that from?' asked Jacob.

'That's what my friend, Tilly, does.'

'I'm sorry, sweetheart, I know things are incredibly tough for you at the moment, but I'm doing my best.'

'I didn't know you wrote poems,' said Jacob, attempting to change the subject.

'Yes. They're rubbish,' said Autumn, folding her arms again. 'And anyway, it's only one gardening job. I mean, that's so lame. It's like Poppy says, you can't have a business with one client.'

Laura tried not to think of their fledgling company – destroyed before it had even got off the ground. And since when had her daughter started quoting Tilly and Poppy? She looked at Jacob.

He shrugged again, grinned and picked up his coffee cup. 'I like this new Autumn. You should talk like that to Levi. That would show him.'

'I don't think it was Levi,' said Laura quietly. 'Jacob's right. It's not something a child would do.'

She noticed that Jacob's coffee cup trembled against the saucer as he put it back. Too much caffeine, nicotine and unprocessed emotion. Autumn slumped in her chair, a sulky expression on her face. She was about to tell her daughter to eat her eggs, but instead found herself saying something quite different.

'You know, you really should try and stand up for yourself. I know it's hard, I'm shy too, but we could both learn to be more assertive.'

'An eye for an eye,' said Jacob, and waved at the waiter, miming that he wanted another black coffee.

'What do you mean?' asked Autumn, sounding a bit more like her normal self.

Laura suddenly flushed and turned away, ashamed. She hadn't told Jacob what she'd done to Levi.

'I'm not a big guy, right?' continued Jacob. 'I mean, for a soldier. I'm smaller than average and some of those men, they're built like a brick… They're quite broad, is what I'm saying. But I had a reputation for being hard.' He put his cup of cold coffee to one side. 'It happened when I started out in the Marines. Some of the older guys were pushing me about, you know, new boy, thought they could intimidate me. And one day, I lost it. I gave one of them a beating he'd never forget and after that it was all cool. No one messed with me.'

'Are you telling me to beat Levi up?' said Autumn.

'That's not what Jacob is saying, is it?' Laura poked his shin under the table with her foot. She didn't believe Jacob's story. It sounded far too sanitized.

He held up his hands and the tattoos on his forearms flexed. 'I'm just saying.'

The waiter handed him another coffee.

'What we need are some skills. For self-defence,' stressed Laura. 'Not for beating anyone up. Just so you can protect yourself if someone attacks you first.'

She and Autumn both looked at Jacob. He glanced from one to the other of them and put down his cup.

'Right, girls, eat up those eggs and beans. You're going to need the energy.'

'What for?' asked Autumn, sitting up straighter.

Jacob smiled and winked at Autumn. 'We're going up on The Downs to teach you some self-defence.'

When they reached The Downs, the frost was beginning to melt, the grass poking, livid green, through its casing of ice. It was still bitterly cold. Jackdaws cawed and squabbled, falling like flakes of soot above black trees strangled by knots of dark ivy.

Jacob opened the back of his Land Rover, which had his gardening tools and a couple of boxes of kit for British Military Fitness. He took out some pads and boxing gloves. The simple act of handling the equipment seemed to change Jacob. He switched into his teaching-soldier mode. He threw the gloves at Autumn and Laura, who put them on slowly, making faces. They stank.

'Right,' he barked, jumping into a semi-crouched stance, the muscles in his thighs raised, his fists by his face. 'Your six senses are here' – he circled a hand around his head, – 'sight, sound, speech, taste, smell.'

'*Six* senses?' said Laura, teasing him.

He scowled back. 'You've got to protect your face, is the point. Even more important, you've got to take care of your brain. It's encased in a thick layer of bone –' He wrapped a knuckle on his shaven head '– but your brain itself is like jelly. If you allow yourself to be hit, your brain will shunt into your skull and that's not good. More than likely, you'll fall backwards, prang your head on the ground, and your brain will smack into the bone again. Not good. So always, always keep a fist up to protect your face.'

He showed them how to stand in the same stance as himself, a bunched fist at his hip.

'If someone comes towards you, back away. Hold out your left arm to create space, keep your left foot forward, this hand, your right, is here, ready to throw a punch. Or step forward and kick.'

He put pads over his hands and made the two of them take turns to punch and then kick the pads. He taught them three types of kick: a heel strike – *directly into the guts* – one into the groin and a side kick – *scorch that artery, girls, you'll give him a dead leg.* They practised moving backwards and forwards in the protective stance, keeping their right foot back, one hand protecting their face, as Jacob aimed slow slaps with the pads at them and they dodged out of the way before throwing a punch or kicking back.

Autumn was much lighter and more nimble on her feet than Laura, easily ducking and rocking backwards and forwards on the balls of her feet.

'Best thing to do is run. Don't engage,' said Jacob. 'But if you have to, do maximum damage and then get the hell out.'

Laura watched as Autumn's punches landed, light as feathers, on

Jacob's pads. She suddenly felt terrified. She thought about what Levi had done to her daughter: taunted her, frightened her, destroyed her paintings, her confidence, her sense of self. Instead of a bright, thoughtful little girl, glowing with good health, Autumn was thin and wan with dark shadows, a pained expression in her eyes; a sickly simulacrum of her former self.

Laura swung her weight forward onto her left leg, twisting from her right hip. As for Levi's father, Aaron, he had effectively isolated her from her friends, cut her off from her mother, father, brother and destroyed everything she owned on her computer. Between the two of them, they had turned every day into one where Autumn dreaded going to school and Laura was terrified of what would be done to them. Her fist, curled at her waist, thumb tucked in, spiralled towards Jacob, the entire force of her body pounding through her shoulder and into the pad, as if she could punch straight through it.

Jacob staggered slightly. 'Good one,' he said, looking at her with surprise.

They stopped at lunchtime and Laura thanked Jacob.

'Any time,' he said, loading the pads and gloves back into the car.

'My hands stink. That's disgusting,' said Autumn.

'Are you okay? About this morning, I mean?' asked Laura.

Jacob hesitated for a moment and then said, 'I could use a drink. What are you doing tonight?'

Laura thought of her dead computer, the cancelled Netflix account, the likely inaccessibility of the Internet, her lost friendships, the report she'd have to give to the police about Ruth's vandalized garden.

'I could use a drink too. Come over for some supper.'

* * *

'I meant what I said,' said Jacob, draining the last of the red wine from his glass.

They were in the sitting room, the fire roaring next to them. Earlier that afternoon, two officers had come round to take a statement about the vandalized garden. Neither of them had seemed particularly engaged, as if they had already concluded that the perpetrator would not be caught and it was a waste of their time and effort. Laura had said Aaron Jablonski was the culprit. Neither officer bothered to hide their scepticism that an IT consultant would be involved in what they considered was clearly a random attack. One of them, PC David King, said they had found a can of spray-paint but it had no fingerprints on it, as if whoever had used it had worn gloves.

They had, though, followed up her lead because, as they were eating risotto, PC King called back and said that they had spoken to Mr Jablonski, who had denied he'd been near the garden or even knew of Laura's garden-design business. He'd shown PC King his time-sheets, which confirmed that he'd been working, and he claimed that he'd taken his son with him.

Autumn had been more confident, less angry, happier, hungrier. She'd eaten lunch and all of the risotto Laura had made for their dinner. As Laura predicted, the Internet had stopped functioning. Fortunately, Jacob had brought the new *Pirates* DVD with him, which Autumn had been pleased about, and they'd all giggled as they watched it. Autumn had gone to bed with a smile on her face for the first time in the past ten days.

After a glass of wine with, an ex-marine in the house, Laura had to admit she felt much safer. Jacob had quietly managed to drink more than half a bottle during the meal and the film. He crouched by the fire and pulled the cork from a new one. Even from across the room, Laura could smell the newly released aroma of black currants and leather.

'If you think you're going to be attacked, do maximum damage. If someone asks you for your phone on a dark night in an alleyway, you must retaliate with a pre-emptive strike: full intensity, all-out aggression. Kick him in the groin or the knee cap. Drive your thumb through his eye into his brain. Punch him in the throat.'

Laura shuddered and then thought, *I have to do whatever it takes to protect my daughter.*

'Course,' Jacob continued, 'you're relying on the shock of what you've done to give you enough time to run for your life. If you attack someone who is used to being hit, who's used to pain – a proper boxer or martial arts expert – he won't be shocked and you probably won't have hurt him that much. But your average civilian mugger is not like that.'

Laura paused, her glass of wine half-way to her lips.

She thought of Aaron, sitting so close to her, her leg accidentally brushing his thigh, saying, *It's a two-thousand-year-old Korean martial art. It means 'the way of the foot and the fist'.*

It wasn't the average civilian mugger she wanted to protect herself and Autumn from.

Jacob smiled at her expression and shrugged. 'Just saying.'

They sat in silence for a while, both of them watching the fire dancing in the grate.

After a few moments, Jacob said, 'You definitely think it was Aaron? Who smashed up the garden?'

She shrugged.

'I don't buy it. It looks like a random, impersonal crime, uncon- nected to you, or even to Ruth.'

'It's too much of a coincidence. Every time I've acted – complaining to the school about Levi, for instance – there's been a response. My emails have been corrupted, the hard drive on my laptop was wiped, Autumn's bike was vandalized, the Internet is down. It has to be Aaron. I gave him my passwords when he was fixing my computer.'

His brow furrowed. 'It could still be a fluke. You got an email virus and that wiped your laptop. Who knows why the Internet isn't working. That kind of technical shit happens all the time. And Autumn's bike – another random act of vandalism.'

'That's what the police said.'

'There you go. You've had a run of bad luck. It's tough, having to watch a kid bully your daughter, but I can't see some IT consultant behaving like a psycho and spray-painting "Bitch" all over a garden we've been landscaping.'

Was it that simple, she wondered? Was it all a connection she'd made in her own mind? She certainly had no proof that Aaron was behind any of the malicious attacks.

'You might be right. But I bought Autumn a mobile, to be on the safe side. Can I give her your number? Just in case she can't get hold of me?'

'Sure.'

After a few moments, to change the subject, she said, 'Why did you leave the Marines?'

He shrugged. 'It was the right thing to do.'

He was still sitting on the floor near the fire, his face half turned away from her, the light from the flames flickering across his sharp features. Eventually he said, 'I was in Northern Ireland. We were staking out a house, way out near Lough Neagh, a deserted, run-down farm house. Looked the most unlikely place, but it was meant to be the headquarters of a terrorist cell. We were waiting for the IRA to turn up.'

As he talked, Laura could picture it: the soft, grey-green dusk in the Northern Irish countryside, the smell of cow manure, bats flitting past, clumps of nettles growing in rank profusion in the unkempt yard. There were three of them, hiding in a ditch beneath a blackthorn hedge, water seeping into their boots, thorns pricking their necks. Jacob said that his mind *had not been quite right* for some time.

'It's not like going to Iraq. There they don't speak your language, they don't wear the same clothes as you, they don't worship the same god, their skin colour is different from yours. You feel justified shooting someone who is shooting at you. It's easier not to think of them as people. You know you're on the right side. But in Ireland our targets were white, they wore Levis, they shopped at Spar, they went to church on a Sunday. I couldn't get my head around it. I thought I might as well be taking pot shots at people in Bristol city centre.'

Jacob and his team waited for a couple of hours. It grew dark. No one turned up. His right foot had gone to sleep and the moon was a thin silver crescent in the sky. And then something happened. The lights came on in the kitchen. To begin with they thought the terrorists had arrived. There were no curtains and through the ill-fitting windows they could see and hear everything. It was soon obvious there were still only two people in the house. The farmer started shouting at his wife. He punched her in the face. The first time he gave her a black eye. The second time he broke her nose. She fell to the floor. The farmer kicked her savagely. After the third kick, she stopped screaming.

Jacob grew increasingly agitated. He said they had to do something. They had to stop the man before he killed the woman. The others said it was no business of theirs. They could not blow their cover. If they did, they might not intercept the cell. Jacob argued that there was no point to it, no point in being armed and highly trained, no point spending hours pumping iron to become some of the fittest men on earth, no point being on the side of the righteous, if they could not save this one woman. Ignoring the others and his orders, he climbed out of the ditch and ran across the yard.

'What did you do?' asked Laura.

'I broke down the door. And I shot the farmer through the heart.'

Laura could no longer see Jacob's face. 'What happened?'

'I was disciplined for disobedience. I went to see the farmer's wife in hospital before I was forced to leave Ireland. She spat in my face. She told me I'd murdered the only man she'd ever loved.'

'It was the right thing to do,' said Laura, 'to try and protect her.'

Jacob shook his head and turned to face her. 'No. It wasn't. The bigger picture – the terrorist cell – was what I should have been focusing on. The IRA went undercover once they knew – thanks to me – that we were watching them. Ten days later they blew up a hotel in Belfast killing five men, two kids and maiming eleven women and children. We – I – could have saved those people. That's when I left.'

Jacob finished his wine and poured another glass. He ran a hand across his eyes. 'I thought I was tough, worthy of being a Marine, but that whole incident showed me who I really was. I'm not capable of being a soldier. I haven't got what it takes.'

'It might not be a bad thing. You have compassion,' said Laura.

'It was all I ever wanted to do,' he said, 'since I was a little kid. And now I'm just, well, drifting. The only reason I get up in the morning is because I thought that we were going to do great things together.'

Laura thought of Jacob's erratic behaviour – the drinking and cigarettes, his obsessively healthy diet, the huge amount of training he continued to do, his wild and impractical ideas for gardens. The one thing that kept him anchored had been their project. Ruth's garden. And she'd ruined that for him.

Jacob grew increasingly drunk and maudlin. Laura was exhausted, physically and emotionally drained. She rubbed her eyes and stood up. 'Come on, Jacob, you should stay here tonight. The spare bed is made up.'

Not by her, she thought. Vanessa had stripped the sheets and remade it while she was at her first British Military Fitness class. Jacob, who was sitting on the floor leaning against the arm chair, clutching his empty wine glass, looked up at her. His lips were cracked and stained burgundy. She realized she'd never gone out drinking with Jacob; she'd no idea what kind of drunk he was. Would he become aggressive, or try it on with her, or simply pass out peacefully? She expected him to protest, to say he could find his own way home, or ask for more wine, but he stood up meekly enough and followed her upstairs, stumbling a little. She held the door of the spare room open for him and went to find a clean towel. When she'd returned, he was lying face down on the bed. She watched him for a moment. He didn't move so she unlaced his boots and slid them off his feet. She folded part of the quilt over him. As she shut the door, she thought of him saying softly, *You feel justified shooting someone who is shooting at you.*

SUNDAY 4 NOVEMBER

AUTUMN

She raced downstairs but there was no one in the kitchen. She ran back up the stairs again. The door to the spare room was ajar. She stood in the entrance and peeped inside. One window was open. The room smelt of frost and fresh air; it didn't smell as if a man had slept here. The bed had been made and the corners were folded unexpectedly tidily and tightly. Without Jacob, the house felt empty and lonely. Autumn lent against the doorjamb and felt the full weight of her dad's absence from her life.

In the kitchen she poured some Shreddies into a bowl. There was no milk so she picked them up and ate them with her fingers, staring out into the silent garden.

Her mum came down a bit later and made a lot of unnecessary noise, banging and bustling around. As if she was making up for Jacob leaving before breakfast. Her mum said they should *do something together* and it would *be fun*. She suggested going to the zoo, like Autumn was a little kid and not nine and a half. Autumn thought about walking past the icy cages and glass houses opaque with condensation, the animals huddled inside, the ring-tailed lemurs all in a shivery burr. Lemurs were meant to live in Madagascar with Uncle Damian, not in chilly Bristol. She shook her head.

She put her bowl in the dishwasher and went back upstairs to her bedroom. As she dressed, she looked at all her pictures on the walls. Levi was right. They were rubbish. Hobbling around, with her tights half on, she tore them down and screwed them up into paper balls and threw them in the bin. She started feeling small and stupid and ugly again and then she remembered what Jacob had said. He said she was strong and beautiful and talented. She would paint new pictures, she decided. Better ones.

Her mum came in as she was getting out her brushes and some paper and said since she didn't want to go out, she'd make a start on assembling her wardrobe. When they'd first moved to Bristol, her mum had bought a whole load of new furniture from Ikea but so far she hadn't got around to putting it together. You can pay someone to do it, but her mum said that was expensive and she was going to do it herself.

It was actually kind of comforting working sort-of together. The day passed so quickly; she felt as if she was bursting with ideas. Her mum, though, did quite a lot of swearing and apologizing and nearly crying and going back to read the instructions again and again and searching for little bits and pieces and getting Autumn to hold things, which she found annoying, but she supposed it was okay because the wardrobe was for her.

Eventually it was finished and they both gave a big cheer and hung all of Autumn's clothes in it. One door didn't quite close properly, but her mum said *it will have to do.* Then she cleared all the cardboard up and carried it and her tools downstairs and said she was going to make a start on the bookshelves for the sitting room. When Autumn went to get a snack in the afternoon, all the tools were lying in the hall and the wood for the bookcases was in the sitting room and all the books were still in boxes.

Autumn looked through all the pictures she'd done that day: a woman carrying a custard white squash like a soup tureen, another waving a maple leaf, a child playing with a conker, shiny mahogany brown, as big as a ball. They were all tiny and precise, smaller than her pictures normally were; they looked like the miniatures in Tilly's house. But it wasn't only that they were so little, she realized when it was time to pack away her paints: the colours were much darker too and everyone had a little black line for a mouth. No one was smiling.

The one she liked best, though, was a self-portrait. It didn't look much like her, but sitting on her lap was her imaginary baby sister. The one she thought of often, the one she couldn't talk to her mum about because, if she did, her mum became upset. Maybe it was her dad's fault: he didn't want another baby so he and mum got divorced. And now there wouldn't be another baby. Ever.

Autumn's imaginary sister was called Emily. Sometimes Emily was a little girl with dark hair and sometimes she was blonde. At other times she imagined her as a small bird, a lost baby soul, fluttering nearby, her downy feathers tickling Autumn's cheeks. Today she drew Emily with light-brown hair and grey eyes, just like her big sister. She pinned the picture to her wall, right in the middle.

MONDAY 5 NOVEMBER

AUTUMN

They drove to school that morning and, as she walked from the car to the playground, she felt as if she were one of the girls in her pictures, tall and thin, holding a sweet chestnut like a giant grenade, spiky and green, ready to hurl it. Her mum kept trying to talk to her but she didn't want to speak to her. She interfered and interfered and made everything worse. And all she went on about was Levi, Levi, Levi.

They were late and when they reached the playground, it was empty, like there had been a calamity and all the people had died. Mrs Sibson was standing at the classroom window and when she saw them, she disappeared. A moment later, she opened the front door and walked towards them.

'Is she okay?' she called from a distance of a few metres, as if Autumn had no voice of her own.

'Like I said on Friday, it was paint. She was extremely frightened, as you can imagine, but she wasn't hurt,' her mum answered. Her mum didn't look at Mrs Sibson. She crouched down in front of her. 'I will be here to pick you up. Do not leave without me. And ignore anything that Levi says to you. We will get through this together. You are beautiful, just remember that.'

Autumn looked down at her toes as her mum made this little speech. She hoped no one was watching them but she knew they would be. Mrs Sibson put her hand on her shoulder and left it there until they reached the entrance. As they were about to go inside,

Autumn turned to look at her mum. She was jogging across the playground and had just reached the gate. Autumn felt bad. Her mum would be late too, and Barney would be cross. She felt guilty that she'd ignored her mum all the way to school. She held up her hand to wave, but her mum didn't look back.

As they went inside and the smell of the school hit her – bleach and oranges and smelly shoes – she tried to remember what her mum had told her. It was something she'd said last week. When her mum was little, she'd travelled backwards and forwards between Namibia and London so Granny and Grandad could carry on studying in Africa. Each time she started again at school, the girls would tease her.

'You're so brown,' they'd say when I was in London. 'You look dirty!' And, 'You're so white!' when I arrived at my Namibian school. It's just because you're new, Autumn. They think you're different. It'll settle down soon, I promise.

What did Granny say? Autumn had asked.

Her Mum had replied, *Granny said I'd just have to 'get on with it'. Sometimes the girls wouldn't let me play with them when I first arrived, but they always forgot about it and let me join in again.*

She'd been trying to make her feel better, Autumn could tell, but the story had made her mum sad. Her mum was not like Granny. She thought about things and wondered what might happen and worried about all the possible outcomes and then couldn't decide what to do. Her mum was right about this though. It *would* settle down.

That afternoon they had Maths. Mrs Sibson clapped her hands together and said they had to put their coats on and line up in pairs, without making a racket. They were going to measure the playground. Autumn stood up slowly, not looking at any of her classmates in case they saw she was frightened of being the only one that no one wanted to partner with. But then Molly touched her elbow and smiled at her and they walked out to the corridor together to fetch their outdoor clothes.

It was cold and their noses ran and their hands went all tingly but it was okay because Autumn liked working with Molly. There was something satisfying about stretching out the yellow tape measure and writing down the numbers and making a little chalk dash on the Tarmac where the tape measure ended and then putting the other end of the tape measure to the chalk sign and starting all over again. When they reached the end of the playground they smiled at one another and rolled up the tape measure and added up the numbers, while around them the other children high-fived and hollered, and Jason ran around the yard twirling his tape measure behind him like a streamer and Mrs Sibson shouted at him.

There were only five minutes to go until afternoon break started so Mrs Sibson collected up their clipboards and tape measures – *Neatly rolled up, I said, neatly rolled up* – and told them to remain outside. She and Molly sat on one of the logs and banged their hands together to warm them up. As soon as the bell rang for the proper start of break, the children from the older classes poured noisily outside. A couple of the boys made faces at her and taunted her about her teeth, but she ignored them and soon they stopped. She turned to Molly and was going to ask about her little brother Jack's fifth birthday and what sort of cake they were going to make, when Levi and his posse sauntered over. She felt as if she couldn't breathe but she said over and over again in her head, *I am strong*, and her heart stopped thundering. She remembered how Jacob taught her to punch and kick.

Don't let anyone push you around, kid, he'd said, and he'd held her hand, sheathed in its boxing glove, and made her corkscrew her arm through the air, shooting all the energy out.

Don't punch the pad. Punch through the pad.

Levi started calling her names. Worse, more hateful than before. Autumn didn't respond. She tried to talk to Molly but Molly was looking frightened and didn't answer about the kind of cake they were making for Jack.

'Maybe a chocolate one? In the shape of a train?' Autumn said hopefully, thinking that would be what a little boy would like.

Levi imitated her in a stupid, whiney voice. Autumn could feel her cheeks beginning to flush. Levi sniggered. He touched her hot face with the tip of one finger. He made a sizzling sound. Everyone in the playground was laughing at her.

She jumped to her feet.

She heard her mum's voice in her head, *You've got to stand up for yourself, love*, and Jacob saying, *Go for the knee or the groin*.

She kicked Levi in the knee as hard as she could.

There was a long moment when time seemed to slow down. She heard Molly gasp and saw her put her hand over her mouth. Levi winced and folded slightly, almost gracefully, at the waist. A couple of the older boys sniggered. Levi stood up straight. His mouth twisted slightly.

'Hey, she's not such a wuss after all,' said one of Levi's gang.

Could she really have hurt him? Perhaps it would stop now, he'd know she could stand up for herself. A feeling of relief swelled inside her. Jacob would be proud.

Levi squared his shoulders and glanced at the other kids. The laughter stopped immediately. He turned to look at her. He gave her a long, sweet smile.

He leant towards her and said quietly, 'You're in trouble now.'

She felt pure terror flood through her body.

All that afternoon she felt anxious, wondering what he'd do, how he'd retaliate. Her insides were like cold, broken-up jelly.

It didn't happen until home time. Her mum hadn't arrived and the playground was nearly empty. *Barney is being really mean to her*, Autumn thought, *not letting her leave on time because she was late for work.* A crisp packet skittered across the concrete and the day had grown grey. Levi must have been hiding around the back of the porch, waiting. Suddenly he was by her side and she jumped. He grabbed hold of her arm and dragged her behind the school building. It was so quick, she didn't think anyone else had seen him. For a moment it was just the two of them, standing on an empty strip of playground, the playing field, grassy and muddy behind them, pocked with puddles of ice like cracked glass. Seagulls picked their way through worm castes across the pitches.

Suddenly his face distorted with hate and she shrank back and turned to run, and that was when he pulled out the scissors.

They were large and she could see how sharp they were, the dull sheen of the metal blades in the sunless light.

She screamed and he put his hand over her mouth, pulling her towards him. He bent forward.

'Don't tell anyone,' he whispered.

He didn't touch her with the scissors. He didn't wave the blades in front of her face. He didn't have to. He held her plaits in his hands and she could hear the shearing sound. Once. Twice. And then there was a sudden feeling of freedom, the tightness released from the back of her head. An icy chill down the back of her neck where her hair had hung.

He ran then. She looked down at the ground, as if her severed plaits might lie there like limbs that could be sewn back on. But there was nothing, just a couple of strands of hair, spiralling gently towards her feet. Slowly, slowly she reached up and touched her hair with her fingertips.

It was worse than she thought.

LAURA

That evening she phoned Jacob. She was shaking with cold. The pavement was coated with black ice and her breath was a frozen fog in front of her face. A loud bang made her jump. Over the top of the park a cloud of pink sparks blossomed and died. Bonfire night. She'd forgotten.

'Please, Jacob. It has to stop.'

She pressed her mobile to her face, her hand numb. She saw her child's white face, the tears she'd dashed away with her fists. And her hair. There was no way Autumn would go to gymnastics tonight looking like that. Autumn had refused to tell her who had done it, although it was obvious. It had to be Levi. She'd spent twenty minutes phoning hairdressers to find one that could fit Autumn in after school – but the earliest appointment was not until Wednesday. She felt at a loss to know what to do, how to begin to rebuild her daughter's shattered confidence.

'If you just talked to him. He won't listen to me. I don't know. Maybe...'

Laura was standing outside the house so that Autumn wouldn't hear her. Another rocket gave an eerie whistle and exploded.

'I'll meet you after school,' Jacob said finally. 'Tomorrow.'

'Thank you. Thank you so much. I'll see you then.'

She tried to ignore the horrid feeling she'd had during the phone call. She hadn't rung Jacob on Sunday to check that he was okay and she could tell by his tone of voice that he hadn't been happy to hear from her. It might be the garden – the loss of their one decent job.

Or it might be that he felt ashamed. He'd told her that he wasn't the man he thought he was. He'd cried in front of her. Jacob didn't seem like a man who could accept feeling weak.

She realized that she was clinging to Jacob, that she'd become too close to him too quickly. The old Laura, the one with her best friend by her side, the network of mums she'd known since Autumn was born, her mismatched assortment of allotment-buddies and fellow students, would never have latched on to someone like Jacob and decided to go into business together on the strength of lunch on an away-day and an assortment of chats in coffee-breaks about planting annuals.

She shut her eyes. She couldn't think about it now. She had to make sure nothing else happened to Autumn. She turned to run back inside the house to the warmth, to Autumn, when she slipped on an ungritted patch of black ice. She had a single moment of clarity as she was falling, the mobile shooting out of her hands, seeing the night sky, lit up by a white comet.

How stupid.

Now, more than ever, she had to concentrate. She had to look after herself for Autumn's sake.

She landed with a jolt and felt her spine jar. A shooting pain ran through her wrist. For a few seconds she was stunned. She was aware of tiny details: her phone lying a couple of metres away in the middle of the street, the muffled sound of traffic from the main road, fireworks exploding above the small park, a pine cone digging sharply into the back of her knee. She stood up slowly and rubbed her back and her wrist, sliding slightly as she did so. She walked gingerly across the road and picked up her phone.

Thank God, it's still working.

She limped the last few metres back to the house, fumbling for her key, the heel of one hand bruised and tender, indented with marks where gravel had dug into her skin.

TUESDAY 6 NOVEMBER

AUTUMN

When she looked in the bathroom mirror, her stomach hurt. Someone she did not recognize was staring back at her. Her skin was pale and puffy from crying the night before and her raggedy hair, without the weight of its length, didn't know what to do with itself. She wet her mum's brush and tried to slick it down. Last night her mum had trimmed her hair. Autumn had cried silently the entire time. She knew her mum was doing her best, but Autumn couldn't help feeling that she was making it even worse. Eventually her mum had put the scissors down and blown her nose.

Autumn felt her breath, rapid and shallow, like the time she had a chest infection, as she walked into school. A few children looked at her and then glanced away. But when she went inside, several of her classmates giggled and pointed at her hair.

Olive said, 'It's a really shit haircut, Autumn.'

Jason jeered and said, 'Did you do it yourself? What did you use, Autumn? The garden shears?' and Tilly wrinkled her nose and said, 'You look like a boy,' which seemed like the worst insult of all.

Mrs Sibson clapped her hands together to get them to all keep quiet, but she didn't tell Tilly or Jason off for being mean or Olive for swearing. Maybe she hadn't heard them? Mrs Sibson gave her a strange look and then said that in Modern Foreign Languages today they were going to examine how stories are told around the world, and then they were going to draw a picture inspired by the story – either the one she told them or a story of their own choosing.

'Gather around, children,' she said, and they sat in a circle on the carpet in the corner of the room where the reading books were. 'Once upon a time there was a little girl...'

Autumn glanced at the other children. Had Mrs Sibson forgotten how old they were? They all knew the tale of *Little Red Riding Hood*. It was for young ones, like Jack, Molly's brother. She rubbed the back of her neck. It felt naked and cold and her back was light without the heaviness of her hair.

'All the better to eat you with!' said Mrs Sibson, and most of the children, even Tilly, laughed. Autumn tried to smile.

Mrs Sibson explained that it was a very old European fairy tale. It may originally have come from France but it was told in lots of different countries. It was first written down by a man called Charles Perrault and it was called *Le Petit Chaperon Rouge*. His ending was different, she said. In his version, the wolf gobbles up Little Red Riding Hood. Mr Perrault said that the moral of the story was that little girls should not listen to strangers.

'But the hunter comes and saves her,' said Olive.

Mrs Sibson nodded. 'The story was told another way,' she said. Two German brothers, called Jacob and Wilhelm Grimm, rewrote it and in their version, called *Rotkäppchen*, the wolf eats the girl but then a hunter with a sharp axe comes along and he slices open the wolf and pulls out Little Red Riding Hood.

'And she's still alive?' asked Jason.

'Yes, he saves her and the wicked wolf dies,' said Mrs Sibson.

'What about the grandmother?' asked Autumn and her classmates turned and looked at her and she could see their eyes straying over her hair. Tilly smirked. She blushed and wished she hadn't spoken.

'In both of those original versions of the story, the grandmother doesn't hide in the cupboard, like she does in ours. The wolf eats her too,' said Mrs Sibson. 'In the Brothers Grimm fairy tale, when the hunter opens the wolf up, the grandmother, as well as the little girl, is alive and well.'

Mrs Sibson smiled at her but Autumn thought there was nothing very much to smile about. Really it was a nasty little tale about a girl who has to walk through a dark forest on her own because she wants to be nice to her sick granny and take her some cake.

Autumn imagined the girl, with long dark hair in plaits and a red cape, running through the wood and stopping because she hears something: soft paws crushing damp moss, an animal breathing. She runs on. She's frightened. She knows what will happen is inevitable. All the while the wolf is keeping pace with her, watching her, its pink tongue lolling over its sharp, white teeth. Waiting for its chance.

No one believes wolves are like snakes, swallowing their prey whole, like it showed you on *Deadly 60*. From somewhere, a phrase drifted into her mind: *Torn limb from limb*. She decided she was not going to draw a picture inspired by *Little Red Riding Hood*.

LAURA

She made sure she was wearing an extra layer of warm clothes and she arrived early to wait for Levi, Autumn and Jacob.

Predictably, Barney had been annoyed. He'd looked pointedly at his watch as she started to pack up her tools at five to three.

'Leaving us already?' he'd said in a voice filled with bluster.

'I'm really sorry, Barney, I'll make it up to you, I promise,' she said and smiled at him.

It had been a difficult day. They'd been laying tiles for a garden path. Normally it was the kind of repetitive, methodical work that Laura liked but it was bitterly cold and hard to keep the tiles level and even while wearing thick gloves. Ted cut the tiles with an axel-grinder; the noise gave her a headache and she could feel his resentment. He'd objected to Barney hiring her from the beginning because she wasn't *a bloke* and therefore wouldn't be any good at lifting or using power tools.

She knows her plants, Barney had said at the time. But in winter there was little planting to do and Ted was right. She wasn't fit enough or strong enough for this job and the cold ate into her bones. She hoped he wasn't going to let her go.

She looked up to see that Jacob had arrived early too. She wasn't sure whether he was a disciplined person or whether he clung to discipline as a way of surviving as a civilian after his years in the army. She was at once relieved to see Jacob and then shocked.

Jacob had parked his black Land Rover a short way down the

street. He jumped out and started walking towards the school, looking around for her. In those few moments before he'd spotted her, she saw him, not as she thought of him – a warm, caring friend with a particular fondness for roses – but as others might see him. Either because he'd just led another fitness class or because he thought it would help, he was still wearing his army gear: combat jacket and trousers, black calf-high boots. His jacket was open, affording a glimpse of a flat, toned stomach, covered by his cotton top. His head was shaved and, as he walked, he practically bounded. His casual glance, searching for her, gave him the impression of a man checking the lie of the land, seeking out his enemies. In spite of his slightness, his small stature, he looked hard, predatory, every inch a soldier. She hesitated and then waved.

Jacob smiled and held up his arm. He darted across the road towards her. She was never sure how to greet him. A double kiss seemed wrong, somehow, with Jacob. Besides, she'd always hated it, going for the wrong side first, bumping noses, spending too much time in another person's space. But equally, one kiss seemed too intimate and they were too close for a handshake. As usual they nodded and smiled awkwardly at one another.

'Thanks for doing this,' said Laura, wondering even as she said it if she should tell Jacob to go home.

Jacob wasn't a malicious person; he wouldn't have calculated the effect of dressing like a soldier on Levi, she thought. As the other parents started to arrive, a few of them looked antagonistically at her and somewhat apprehensively at Jacob. To stop herself feeling even more awkward, she described Levi to him. Jacob stared fixedly at the school as she spoke and bounced on his toes. She started to feel as if she might be sick.

Would it be better if Levi was first? What if Autumn came out of school before him?

She'd have to go to her straight away and then maybe she'd

miss Levi, or miss pointing him out to Jacob. But she couldn't risk Autumn thinking she was going to be late.

She was about to say, apologetically, that she'd have to go inside the school gates to wait for Autumn and that they should leave it, when Jacob suddenly said, 'There he is.' He turned to her. 'Am I right?'

She peered between the shrubs growing around the edge of the wire mesh and the low stone wall that surrounded the school yard. Levi, blazer undone, laughing, was crossing the playground with his friends. She nodded.

'Good description,' he said, smiling at her. 'Go. I know you need to meet Autumn. I can take care of myself.'

Keen as she was to reach Autumn, she left him reluctantly. The traffic was bad and she had to wait what seemed like an age for the lights to change before she could reach the other side. She entered the playground as Levi came out. He looked coolly at her and spat on the pavement, just missing her shoes. Laura felt her heart beat faster. She hurried uphill towards the school.

Autumn emerged. Her shorn hair, hacked into an uneven and old-fashioned cut, made her pale face appear gaunt. Her eyes, as they flickered across the playground, had a hunted expression and she walked with a quick step, her shoulders hunched. She looked like a refugee.

'Jacob's here,' she said to Autumn when she reached her. 'Come on.'

She took the girl's satchel and tried to take her hand, but Autumn pulled away. She trailed sullenly after her mother.

'How was school?' Laura asked over her shoulder.

Autumn, as if sensing that Laura was only partly paying attention to her, said nothing.

'Autumn, I asked you a question.'

'Mrs Sibson wanted to know who cut my hair,' muttered Autumn.

Laura stopped walking. 'And what did you tell her?'

Autumn shrugged and scuffed the toe of her shoe on the pavement. 'I told her you did but I'm going to a proper hairdresser tomorrow to fix it.'

'Oh, love, why didn't you tell her who really did it?'

Autumn walked on, ignoring her. After a moment's hesitation, Laura followed, wondering how much worse the Social Services situation was going to be, now that Mrs Sibson thought she'd bruised her daughter's arm and hacked off her hair. They reached the main road. Jacob, who had been leaning against a wall, watching Levi, pushed himself upright and started to follow the boy. Laura, a few metres behind and on the opposite side of the road, hurried after them.

'Where are we going?' asked Autumn. When Laura didn't answer her, Autumn said, 'We're walking the wrong way.'

Levi had passed the turn for Briar Lane and now only had two other boys for company. He sauntered along, his hands in his pockets. Jacob, who was going slowly for him, was quickly catching up.

'What's happening, Mum?' asked Autumn.

'Shush,' said Laura. 'Let's just keep going.'

She wondered whether she should take Autumn home as fast as possible. It wasn't that she didn't trust Jacob. She didn't think he would touch the boy. Nor did she think he would back out and not speak to him. So why was she following him? Was it morbid curiosity? No, she thought. She needed to know that whatever Jacob said to Levi would work – and then she would be able to relax knowing that the boy would finally stay away from her daughter.

She became aware that Autumn was no longer with her. She spun around. Autumn was standing in the middle of the pavement. There were tears in her eyes and she looked furious. It reminded

Laura of when Autumn had been a toddler: there was that same anger and despair at what felt like a lack of control for most of a small child's life. Only this time her daughter was older and could manipulate events much more effectively. She hurried back.

'Jacob is going to speak to Levi,' she said quietly. 'I want this to end. I want him to stay away from you.'

They both turned back. Diagonally opposite, interrupted by the cars speeding past, they could see Jacob leaning over Levi. Jacob, for all that he was lean and wiry, was a threatening figure, a good several inches taller and broader. Levi seemed to have diminished in his presence. Laura became acutely aware of what he was: a boy, with ink stains on his hands, his trousers ever so slightly too short, a grass stain on his sock, a streak of mud on one trainer.

The other kids had shrunk back. She couldn't hear what Jacob was saying. The cars going past were loud and Jacob was speaking quietly. Though he was uncomfortably close to the lad, he didn't touch him. Laura wasn't sure whether it was the uniform or Jacob himself, but something violent shivered in the air.

For the first time it struck her forcefully that Jacob had killed a man, quite possibly many men, maybe even women and children. Jacob's role had literally been one where he was required to kill and maim other human beings. He had signed up to be a marine knowing that he would have to take lives and watch men die.

She should stop him, she realized. With a dreadful certainty, she knew she should go over there right now. It had been a mistake to ask Jacob to speak to the boy. She looked from side to side but the cars were coming so fast and there wasn't a gap in the traffic. And then Levi glanced over and saw her and Autumn watching. For a moment she could see the fear in his face; the whites of his eyes shone vividly, his nostrils flared. He was holding himself unnaturally rigid. A muscle in his jaw jumped. Laura felt a rush of shame, hot and intense. She flushed, a painful burn that spread across her cheeks, down her neck, prickled in her ears. She could see the comprehension dawn in Levi's face.

There was a scraping sound as Autumn's boots slid on the Tarmac and then she was running, running as hard and as fast as she could, her red coat flying out behind her, running away from Laura.

Laura caught up with Autumn at the corner of Wolferton Place but only because her daughter was now standing staring down the street. Laura stopped to see why. Outside their house were two police officers.

'Are they waiting for you?' asked Autumn, as Laura rested her hands on the child's shoulders.

One of the officers looked up and the other noticed and turned to face them too.

'I'm afraid they might be,' said Laura.

She wasn't sure if the police had been given a description of her, or if she simply looked guilty, but they both started to walk purposefully towards her and Autumn.

'Why are they here?' asked Autumn. 'Is it about Levi?'

'I expect so. Aaron has reported me to the police. It's not your fault, Autumn,' she murmured, taking the child's hand.

'Will you have to go to prison?'

The two officers reached them in time to overhear her.

'Mrs Wild?' asked one officer.

Laura shook her head. 'That's my daughter's name. I'm Laura Baron-Cohen.'

'Do you know why we're here?'

The officer was in his early fifties, jowly, with grey hair, his stomach stretching the fabric of his shirt. In contrast, the other officer looked as if he was barely in his twenties, with short, dark hair, artfully spiked and ruffled, pronounced cheekbones and pale skin. He was small and slight and could have been in a boy band.

Laura nodded and the officer continued.

'I'm Police Constable John Willow and this is PC Alan James. We are here to inform you that Mr Aaron Jablonski has reported you for causing actual bodily harm to his son, Levi Jablonski. It is alleged that you knocked the victim to the ground and caused him to cut his face and sustain a blow to his head. We assume that you will not be leaving the country for the foreseeable future so there is nothing that you need to do at this moment in time. We have begun interviewing the witnesses; once we have all their statements, you will then be arrested. At that point it would be advisable to bring a solicitor to the station with you. Do you understand?'

Laura nodded. Autumn started to cry.

'I don't want you to go to prison,' she said.

'Let's hope it won't come to that, eh?' said the younger officer, crouching down so that he was at eye level with her and smiling.

'This is Autumn Wild, I take it?' said PC Willow. 'We will need to take her statement too, with an adult present. You will be unable to attend her interview. Perhaps your husband can accompany her.'

Laura shook her head. 'We're divorced.'

'I suggest you decide now who will be present. Her grandmother? Someone she knows and trusts.'

He was trying to be kind. Laura walked unsteadily past the two officers. It was only once she was inside the house, and had locked the front door behind her, that she realized she hadn't asked PC Willow how long it would take to gather statements from the six boys who'd seen her push Levi.

WEDNESDAY 7 NOVEMBER

AUTUMN

This morning she'd held the phone in her hand on the way to school. It was shiny and smooth and reassuring. It was like a talisman to ward off any more comments about her hair. Her mum had shown her how to switch her new phone to silent. She'd put her mum's mobile, their landline and Jacob's number into Favourites so Autumn could call her mum or Jacob just by pressing one button.

When she reached school she put it in her trouser pocket so it would be with her all the time. She thought no one else knew about it but at break-time, Tilly said to her, 'Can you get Facebook on your new mobile?'

Autumn had been too shy to speak. You weren't meant to use phones at school. But she was overwhelmingly grateful – Tilly wanted to talk to her again! She was smiling. Tilly must believe that she hadn't copied her work after all.

Tilly held out her hand and Autumn reluctantly passed her the phone. The girl swiped the screen and tapped it a few times, pushing her hair out of her eyes with her thumb. Smirking, she handed the mobile back.

On the screen was Facebook. It showed a picture of Autumn. She was looking like a deer they'd startled one night on the way home from a trip to Epsom Forest: caught in the glare of the headlights, it had flared its nostrils, its eyes wide and retinal-blue. Autumn couldn't understand it. She hadn't made a Facebook page for herself.

She'd never seen the picture before. And then she read the title. It said: We Hate Autumn.

Underneath it was the newsfeed. There were already several status updates. Autumn started reading them and blushed. She looked up at Tilly in confusion. Tilly smiled sweetly and tossed her hair over her shoulder. The words became jumbled up in her head. There were so many of them: teeth, dumb, ugly, stupid, bitch, hate, name, emo, hate, hate...

She switched the phone off and put it in her pocket. Her throat had grown dry and she could hardly swallow. Her face was burning. Her classmates all knew. They were all in on this. They were all writing on the Facebook page.

At lunchtime she went into the toilets by herself. The page was still on her mobile but there were many more messages now. She turned it off and put it back in her pocket. She felt the mobile burning against her leg, churning out more vile words: copy, stole, thick, stuck-up, thief, hate, whore, hate, bitch, hate. Die.

She stayed in the toilets until lunch was over and then crept slowly out, as if her whole body ached, checking the corridor to see if anyone was watching.

In the afternoon lessons she couldn't concentrate and Mrs Sibson told her off three times. Her voice was a nasty teacher's voice, but her expression didn't match. She looked worried. The mobile buzzed against her thigh. She thought it was more messages, pouring into Facebook. But it wasn't. She checked at afternoon break.

There were three of them. There was no number and no name.

The first text said, *Everyone hates you, Autumn Wild.*

The second said, *Fuck off back to London.*

The final one said, *Go kill yourself.*

LAURA

Laura hadn't been able to concentrate on her lectures today. She'd left the university even earlier than last week to make sure that no matter what the traffic was like, she wouldn't be late. Autumn, though, was one of the last children to leave the school. Laura had been on the point of going inside to search for her when she came running out across the empty playground.

Laura felt her chest tighten. It was the shock of seeing her look like a child from the seventies, instead of the image she carried of her daughter: laughing, her grey eyes sparkling, her plaits tumbling down her back. Laura wasn't sure the hairdresser was going to be able to do much with her hair.

Just before Autumn reached her, the child stopped. She was staring straight ahead with a fixed expression. She reached out and seized her mother's hand.

'What is it, sweetheart?'

Autumn didn't reply. Laura looked behind her to see what she was staring at. Blocking the entrance to the school gates was a man. He was dressed in a long, black coat. As they paused, he lifted his head and stared at them. She couldn't see his eyes but a thin bead of light from the street lamp ran down his cheek, curved under the bone. His jaw was clenched tight. Laura stiffened and felt her pulse race, the hand holding Autumn's grow slippery with sweat.

Nothing can happen to us here; the head and some of the teachers are still in the school, cars are going past, there are people all around.

She gripped Autumn's hand tighter and strode forward to meet Aaron.

'How dare you?' he shouted as they approached, immediately on the offensive.

Autumn half hid behind her mother.

'You are fucking unbelievable. You hired a soldier to beat Levi up!'

'I did not,' said Laura. 'He is not a soldier and I did not...'

'A fucking Marine! You paid a Marine to assault my boy!'

'He isn't... I didn't...'

Laura's bravado disintegrated now that he was only a few feet from her, so much taller, leaner and more threatening than she remembered him from their evening together. The whites of his eyes glistened and the tiny charm angled on his wrist bone flashed as he spoke. She felt queasy as she remembered how she'd almost fallen for him the evening he had come to her house and softly spoken to her about a planet born from the sun's remains. How close they had been to each other in the confined space of her office. What might have happened if... She pushed the thought away.

'I've reported you to the police for the original assault. I'm considering giving them a further statement about your latest crime. I can only tell you one last time: stay away from my son.'

He turned and flung open the door of his car, illegally parked facing the wrong way on the zigzag lines outside the school, and drove away with a screech of tyres.

Laura was trembling. Did that mean, she thought, that there was a chance, even the slightest of chances, that he was not going to go to the police about Jacob speaking to Levi? Jacob would back her up; he was innocent, after all. But it would be awkward and embarrassing for both of them if Aaron did report her. And it would make the police case against her even more damning. It looked as if he was going to hold this as a threat over her for now.

Autumn let go of her hand and Laura felt her palm fill with cold air as if an icy ball had been pushed into her skin.

'Levi had a black eye today,' she said quietly.

'You don't seriously think Jacob did it, do you?' Laura said quickly. 'We were there, remember? He must have got into a fight with one of the other boys.'

'But then I ran off. You followed me. You didn't see Jacob leave.'

'Jacob wouldn't have touched him, let alone hurt him.'

'You did,' said Autumn.

Laura bit her lip. 'Come on, we're going to be late,' she said, opening the car door.

The hairdresser's was an expensive salon in Cotham, but it was the only one Laura could find at short notice. From the darkened street the windows glowed and were garlanded with strings of fairy lights. There were velvet sofas and a giant chandelier, sparkling with cut glass hanging above a semi-circular desk in the centre of the room. A white waxy orchid in a gold pot stood next to the till and against one wall was a tall, thin mahogany set of shelves with hair products in minimal and tasteful packaging.

She expected the hairdresser wouldn't be able to do anything with Autumn's hair. She felt guilty although she knew that was ridiculous – it was not as if she could have prevented a malicious boy from chopping Autumn's plaits off at the roots. Autumn was still refusing to say that Levi had done it.

A young man led Autumn to a chair in front of a mirror and pulled another over for Laura. She assumed he was an assistant but, after he'd wrapped a gown around Autumn, he ran his hands through her hair a couple of times.

'You have beautiful hair,' he murmured, and Autumn almost smiled.

The man, who introduced himself as Sam, was thin and pale with floppy, dark hair in a rumpled quiff.

He nodded a couple of times and then looked at Autumn's reflection. He had light-blue eyes with a dark ring around them and a lopsided smile.

'I think you'll look really cool when we're finished,' he said quietly. He glanced at Laura and added, 'I'll just tidy up these ends and shape it a little, shall I?'

Laura nodded. Sam sprayed Autumn's hair so that it was damp and then bent his lanky form over her daughter. For the next twenty minutes, he worked with the utmost concentration, before spraying her hair again and blow-drying it.

When he'd finished, he handed Autumn a hand mirror and twirled her around so that she could see the back of her head. Laura, watching Autumn looking at herself, felt tears well up. All that lovely, long, thick hair. Autumn had an elfin cut now. It accentuated her sharp chin and wide cheekbones, highlighted the fragility of her neck, the bones standing out, the hollow at the nape. She looked like a changeling-child, immortal, ageless. It made Laura feel uncomfortable, as if her daughter's innocence had been stolen.

Autumn nodded and smiled up at Sam. At least it was better than it had been before.

'If you want to grow it again, leave it for a couple of months and then come back for a trim,' Sam said to her.

Laura winced when Sam told her how much it was going to cost. She'd thought about asking if he could trim her hair too, but at these prices she could barely afford Autumn's haircut. She swallowed. They'd have to economize somehow. She handed him her credit card. She'd phoned the bank about her debit card and the woman she'd spoken to had said the password had been altered and she'd need to come to a branch with some ID to reset it, but Laura hadn't had time so far. She dug her fingernails into her palms as Sam put through the extortionate amount and then they both waited.

'It's been rejected,' he said.

In the mirror Laura saw Autumn's face fall. Sam seemed almost as nervous as she was. He wiped his hands on his trousers and said from under his curly ruff of hair, 'I've got dyslexia, I'm no good at this kind of thing. Hang on and I'll get someone else instead.'

A couple of minutes later, he returned with a bored-looking girl whose platinum-blonde hair was interspersed with pink streaks. She popped gum loudly as she put Laura's card in the machine again. Laura wondered what she could do – she might have to go home and find her cheque book. A cheque would take a few days to clear and give her time to unlock her current account.

There was a whirring sound and the girl tore off the receipt and handed it to her.

Thank God, she thought, smiling brightly, as if nothing had been wrong.

They were late returning home after the hairdresser's and the van with the security company logo was already waiting outside for them. Laura had called the company yesterday after the police had spoken to her. She had to face up to what was happening. It wasn't simply that Autumn was being bullied in a particularly brutal way, it was everything: the destruction of her bike, the vandalism of Ruth's garden, the corruption of her emails and Skype, her bank account, which had been hacked into, her passwords for Netflix, Amazon and the Internet all reset, her laptop destroyed. There was no question about it, she felt increasingly unsafe.

A man, seeing them approach, opened the van door and climbed out.

'Who's that?' asked Autumn.

'He's going to fit a burglar alarm,' said Laura.

She hadn't told Autumn in case she felt worried about them needing a security system, but when she glanced back at her daughter, who was unclipping her seat belt, she didn't seem concerned.

Steve, from Cannongate Security, worked quietly and efficiently as Laura cooked dinner for herself and Autumn, fitting the alarm and also a panic button. When he'd finished, he called downstairs to her.

He showed her how to set the code for the alarm. The high-pitched beeping, signalling the alarm was about to go off, made her pulse elevate.

'If someone breaks in then we and the police will automatically be notified,' he said calmly as she put in the code, her fingers trembling. The beeping silenced immediately. 'We'll call you and if you don't answer, the police will be sent round. To set the alarm, you punch the code in when you're leaving the house and you'll have forty seconds to get out and shut the door behind you. When you re-enter the house, you'll have forty seconds to put the code in before the alarm goes off. You also have another option,' he said, turning to her. She noticed how patient he was, taking care to make sure she had understood. 'At night, before you go to bed, use this code.' He showed her on the key pad and then wrote it down on the Cannongate contract. 'Now you can go to your bedrooms and the bathroom – basically anywhere from the bottom of these stairs to the attic – but if someone breaks into either the sitting room or the kitchen, the alarm will be triggered. It means that you'll need to cancel the code when you get up in the morning – or if you want to go downstairs during the night.'

Laura nodded. 'Thank you.'

'If that's everything, I'll need to take payment from you now and set up a monthly direct debit for the alarm,' said Steve.

Laura sat on the stairs to fill in the forms. Autumn, who had been hovering behind her, disappeared back to the kitchen. She hesitated once the form was completed and only required her signature to validate the contract. She wasn't sure she could afford the extra expense. Still, since she no longer had access to her bank account, thanks to Aaron, she'd have to pay for it using her credit card. She'd worry about it later. She signed the form, pressing harder into the paper than she normally would.

After Steve left, she found Autumn sitting silently at the kitchen table, staring at the wall. It was as if some vital spark had been extinguished; her silent rage against her mother had turned to limp apathy. There was a blankness behind her eyes. She hung her head over her dinner. To Laura, this abject resignation – in spite of the new haircut, which Laura had thought would cheer her up – was more frightening than the anger Autumn had previously directed towards her. As soon as they'd finished eating, Autumn walked away from her, leadenly climbing the steep stairs towards her bedroom.

THURSDAY 8 NOVEMBER

LAURA

Autumn did not appear that morning. Eventually Laura tiptoed into her room and saw that she was still sleeping. She looked so peaceful, her pale face smooth and free of her perpetually anxious expression. Laura couldn't help smiling but then she noticed that her daughter's hands were twisted into her duvet, her fingers white from gripping so tightly. Laura laid out her school uniform on the end of the bed and, when the child still did not stir, she kissed her on the tip of her nose and whispered her name as she used to do when her daughter was young enough to have naps during the day. Autumn frowned in her sleep and then sat bolt upright, her eyes wide with fright. Laura put her arms around her to soothe her. Autumn remained rigid for a moment before pushing her mother away.

'How are you feeling?' she asked as she knelt on the floor in front of her child.

Autumn looked at her school uniform with disbelief. 'I don't want to go to school.'

Laura thought of the call Dileep George had made to Social Services. She couldn't risk keeping her at home – and she couldn't annoy Barney even more than she already had. She silently handed the uniform to Autumn, who snatched it out of her hands and stalked out of the room, slamming the door behind her. She refused to eat anything before they left. Laura didn't push her. There was almost nothing in the house anyway and she thought that at least

Autumn would be able to have a decent lunch at Ashley Grove. She wondered if her daughter was eligible for free school meals; she made a mental note to look into it once this was all over.

Autumn neither spoke nor made eye contact with her as they drove in. After she'd dropped her off at the school gates, Laura drove recklessly fast to reach the garden she was working on with Barney and Ted. It was as she was approaching the blind bend on Frenchay Road that she saw the flowers. She slowed down. There were three bunches tied to the wall, still wrapped in cellophane: carnations and chrysanthemums, harsh, cheap flowers, garish in the grey light, already frost-bitten and wilting. A few metres further on was a yellow road sign asking for information about the accident.

Sweat pricked her palms. The young girl she'd seen the week before – the one with the blue nail varnish and long, unblemished white legs, lying on the pavement – she must have died after she was hit by the car. Laura was now crawling at ten miles an hour. The car behind her hooted its horn. There was a homemade banner fluttering from a lamp post, the stitching uneven. Ribbon had been sewn on to create words: *We love you Joanna.*

Laura's eyes filled with tears. She put the car into second gear and slowly accelerated away.

AUTUMN

Autumn had had many bad days at school since she moved to Bristol, but this one, this one was the worst.

She walked into the classroom and found that she no longer existed. No one looked up. No one spoke to her. She felt as if a chill wind had blown through her and made her all shimmery and invisible. She tried to speak but all the words had been taken away.

'Maths homework was really tricky. Could you do the partitions?' she finally managed to say to Molly and Olive.

Her voice was croaky, as if it had not been used before.

Both girls looked at their notebooks. Olive lined her pencils up in a row. Autumn pulled out the empty chair next to Olive but the girl smacked her hand on the table.

'This seat is taken,' she said.

Autumn moved to the next chair, but another girl, Katie, pulled it away from her. She tried one more time, moving towards the only spare place left next to the other pupils, but Tilly dropped her bag on the chair, just as she was about to sit down. She was forced to sit at a table on her own.

In Literacy Mrs Sibson put them into groups of three. They were supposed to discuss friendship and write a story together on what the best part of being friends was. Mrs Sibson placed her with Olive and Tilly. Tilly asked if she could move to a new group because everyone knew that Autumn copied people's work. Mrs Sibson said no, it was *a collaborative venture*. Autumn felt her cheeks glow. Mrs Sibson had not said, *Autumn did not copy you, Tilly*.

Tilly made a face and some of the other girls looked sympathetic. She and Olive whispered to each other, glancing back at Autumn, cupping their hands around their mouths so she couldn't hear what they were saying. They half turned so she couldn't speak to them or see what they were writing either.

At break-time she went to sit next to Molly. As she sat down, Molly walked over to the other girls. There was no more room on the log they were perched on, but they all budged up and Molly squeezed on the end. They looked at her and tossed their hair and sat forward and whispered.

Autumn was acutely aware of the space that had opened up around her. She was alone. No one spoke to her. It was difficult to breathe. She stared down at her shoes on the cracked Tarmac of the playground, a tree root visible beneath the asphalt.

She hoped no one noticed how alone she was. Levi was leaning against the climbing frame with his friends. He looked up, an egg sandwich, part of it still in its corner shop wrapper, spilling in creamy clots from his mouth. He gave a wolfish grin.

LAURA

At lunchtime, Laura went to sit in her car to eat the leftovers from last night's meal and shelter from the rain. She turned the engine on and the heat as high as it would go to try and warm herself up. Ted and Barney were in Barney's Land Rover but there wasn't enough room for all three of them in the front, even if she had wanted to join them.

As she was eating, she noticed a flash of bright pink. She reached forward to see what it was. Tucked in the pocket in the passenger side of the door was Autumn's mobile.

She must have forgotten to take it to school, Laura thought.

She wiped her hands on her army trousers and reached over to retrieve it. There was a spiderweb of cracks on the screen. Autumn had dropped or thrown it. Before she could stop herself, Laura turned on the phone. She felt dreadful, as if she was spying on her daughter. Immediately five texts appeared on the home screen. Laura pressed the Message button to look at them properly.

They were all from the same person. The caller's number was blocked and there was no name, only the messages, each worse than the previous one. She read them over and over again. She couldn't believe how vicious they were, how foul the language.

She was going to kill the person who had done this to her daughter.

At least now she had proof. She could take the mobile to the police and show them. Surely they could unbar the number? She clicked on the first text to see if there was any more information, any way to trace the call, but it said, *Caller ID withheld*.

She remembered the article she'd read in *The Washington Post* about the father who'd hired a teenager to beat up his son's bully. The journalist had described how bullying had become more Internet-based – cyber-stalking and trolls posting hateful comments on social networking sites.

Surely that's too advanced for Autumn's age group?

And then she thought of Levi's father.

She touched the Facebook icon. The screen opened and slowly loaded. She jabbed at the phone, to scroll through the newsfeed. She stared at it in disbelief. She sat, stunned, the phone in her hand, its blank screen slowly dimming. She threw the mobile on the seat and put the car into gear. She pulled out and slowed next to the Land Rover and wound the window down. Ted started to lower his window but, without waiting for it to fully open, she shouted at the two of them, 'Got to go. It's an emergency,' and drove off before they could respond.

Within a few seconds, her phone started to ring. It was Barney. She dropped her phone on the seat next to Autumn's and pushed the car into third gear.

AUTUMN

She told Mrs Sibson she wasn't feeling well and she didn't want anything to eat. She said maybe she was coming down with flu. She could tell Mrs Sibson didn't believe her because she had that sceptical expression her dad used to have when he said, *Pull the other one.* But she must have felt sorry for her because she said she could stay inside during lunchtime.

At first she was relieved. She watched the other children playing outside, as if they were dangerous animals in a giant enclosure and she was safely on the other side of the thick glass walls. She didn't turn the lights on. She took out a pad and a fine-tipped black pen but she couldn't think of anything she wanted to draw. She opened *The Amber Spyglass*, the book that Granny had been reading to her – but Lyra's dreams of the Land of the Dead made her frightened and she closed it again.

And so, with nothing to occupy her, and her thoughts skittish as the pond skaters in their garden back home, in their *real* home, she started to think about the Facebook page. She wondered if it was still there. If the children in her class were still posting messages. She'd have a quick look, she thought, just to check. Then she'd know who she could trust. She turned on one of the computers and clicked on Facebook. It opened at the We Hate Autumn page. There were so many new messages. A kind of panic seized her. She couldn't read them properly. The sentences and names were jumbled up, the words black and rotting, like decaying liquorice allsorts. She backed away.

It was the noise that caught her attention. A strange kind of panting and moaning, like an animal in distress. She turned around slowly. It was a video posted on the Facebook page. Autumn didn't understand it but she knew straight away that it was shameful and disgusting and she could never tell anyone about it, not even her mum.

The video was of a naked man and woman. He was doing something to her and it looked as if he was hurting her. She was a proper lady, with boobs that wobbled every time he pushed her, although she didn't get up and run away. But the terrible, terrible thing that she would never be able to tell anyone about ever, was that this grown woman had *her* face.

LAURA

As she drove back through Frenchay, she noticed that there were more flowers for the dead girl and, stuck between the railings was a teddy, limp with damp. The rain grew heavier. She slowed down as a cyclist wobbled in front of her. Laura couldn't risk overtaking her; the streets in Bristol were so narrow and the girl was almost in the middle of the road. She was dressed entirely in black, with a short skirt and lace tights. Her hair had turned into fat, wet ropes. She wasn't wearing a helmet and with one hand she shielded her face to see through the rain. Laura felt worried and annoyed at the delay; at the same time, she couldn't help but admire her insouciance, the attitude that allowed a young woman to ride fast and dangerously in inappropriate attire in inclement weather and trust the world to keep her safe.

She overtook the girl as the road widened and drove as fast as she could to the school. She parked illegally at the edge of the road on double yellow lines and ran across the playground, clutching Autumn's phone. For a moment she thought she glimpsed Autumn in an empty classroom, but it couldn't have been her because all the children in her year were in the canteen finishing their lunch. Some were beginning to leave the cafeteria, noisily filtering down the corridors and bursting into the playground in a multi-coloured jumble of waterproofs and wellingtons.

Laura raced past the school secretary, who called out to her, and ran down the corridor towards Dileep George's office. She knocked once on his door and then walked in. He looked up, startled. She strode across the room and threw the pink mobile on his desk.

'It's Autumn's,' she said, when he made no move to pick it up.

'We don't allow children to have...'

'There were five nasty texts on her phone, from a barred number. And then this.'

She swiped the splintered screen and handed it back to him, open at the Facebook page. 'I haven't been able to refresh it. Either there's no signal or the phone isn't working properly – it looks like Autumn tried to smash it – but you can see what was written up until yesterday.'

Dileep George swallowed uncomfortably, his Adam's apple pushing out the grizzled skin of his neck. 'Do you have any idea who created this? Or is writing these messages? This is a primary school, Mrs Baron-Cohen. The pupils here would simply not have the kind of skills...'

'To create a Facebook page and then post status updates from fake accounts? I'm sure some of them do. Particularly the son of your IT consultant. Who happens to be twelve. A year too old to be attending a primary school. A little fact that seems to have slipped your mind when I first reported his bullying of my daughter to you. But you're right, it does seem a bit advanced for a kid. I assume Aaron is behind it – he could even be helping Levi.'

'This website *is* shocking but it's a matter for the police. It is not—'

'I can't believe that, even with this proof, you're unwillingly to believe what is taking place in your own school.'

'These posts could be from anyone,' said Mr George.

'I've had enough,' said Laura, snatching the phone out of his hands. 'I'm taking Autumn out of this school right now. She's not safe here.'

He sat back in his chair and looked up at her. His unease seemed to have dissipated. 'I very much doubt that Social Services will look on such an action favourably.'

Laura turned and walked out, almost knocking over the secretary, who had come, presumably, to say she should have made an appointment, tell her off for running in school or to remonstrate with her about the mud she had tracked into the headmaster's room. Laura marched down the corridor. She could hear the secretary asking Mr George if everything was okay. She angrily shoved Autumn's phone in her pocket and wondered where to start looking for her daughter.

Autumn would probably be outside with the other children, but it wouldn't hurt to check the classroom, just in case. She had an after-image of her pale face, as if she were underwater.

'Wait.'

She turned to see Mr George hurrying after her, his blazer flapping, his brogues so worn that his steps were almost soundless.

'I can understand your concern, Mrs Baron-Cohen. Let me speak to Mr Jablonski about this. I can't accept your accusation that he would be behind it, and I don't believe Levi is either, but if – *if* Levi knows anything about this site, Aaron would know.'

'How?'

'He told me once that he monitors Levi's Internet usage. Something to do with—'

'Being able to hack into his laptop or computer remotely?' Laura interrupted.

Mr George nodded. 'I don't understand the technology – he has a mirror of Levi's hard drive on his own computer. I don't think he looks at it much – he says it's more of a precautionary measure. I'm sure you'll find that Levi is not implicated, but Aaron will be able to help us trace who could have set up this Facebook account and is posting those awful messages.'

Laura stared at him silently. His sallow skin looked greasy under the strip-lighting in the corridor. She assumed that Aaron was ultimately behind the troll page and had either set it up himself or shown Levi how to. Either way, he would naturally deny all knowledge and would have covered his traces effectively. And, if he hadn't, why would he help her? The woman who'd pushed his child so hard he'd fallen and cut his cheek open on a rock. The woman he'd been cyber-bullying for the past ten days. She started walking away from Mr George.

To her surprise, the headmaster followed her.

'Mrs Baron-Cohen.' He held out his arm as if to touch hers, but withdrew his hand awkwardly. 'Let me accompany you.'

'I *am* taking Autumn out of this school,' she said, quickening her stride.

'I understand. I think it's the right thing to do.'

'What?' She swung around to face him. 'A minute ago you...'

He bowed his head in acknowledgement and held out his hands towards her palms up, as if in supplication.

'I can see you and Autumn are both upset. I don't want to lose her as a pupil. Take her home today. You have had quite a shock. Keep Autumn at home tomorrow too. I'll mark it down as sick leave. In the meantime, I'll speak to Mr Jablonski. But please, think about what you're doing. This isn't a long-term solution. Bring Autumn back to school on Monday. It won't do you any favours when you have to appear in court if you have hindered your daughter's education. After all, you do not have another school ready and willing to take her. I know, for a fact, that there are no places in any of the schools you are in the catchment area for. Your only other option would be to send her to a fee-paying school.'

'How do you know that I'm not going to do that?' She wondered if his sole concern was still only for the school's reputation.

'That is entirely up to you, Mrs Baron-Cohen, if you should chose to do so... and can afford it. But it is not why you're removing Autumn at this point in time. She has, in many ways, settled in well here and I can see that she is an asset to the school. As I say, I do not want to lose her, nor do I wish her education to be jeopardized.'

He half-smiled at her, although his eyes remained cold. She could see the glint of his bridge-work. How on earth had he come to be in charge of a primary school, she wondered? She couldn't imagine him making a child feel at ease.

They were standing a few steps away from Autumn's classroom now. The noise from the playground seemed to boom and echo in the confined space.

'She'll be outside. It's still lunch break,' said Mr George.

Laura opened the door and stepped inside.

Autumn was in the classroom on her own, bending over one of the monitors. There was a faint flash of light, as if she'd just switched it off. The other monitor screens were dark. When she looked up at them, her expression was guilty.

'What are you doing in here?' asked Mr George, turning on the light.

'Mrs Sibson said I could stay inside,' Autumn whispered. 'I don't feel well.'

Laura held out her arms. 'Autumn, we're going home.'

The girl flew across the room and hugged her.

'Is there anything you need to get?'

Autumn shook her head, still buried in her mother's embrace. Laura disentangled herself and strode across the room to pick up Autumn's satchel.

'I'll call you when I know more,' said Mr George, opening the front door of the school for them.

Autumn grabbed her coat and ran after her, bowing her head so she wouldn't have to make eye contact with anyone.

In the car she looked almost cheerful again.

'What were you watching on those computers?' asked Laura, putting the key in the ignition.

Her daughter's expression clouded and she turned to stare out of the window.

'Are we going home?'

'I have to go to work,' said Laura. 'I saw your phone, Autumn. I'm so sorry, sweetheart.'

'You looked at my phone?' She was suddenly furious.

'I thought you'd forgotten it. I was going to give it back to you but then I saw... I wish you'd told me, love. I couldn't leave you there for another minute.'

'But what will I do while you're working?' She had her arms crossed and was resolutely turned as far away from Laura as she could within the confines of her seat belt and booster seat.

'Do you want to talk about it? Some of those texts were awful. Did they frighten you?'

Autumn said nothing and refused to meet Laura's eye in the rear-view mirror.

'Are they from Levi? Do you think he's behind the Facebook page too?'

'You saw the Facebook page?' Autumn snapped her attention back to Laura.

'Yes. I'm sorry, love. I just wish I'd been able to stop this earlier. Or that you'd told me. How long has it been going on for?'

'Facebook is private. You shouldn't be looking at my stuff – spying on me like this.'

'I wasn't spying! I saw the Facebook icon on your phone, when I was looking at the texts. I guess it was logged in as you already. All those awful messages.'

'Messages? Just messages?'

'Yes, messages. Written on your wall.' Laura looked at her in confusion. She must have seen them. She knew they were there – so why was her reaction so odd?

'They're obscene. You must never think any of that stuff those kids have written is true. Not for a minute. You are beautiful and kind and smart.'

Autumn sat back in her booster seat. 'You still haven't told me what I'm going to do when you're working.'

'I'm not sure,' said Laura, pulling out into the main road. 'I hadn't thought that far. Maybe you'll be able to sit in a café. You could do some drawing. Or read a book.'

'I didn't bring my pad with me. And I don't like my book,' said Autumn sulkily.

She resumed looking out of the window and didn't say another word until they arrived at the garden in Frenchay. Laura pulled over behind Barney's Land Rover, his Bronze Beech logo emblazoned on the side.

Barney and Ted looked up and then did a double-take as Autumn climbed out of the car.

'What's going on?' asked Barney, walking over and looking from her to Autumn.

'There was an emergency. I had to take her out of school.'

'What kind of emergency? Doesn't look as if she's bleeding to me,' said Ted.

'Look, I'm sorry about this, Barney, but—'

'She can't stay here,' said Barney quickly. 'Health and Safety would have a field day. We're working, in case you haven't noticed. Laying tiles. It's no place for a child.'

'I know that. It's far too cold for her to hang about here anyway. I thought she could maybe go to a nearby café – there must be something around the corner – and I'd check up on her every hour. Maybe every half hour. Just for the rest of the day.'

'Laura.' Barney rubbed his face with his hand. He wasn't wearing gloves and hardly seemed to feel the cold. 'It's Frenchay. There are no chi-chi cafés. The nearest place to grab an instant coffee is the Texaco garage.'

'Then I'm sorry, Barney, but I'll have to go home. I wanted you to know it was serious. I wouldn't have left otherwise.'

'Frankly, you've been having a lot of "emergencies" recently. And when you have been here, you haven't been pulling your weight. Your mind has been elsewhere. I don't know what is going on with you, but I'm afraid this is your last chance. You'll have to go home now, you can't stay here with the kid, and I'm not paying you for today. At all. But you need to sort yourself out. If you don't turn up tomorrow, or you show up with the kid, then you're fired.'

Over Barney's shoulder Laura could see Ted smirking. She was about to argue – she had, after all, put in a morning's work – but then she thought Barney might fire her on the spot. Instead, she held the car door open for Autumn and got in the other side.

'Are you going to make me go back to school tomorrow?' asked Autumn as they drove off.

'No.'

'Are you going to leave me at home?'

'No, of course not,' said Laura, thinking that there really was no one Autumn could stay with.

'But you'll lose your job. That's what Barney said.'

'We'll see. He's feeling cross right now. By tomorrow he'll have calmed down. Anyway, I'll have my own garden company soon. And I'll be the boss. I'll be the one hiring and firing people.'

At home, Autumn raced up the stairs to change out of her uniform, running faster than Laura had seen her move all week. Laura was about to make herself a cup of tea when she realized that there was no milk, not even a spare pint tucked in the freezer for emergencies. In fact, the cupboards and the fridge were almost empty. She still hadn't been able to reinstate her debit card.

Tomorrow, she promised herself, she'd go to the bank and sort it out.

'Autumn,' she shouted up the stairs. When her daughter didn't appear, she started searching for her and found her in her bedroom. 'Sorry, love, we're going to have to go out again. There's no food in the house. We'll have to do a shop.'

'No way, Mum. It was too embarrassing last time when the lady at the checkout wouldn't take your card.'

'I'll put it on my credit card. Come on. It'll be fun. You can choose some nice things for dinner.'

Autumn shook her head. She looked utterly exhausted, her face was pinched and the circles beneath her eyes greenish. Laura hesitated. She didn't want to drag Autumn around the supermarket but, on the other hand, she was reluctant to leave her alone, even if it was only for a short time. And they literally had nothing to eat in the house.

'Come on, sweetheart. I don't want you to stay here by yourself.'

'I'll be fine. I really, really don't want to go, Mum.'

'What if...' She paused, wondering if she was being extreme. 'What if I put the alarm on? You know, like we did last night. You'd have to stay up here though, and not go downstairs to the kitchen or sitting room. Or answer the door. Not that you should answer the door if I'm not here.'

'Yes,' said Autumn, her voice slurring with tiredness. 'That's a good idea. I'll stay in my room.'

'And I won't be long.'

'Just go, Mum.'

Laura drove to Waitrose. Normally she shopped at Lidl – Waitrose was too expensive – but it was the nearest supermarket. She could do a quick shop and be home in half an hour.

She felt nervous, leaving Autumn by herself. She imagined what Vanessa would say, or rather, wouldn't say, merely arching an eyebrow in lieu of commenting. Vanessa had frequently left her on her own to *run errands*, as she put it, when she was as young as seven. No, that wasn't quite right, she corrected herself. Damian had been with her, the responsible nine-year-old, who would disappear into his room, shutting the door behind him, to work on his latest science project. Anything could have happened to her, Laura thought wildly. She'd felt frightened in their large London house, unable to even hear Damian, and so she wouldn't move from wherever her mother left her – usually curled up with a book by the radiator in the front room, watching out of the window for her mum to return.

Once she'd reached the supermarket, she scanned the Waitrose essentials range and bought the cheapest items she could find, enough to tide them over for a short while. They were out of all the basics: milk, bread, cereal, orange juice. At the last minute, she tossed in a large marbled bar of milk and white chocolate studded with raspberries because it reminded her of the birthday cake she'd once made Autumn, the photograph of it and her daughter blowing out the candles now irretrievably lost. At the checkout she handed the cashier her credit card.

The woman's brow furrowed. Laura stopped packing her bags.

The woman shook her head. 'I'm very sorry. I've tried your card twice now and it's been declined.'

Laura put the bag she was filling down and walked out of the shop. In the car she buried her head in her hands and cried. She was exhausted. Her eyes felt raw.

There had to be a way to stop him.

There was a sharp rap on the car window. A woman stood outside with a baby balanced on her hip. Laura wiped her eyes and opened the window. It was Amy with her youngest, Tom.

'Are you okay?' she asked in her high-pitched and oddly child-like voice.

Laura nodded. 'Yes. Fine, thanks.'

Amy lifted Tom up and hitched him onto her other hip. 'I saw you inside. At the till.'

Laura could feel a blush beginning to spread across her cheeks. She hated the sound of Amy's voice. It set her teeth on edge. She hadn't even changed and she was still in her mud-covered trousers. Amy, on the other hand, looked petite and perfect. She was wearing a diaphanous dress over thick woollen tights, with knee-high boots and a shearling aviator jacket. As if she'd stepped out of an advertisement.

Amy balanced her handbag in the crook of her arm and tucked a strand of hair behind her ear. She said, 'I could pay for your shopping.'

'What?' said Laura, turning back to her.

'It's what credit cards are for. Come on. If we hurry, they won't have unpacked your bags yet.' She started walking towards the supermarket, leaving Laura no option but to jump out of the car and follow her.

'Really, Amy, there's no need. I'm going to go to the bank tomorrow.'

'Well, when you do, you can pay me back. Silly to waste a trip.'

Laura felt utterly mortified and also relieved. She wasn't sure what she would have done if Amy hadn't shown up. Amy stopped a woman in Customer Services and swiftly had Laura's shopping, which was just being unpacked, put back in a trolley. Tom gurgled and pointed at the shoppers, trailing a string of drool from his chubby fingers.

'I can't thank you enough,' said Laura, as they walked back to the car.

'It's no problem. I'm parked over here,' she said, gesturing to a Volkswagen three spaces away from Laura's battered Toyota.

Laura was thinking that not one of the other mothers would have stopped to help her. No one had even asked her if Autumn was all right. Not one of the other mothers had even questioned what had happened between her and Levi, preferring to believe Aaron and the gossip circulating the playground. She was about to say goodbye when Amy, as if guessing her thoughts, spoke.

'I don't know if you know this already, but the police are just over halfway through interviewing the boys. You know, the witnesses to the incident between you and Levi? They've collected four, maybe five statements so far.'

A spot of rain landed on Laura's eyelashes and she blinked. She was thinking how tactful Amy's phrasing was when she continued.

'I thought you should know – I heard a couple of the parents talking about it and it seems that all the statements so far back up your version of events.'

'*My* version?'

Another spot of rain landed on her cheek and Laura squinted up at the grey sky. Amy gave a little shrug and jiggled Tom up and down. The child was starting to grow impatient. She glanced at Laura out of the corner of her eye. 'Everyone has their own version, their own memories.'

Laura tried to stop herself from becoming annoyed by Amy's prim tone.

'True,' she sighed. 'But in this case, there can be no doubt. I did push him. And he did fall and cut his face. All those kids, including my own daughter, saw me do it.'

It was a relief to finally say it out loud to another adult. Amy's response was not what she was expecting though.

'Yes. And that's what the boys are saying so far. I always thought that Aaron's version was unlikely.'

'Aaron's version?'

It started to rain properly, a light patter of large drops. Tom's face crumpled. Amy pulled a dummy out of her handbag and popped it in his mouth before continuing.

'I mean, I can imagine losing my temper. Especially if I thought my children were threatened. Levi is a big kid and the boys that were with him are intimidating – they're all from the local secondary school. I feel threatened by them. But I couldn't picture you beating Levi like that.' Amy turned to face her properly. 'Apparently Aaron told the police you hit Levi several times, on his back and across his chest too. With a stick.' She fished her car keys out and held them in a tight fist.

Laura frowned. *Why would Aaron lie?* She was going to get into enough trouble as it was without him making it sound worse.

'Thank you,' said Laura. 'Thanks for letting me know.'

She opened the boot and started to put the groceries in. Amy ran, her head bowed, towards her car. A couple of minutes later, she gave Laura a tiny, stiff wave as she drove past, the baby waving his fat fists and howling in the back.

On the way home, Laura thought of the upmarket bar of chocolate. It felt like a long time since she'd treated herself, or even eaten decently.

On her front doorstep, she took a deep breath before unlocking the door. This was only the second time she'd had to switch the alarm off. The beeping, signalling that the alarm was about to trigger, frightened her. But it would be okay, she told herself, she'd done it before and she knew the code. She opened the door and rushed inside to turn the alarm off. Nothing happened. There was no sound. She looked at the security box, newly mounted on the wall by the front door. There were no lights on. The system was dead.

Her first thought was of Autumn. Could she have switched off the alarm? No, that would be impossible, she hadn't taught her the code. And even if she had somehow managed to silence the alarm, the system would still be active.

'Autumn?' she called up the stairs. Her voice echoed in the stillness. She shouted her name again, louder.

There was no reply. Could Aaron have somehow hacked into the system and overridden it? What if he was inside the house now? Leaving the shopping bags where she'd set them down on the step, the door open, the car boot gaping wide, she raced up the stairs. She ran up two flights and burst into Autumn's room, her heart pounding. The bedroom was empty. She ran out and across the landing to the spare room. She wasn't there either.

She hadn't checked the bathroom, she thought. She ran back down the narrow stairs. She slipped and had to grab the banisters to stop herself from falling. The bathroom door was ajar. Autumn was not inside. She hurriedly searched the spare room. It was also empty. Standing outside her own office, still in the hall, she had a glimpse of the end of the garden. She couldn't have gone outside, Laura thought – she'd have triggered the alarm by even entering the hall, let alone the kitchen.

And then she realized that, of course, the alarm wasn't working. Autumn could be anywhere. But the child didn't know the alarm had been switched off, so Autumn wouldn't have tried to go outside or even down to the sitting room. Unless... Her mind was whirling in frantic circles... Unless someone had cancelled the alarm and broken into the house while Laura was out and forced her...

'Autumn!' she screamed at the top of her voice.

There was no reply.

She ran back to the hall and grabbed her phone out of her handbag. She'd call the police. But first, she had to double-check that Autumn really was not in the house. She'd start at the top, she thought, and be methodical about it. As she was running up the stairs, she felt as if she was wasting time. If Autumn had already been taken...

When she reached the attic, she flung open the door of her bedroom. Autumn looked up at her in surprise. She was lying on the bed, listening to music on Laura's iPod. She pulled off her pink headphones.

'Did you get any biscuits, Mum? I'm starving.' She sounded grouchy and tired.

Laura thought she was going to burst into tears. She rushed over and hugged her.

'Mum, you've only been gone an hour,' said Autumn, wriggling out of her embrace. She slowly eased herself off the bed, casually tossing Laura's iPod behind her.

As Laura retrieved the shopping and locked the house, she realized why the alarm wasn't working. She hadn't been able to use her credit card in the supermarket – Aaron, presumably, had done something to it, just as he'd managed to cancel her bank card, the Internet, Skype, Netflix... The list seemed endless. While she was unpacking the shopping, she phoned the security company to check.

'Mrs Baron-Cohen? I've been trying to reach you. I left a couple of messages on the landline,' said the man on the other end, when she'd introduced herself.

As she suspected, the payment had not gone through so the system had been deactivated.

'We can have it up in a moment, as soon as the payment is processed,' he said.

Laura hung up.

'Let's have some hot chocolate with our biscuits,' she said brightly to Autumn.

Autumn shrugged in response and listlessly sat down at the kitchen table.

Tomorrow Laura could visit the bank and reactivate her cards – she had no way of reinstating the burglar alarm otherwise. The money she earned from Bronze Beech all went straight into her current account; the only other cash she could get hold of would have been her payment from Ruth but Laura didn't have the heart to ask her for it.

First, though, she'd ring Jacob. She went into her office to call him so that Autumn wouldn't hear her. The grey light, filtering through the sheets of rain, made a watery pattern against the wall. Jacob didn't sound particularly happy to hear from her but he listened patiently.

'It's got to be him. I mean, who else could it possibly have been?' she said, when she'd explained about the Facebook troll page.

'What do the school say?' asked Jacob.

She hesitated. She didn't want to tell him that the head teacher had said he would speak to Aaron, because she knew Aaron would deny it and Mr George was bound to believe him.

'I can give you his phone number. You could arrange to meet him on the pretext of having your laptop repaired,' she said.

'And then do what?'

'Just talk to him. He won't listen to me. Tell him to stop. To leave me alone. To leave *us* alone.'

There was a long pause. Laura could hear people talking, but their voices didn't sound hollow as they might if Jacob was in a café.

'Where are you?' she asked finally.

'On The Downs. I'm about to teach a class. Look, Laura, I'm really sorry about what happened. It must have been, well, frightening. But you're okay. Autumn is safe. You've taken her out of school. I've got to go, Laura.'

He hung up.

Sometime in the night she woke, suddenly and completely. Her first thought was of Autumn. Perhaps her daughter couldn't sleep and had risen and that was what had woken her. Laura sat up and listened. She couldn't hear anything but the house felt different. There was a thin wind that rattled the panes of glass and moaned around the gable wall. Something banged loudly, making her jump. It sounded as if it was coming from outside the back of the house. She climbed out of bed and wrapped her dressing gown around herself.

Before she'd gone to bed, Laura had double-checked that the garden gate, the doors and windows were locked. She tried not to think about the alarm, now simply a dead, white plastic box stuck on the wall in the hall.

There was another crash from outside the house. Laura automatically looked towards the landing window but, in the darkness and from this height, she could see nothing save the stars and a moon-rimmed grey cloud. It sounded like the garden gate, swinging open and beating against the wall. It had been locked though, she was sure of it. Perhaps it was the neighbour's, she thought. She felt her heart turn to ice.

She crept downstairs and peered in at Autumn. She was asleep. She could hear her breathing; it was fast and slightly nasal. Looking down at her daughter in the dark, she remembered the feel of Autumn's soft skin just after she'd been born, her baby hair, as downy as a fledgling's, the gentle dip of her fontanelle where her cranium had not yet fused; how noisy she was, like a hedgehog snuffling in its sleep.

She tiptoed through the rest of the house. She took the last steps down into the kitchen without turning the light on, hands balanced on the wall on either side of her, as if they were closing in on her and she had to push them away. She stood in the entrance to the kitchen and looked out towards the garden. She could see nothing. She waited until her eyes adjusted and the trees and the shrubs and the fence at the back became cut-out silhouettes against the dark of the sky. She decided it was too much of a risk to open the door to the garden but it didn't look as if there'd been a break-in and she couldn't hear or see any movement.

She started to shiver and, after a while, she crept slowly back upstairs and climbed into bed.

FRIDAY 9TH NOVEMBER

LAURA

She slept fitfully, half listening for any noise. Early, before her alarm went off and Autumn woke, she rose. She went downstairs and opened the kitchen door. A thin, milky-yellow light spilt over the horizon. Venus shone brightly to the east. The first birds were beginning to sing. During the night, thanks to the freakish wind, all the leaves from the ash tree next door had blown down and the entire garden was covered with dead brown drifts, as thick as snow. She walked through the freezing garden, the leaves crunching beneath her feet.

The garden gate was shut and locked. She rattled it to make sure. As far as she could tell, it hadn't been damaged. It must have been next door's, crashing open and closed in the wind. She felt as if she'd suddenly grown lighter, as if a steel weight had slipped from her shoulders. She turned to go back inside the house and that was when she saw it.

In the feeble dawn, part of the wall of the house was illuminated. She recognized the colour of the paint. It was scarlet-red, exactly the same shade of spray-paint that had been used on Autumn's bike and to scrawl *Bitch,* again and again, across Ruth's garden. On the wall between the kitchen door and the window someone had written:

Bone by Bone

Laura froze. She heard Aaron's voice, so quiet it was barely more than a whisper *It's the best place to see the stars in the city.*

He had wanted to walk home through the nature reserve so that he could watch Jupiter's raging red-eye from Narroways' hill. And she had given him the key code to the garden door. And now he had let himself in, painted on her house and left, locking the gate behind him.

The police arrived half an hour later. Laura, who didn't want to wake Autumn, was waiting for them at the door. A young woman and a middle-aged man got out of the police car and came over to the house. The woman, small and stocky in her tight black trousers, introduced herself as PC Rachel Emery and her companion as PC Sebastien Jones.

She led them downstairs to the kitchen. PC Emery had a heart-shaped face and she inclined her head towards Laura as she listened. When she took her hat off, she looked younger, more vulnerable. She had creamy skin and freckles and brown hair which had recently been highlighted and was now pulled back from her face in a low ponytail. On her left hand was an engagement ring; a single diamond dug into the flesh, as if her fingers were a little swollen. Laura, looking at the woman's plain face and her soft body, realized that she had no faith in PC Emery's ability to protect her or her daughter. PC Jones stood a little behind her, as if distancing himself from the proceedings.

'So, let me see if I've understood this correctly,' said PC Emery. 'There has been no break-in. You think someone let themselves into the garden from the lane behind the house, using the key code on the garden door, and then left again, locking the gate behind them.'

'Have you checked if anything is missing?' asked PC Jones. 'Bikes, the TV, the DVD player, camera equipment, your laptop – anything valuable?'

He had a doughy face, fleshy bags under his eyes, which were of an indeterminate colour. His grey hair was cropped closely at the sides of his head and stood straight upright from his crown, bristly, like a scrubbing brush.

'No!' said Laura. 'I know who did this. And he didn't come here to steal anything. It was a computer repair man. He was in our house – to fix my laptop – about ten days ago. I gave him the key code so he could let himself out the back.'

He and PC Emery exchanged a look, as if they were suddenly unsure what or who they were dealing with; as if Laura's claim that it was a break-in was a lie.

She took them outside.

'It's a line from a poem by Emily Dickinson,' Laura said to the police officers as the three of them stood and looked at the words, each letter in garish red smudged across the white wall.

'A literate vandal?' said PC Jones.

She shook her head. 'I told you. The computer guy. He hacked into my laptop after he'd fixed it. So he knows that I wrote my dissertation on Dickinson.'

They don't believe me, she thought, her face starting to burn.

PC Jones coughed and looked down at his feet. PC Emery was examining Laura carefully.

Still standing outside, staring at the defaced wall, her feet numb with cold, Laura quoted:

There is a pain – so utter –
It swallows substance up –
Then covers the Abyss with Trance –
So Memory can step
Around – across – upon it –
As one within a Swoon –
Goes safely – where an open eye –
Would drop Him – Bone by Bone.

When she stopped, they both stared at her and she felt a surge of embarrassment. It used to be so natural to quote poetry when she was a teenager at university and now, here she was, in her thirties, her feet bare, sounding like a Victorian lunatic. She still couldn't tell what colour PC Jones's eyes were.

'It was the poem on the first page of my essay. It's about death. And rage. Violence, grief, pain. Pain above all else. Pain beyond measure. A pain that is impossible to endure. The body can't deal with suffering on that scale so it closes down, goes into a trance... She – Emily Dickinson – had nervous breakdowns.'

She tucked one foot behind her calf, trying to warm her toes.

PC Jones stared up at the scarlet letters. 'Could be a line from a rap lyric. A graffiti artist's tag. Or a threat from someone who's never read a line of poetry in his life.'

'No! I told you who did it. He's trying to scare us.'

The dawn light picked out the warm chestnut streaks in PC Emery's hair. She walked towards Laura and took her arm. 'Let's go inside, shall we? You could do with a cup of tea to warm you up.'

Later that day, Laura found herself in Autumn's room. She wasn't quite sure what she was doing there. She thought she might lie down for a moment, stretch out on Autumn's bed, inhale her daughter's scent. She was bone tired.

Autumn had risen late that morning, well after the police had left. Laura didn't tell her about the break-in. She'd been lethargic and uncommunicative, silently eating a bowl of Frosties. At least she was eating, Laura thought. She'd made her a cup of hot Ribena and put CBBC on and now Autumn was sitting in front of the TV, still in her pyjamas.

Laura thought she should change the sheets – it had been ages since she'd last done it – when she remembered Autumn had stuck one picture back on the wall. She walked over to look at it. It was of a girl. She had grey eyes and long brown hair in plaits. She was smiling and she had a gap in her teeth. On her knee was a baby. The child was gurgling, open-mouthed. She had the same pale-grey eyes and light-brown hair as her big sister.

Autumn and her imaginary little sister, Emily. Autumn had told her about her once. She used to draw pictures of Emily all the time. Laura had hoped Autumn had stopped wishing for a sister or a brother. Maybe because she was feeling so vulnerable, she'd started thinking about Emily again.

It wasn't too late, Laura thought. She could meet someone. It was still possible.

The phone rang. Laura ran down the stairs and into her office.

'Laura! I've been trying to reach you.'

She had an image of Matt, snow-clad Himalayas in the background, five stunning athletes flanking him as he strode down the mountain. He must be ringing because he couldn't get through on Skype, she thought, but it was too early for his call with Autumn – and it was not like Matt to waste money using the satellite phone unless it was an emergency.

'What's the matter? Where are you?' she asked.

'That's the problem. We're stuck.'

'What? Where?'

'In Simikot. Our connecting flight to Kathmandu has been cancelled. I've been going spare. Someone phoned and cancelled our seat reservations. I gave our PA hell, but she's no idea who did it. There are flights leaving, but not many and they're all booked. There isn't another one until Saturday night and even then there aren't enough seats for all of us.'

Laura looked down the narrow length of the garden. The dead brown ash leaves that had shrouded the strawberry tree had blown away and the berries had all turned scarlet. She did a swift mental calculation. If Matt and his crew couldn't fly out of Simikot until Saturday, it meant they wouldn't be able to leave Kathmandu until Sunday. Then they'd have to reach India and from there fly to London via Amsterdam or Paris before driving back to Bristol.

'Tuesday,' said Matt. 'It means the earliest I could be home won't be until Tuesday but I'll probably need to give those seats to the athletes and catch a later flight. I can't believe how much money we're losing – booking all the new tickets plus excess baggage. The athletes' agents are saying we need to pay them for the extra time,' he said. 'And I'm sorry, it means another few more days until I can see Autumn. I can't think who could have done this to me.'

'I can,' said Laura. 'Your schedule was on my laptop.'

'So?' said Matt.

She could picture him clearly now, dishevelled, sun-burnt, running his hand impatiently through his windswept hair. Laura started from the beginning, explaining what had happened. She told him about Aaron sitting in their house, drinking red wine and resetting her password, how he had threatened her at the gates of the school playground, about Autumn's mangled bike, the lost photos, the infected emails, the pornographic virus, the copied essay, the boy who had attacked Autumn in the nature reserve, the vandalized garden, Autumn's shorn hair, how her bank cards had been stopped, the alarm disabled. She didn't care how much the call would cost Matt or his company or the BBC, whoever would foot the phone bill and the use of the satellite phone – or what he would think of her. He had to know what was happening to his daughter.

'He actually let himself into the garden and wrote *Bone by Bone* on the wall of your house?' said Matt. 'Jesus. Is Autumn okay?'

She stared straight ahead at the grey clouds drifting past, the branches of the trees shaking, stark against the white sky.

'She will be. I've taken her out of school.'

There was a pause and she could tell he was debating whether to argue with her. He took a breath and said, 'Tell her I'm sorry I can't Skype her tonight and give her a bear hug from me. You were right – I mean, about her travelling to London. I'll come to Bristol as soon as I get back and stick around. Take her out for the day. Maybe to the zoo? She'd like that, wouldn't she?'

As soon as she'd hung up, the phone rang again, startling her.

'Laura.' Jacob said it tersely, as if she were a bank manager or a sales person, someone he had no desire to speak to. 'I changed my mind after you spoke to me. I thought about how frightened you must feel. So I Googled him. Aaron Jablonski. I found his mobile number.'

'Oh.' She wanted to feel relief – Jacob had decided to help her – but his tone was so ominous, her whole body tensed.

'I don't think you've been completely honest with me,' said Jacob.

She was stunned. Of all the people who might turn against her, she'd never considered Jacob to be one of them.

'Aaron tells me you assaulted Levi. You knocked him down and he cut his head open! Laura, how could you? He's a child.'

'I didn't—'

'Aaron showed me the photographs of the bruises and the gash on his cheek.'

There was a heavy crack and boom of thunder, alarmingly close, and a fresh squall of rain. Laura said nothing. Was she going to have to defend herself to Jacob too?

Yes, she thought, squeezing her eyes tightly together and rubbing her sore wrist. *Yes, I have to. He's the only friend I've got.*

She took a breath and was about to explain when Jacob cut across her.

He said that he'd made an appointment to speak to Aaron last night. He'd been surprised to find that the address he'd given him was for a flat on the main road through Filton, in an impoverished, run-down area. The apartment was above a place that sold reptiles; next door was a sex shop called My Only Vice. Both establishments had their windows blacked out.

'I own a house in Montpelier,' said Aaron bitterly, when Jacob had stepped out of his Land Rover and introduced himself. 'My bloody ex-wife still lives there. I'd rather have come to you,' he'd added. 'It's not a fit place to receive a client.'

Inside it was dark. Damp bloomed on the walls. A pile of dirty laundry, including a school uniform, was heaped in one corner and there was a tower of take-away cartons next to the sink.

Levi was there, in the dismal sitting room on his own, watching TV with the lights turned off. He barely looked up when his father and Jacob arrived. Perhaps because it was dark, and since Jacob was wearing jeans and a jumper, Levi didn't recognize him at first.

They sat down at a greasy table behind the sofa.

'Let's see your laptop then,' said Aaron.

'I haven't come about a computer,' said Jacob.

Aaron's whole demeanour changed then, said Jacob. He couldn't explain it, he didn't move a muscle, but Jacob had the impression that he was suddenly different. Laura could imagine it: Aaron sitting opposite Jacob in his waistcoat and shirt, neatness sprung from this den of mess, watchful, his martial-arts-honed body poised.

Jacob explained that he'd come because he was Laura's friend and her daughter, Autumn, was being bullied by Levi. At that point Levi had spun around and pointed at him.

'That's him, that's the soldier I was telling you about, Dad.'

'Is that true?' asked Aaron. 'Are you the man Laura hired to beat my son?'

Jacob shook his head. He said that Laura had asked him to talk to Levi but that he hadn't touched him. Aaron turned the TV off and switched on the lights and then sat back down at the table.

Jacob had been about to go on to say that Aaron was now cyber-bullying Laura when Aaron interrupted.

'My son is innocent,' he said fiercely. 'I know, I swear, there is no way he would hurt a girl, a little girl like Autumn.'

That was when he'd told Jacob about Laura's attack on his son and shown him the photographs of Levi's injuries. Aaron said he'd been about to go to the police regarding Jacob's assault on his son, but now he'd met him, he believed Jacob hadn't hit him and he wouldn't report him.

'She's hounding me, Jacob. She's gone to the school, God knows how many times, to complain about me and my son. She's reported me to the police for *vandalizing* her little girl's bike. That garden you two were working on – the police came round here, accusing me of destroying it. I mean, do I look like the kind of man that would trash a lady's garden? All I want,' he said, his voice trembling, 'is to care for my son. I'm working flat-out to gain custody of him. That woman's accusations could jeopardize my case.'

Jacob cleared his throat. His voice sounded louder – as if he'd put his mouth closer to the receiver. He said, 'The bottom line for me is how can you trust a person who beats a child? I want you to know that going to speak to Aaron was the last thing I was willing to do for you. I don't want you to ask me for help again. I don't want to work with you. I don't want to run a business with you. When you're in college, I don't want you to speak to me. If you ever go back to British Military Fitness, I will act as if I have no personal connection to you. You no longer exist for me.'

There was a click as he hung up. For several minutes Laura simply sat in her office, watching the strawberry tree tossing in the wind, holding the phone in her hand.

AUTUMN

When she woke, it was as if she'd been transformed during the night. Her bones were made of lead. Her head was filled with dandelion seeds, soft as thistledown, like the clocks her mother had taught her to blow, telling the time as the seeds drifted away: *what's the time, Mr Wolf? One o'clock, two o'clock...* Her mouth was dry and she felt nauseous. She thought she'd feel better, knowing that she didn't have to go back to school, but she was worse.

She lay in bed and thought about her mum. She could hear her bustling around downstairs; the smell of coffee and burnt toast drifted up to her room. Because of her, her mum had lost her job. She didn't believe her mum thought it was all fine and soon she'd be some big-shot boss, hiring and firing employees at will. She couldn't imagine her like Barney, all red in the face, telling people off: *and if you bring that kid again...*

Her mum had been saving up to start her own company with Jacob and now that wouldn't happen. Her mum would return to being at home and she'd be sad, like she used to be; that time when she was a colourless version of herself and nothing had been fun. And it was her fault.

She thought of all the things she hadn't told her mum: about Levi following her to school and what might have happened if the man and the dog hadn't appeared, or she hadn't seen the other children in Briar Lane. About Levi sitting in the park, late at night, watching her and how he knew she knew he was there. How he was really behind the paint-attack. That he'd cut off her hair. And that terrible... *thing* on Facebook. It made her stomach twist in knots and she couldn't breathe properly, but she couldn't tell her mum because she'd be even more worried than she was already. And what would happen when the police came and took her away? Would she have to go to prison? Who would look after her then? Her dad? He'd only ruffle her hair and tell her to *stand up for herself.*

Her mum was always there for her. She didn't disappear off to Nepal or Namibia. Her mum loved her, even when Autumn hadn't been nice to her. Actually, she thought, with a hot rush of shame, she'd often been angry or sulky. Mum had taken her away from school and those horrid girls and Levi. Her love for her mum was so big it hurt to think about it. It was like a sharp-edged disc inside her chest. She'd paint an extra-specially nice picture for her, she decided.

She rubbed her eyes and stumbled downstairs to attempt to eat some breakfast. She didn't want her mum to be anxious.

She lay on the sofa, sipping hot Ribena and watching CBBC. She couldn't even bring herself to get up and put *Deadly 60* on or set out her paper and inks. Her stomach was sore, a dull but sharp ache, as if she'd swallowed a bag of nails, all heavy and spikey, and so, when her mum was on the phone, she crept outside to the garden for some fresh air. She still wasn't dressed and it was cold. The air was like needles piercing the back of her throat. She took deep, raggedy inhalations and watched her breath freeze in clouds around her. She was a dragon from a fairy story. She gave a little roar. After a few moments, she felt calmer, and the pain in her stomach eased but her fingers and toes started to go numb.

She turned to go back inside and that's when she saw it. The words in the white-grey dawn, livid and blood-thirsty, scrawled unevenly over the house.

Bone by Bone

She didn't know what it meant but it must be a warning, a grisly message to her and her mum, of what might happen to them if they didn't leave it be, if they didn't stop complaining about Levi and his dad to the school, to the police... The words were spray-painted, the edges blurred when you got up close, the paint gloss-smooth over the little lumps in the wall, like the house had goose bumps. There were some drips, shiny-sticky.

She thought she was going to retch. She put her hand over her mouth and backed away. She looked up and saw her mum in the window of her office. She was on the phone, holding the receiver with one hand and gesturing with the other. Her face was a pale smudge through the condensation and the tangle of ash branches. She might turn around at any moment and see her.

Autumn was frozen to the spot. It was her fault that this had happened too. It must have been Levi. She could imagine him wielding a spray can, dreaming up the words that would terrify her, the small, secret smile he had when he was hurting her, the frightening light in his eyes. He knew where they lived. If she'd told her mum about him waiting for her that morning, or about the times he'd sat on the swing and watched her, maybe she could have stopped him. Maybe this wouldn't have happened. Did her mum even know about the words on the wall? She hoped not. She'd be afraid, knowing that Levi had, somehow, climbed into the garden. He was so agile and athletic, maybe he'd scaled the fence using the strawberry tree like a rope and a ladder.

She looked up one more time and, averting her eyes from the message, she ran back indoors and locked the kitchen door behind her. She would have to make sure her mum didn't go into the garden.

LAURA

Laura thought Autumn would be her old self now that she didn't have to return to school, but she seemed even more unhappy. She was tired, withdrawn, almost catatonic. She spent most of the morning lying on the sofa and groaned and flat-out refused when Laura asked her to come to the bank with her. Laura gave up. She'd go later, when Autumn felt up to it.

As soon as she got the Internet up and running again, she could set up a new email address and start searching for schools outside their catchment area. And she had all the time in the world now that she had no job to go to, or school run to do. She'd start right now, by phoning their Internet provider – and then calling Barney to see if he'd calmed down. Maybe she could persuade him to let her take unpaid leave?

As she waited for the call centre to take her off hold (there were three people in the queue ahead of her), she wondered how she was going to afford the mortgage. She'd have to find a tenant. A new job if she couldn't talk Barney round. And what was she going to do about Autumn's education? The council was unlikely to support her plea to place her daughter in another school when they heard Social Services had been notified and she was facing a court case for assaulting a child. In the meantime, what should she do about Levi? Mr George hadn't phoned her back. There seemed to be no end to the lengths Aaron was prepared to go to bully her and Autumn. The school hadn't intervened. Neither had the police.

PC Emery had rung that morning. She'd sounded kind, asking her if she was okay, if her little girl had heard anything in the night, if Laura had managed to switch the alarm back on (*Yes, No, Not yet*). Then she'd cleared her throat and said they'd gone to see Aaron Jablonski, who'd denied using the key code to her garden, letting himself in, and spray-painting poetry on the wall.

'He said, "I don't even know who Emily effing Dickinson is,"' said Emery. 'At any rate, he couldn't have been responsible. Mr Jablonski had an emergency call-out last night. For IBM. He showed me the paperwork. He clocked off at 5 a.m. Got an hour's sleep before we arrived on his doorstep.' There was a pause and Laura expected the police officer to wind up the conversation. Instead, she said, 'While we were there, we went through Mr Jablonski's records. He keeps a hard copy and a computer record of all the call-outs he makes, his time-sheets and his invoices for the work. There was no record of him ever visiting you at 6.30 p.m. on the twenty-sixth of October to mend your laptop. On the day in question, he made two call-outs to private residences in Filton and Abbey Wood and then he drove straight to the MoD's site, also in Abbey Wood, where he worked until 8 p.m.'

'He's lying,' Laura had said, before hanging up.

She had no evidence to back up any of her claims. There was no one on her side.

Laura, standing in the hall glaring at the phone, realized that she only had one option left. There was one thing she hadn't done – spoken to Levi's mother.

At three in the afternoon, she packed a bag with some of Autumn's books, a pad and felt tips, a couple of apples and a carton of juice. She tossed some clothes towards Autumn, who was still lying on the sofa.

'Come on, Autumn. Put these on and let's go.'

'Where? I don't want to.'

'You won't have to even get out of the car. Come on, hurry.'

'I'm not wearing these!' she said disgustedly.

It seemed to take forever for Autumn to return from her bedroom dressed in a different outfit and put on her shoes.

'Where are we going?' she asked again.

'It's a surprise,' said Laura.

'I don't like surprises.'

As they pulled over on the kerb, a hundred yards away from Ashley Grove, Autumn sat up straight.

'You promised I wouldn't have to go back to school.' Her voice was high-pitched, bordering on hysteria.

'It's okay. School's almost finished. Everyone will be coming out and going home in a minute.'

'Why are we here, then?'

'I'm going to find out who Levi's mother is.'

Autumn stared straight ahead. 'You're not going to ask him, are you?'

'I brought some things for you to do. In that bag. It could take a while. We don't know if he'll go straight home or not.'

Laura, who hadn't taken her eyes off the children starting to filter out of school, spotted Levi. He was unmistakable. Taller and broader than the other kids, there was something polished about him. In the dull light, his skin gleamed. From this distance, she could see how like his father he was – the same spare figure, the square shape of his jaw, the jut of his chin were all Aaron's. As he came out of the school gates, he pulled a black woollen cap over his head and slouched, his gait rolling, down the road. With a lurch, Laura recognized the hat. It was the one he'd been wearing when she'd pushed him and he'd hit his head.

She put the car into gear and pulled out. It was a long shot, trying to follow the boy, but it was the only option she had left. She didn't dare go after him on foot as he'd easily see her and Autumn. In any case, she thought he might have some activity, an after-school club to attend; he might be heading to Filton to see his dad, or hang out with friends, and they could be waiting for a while. At least they could stay warm in the car.

At first, it wasn't difficult to follow him. He walked along the main road with a couple of other boys, on the opposite side from her. The traffic, as usual for this time of day, was heavy and they crawled along. But, at a roundabout, Levi took a right and when she followed, the road cleared. She pulled over, waiting for him to catch up and pass them, hoping that in the poor light, he wouldn't notice them sitting in a parked car across the street from him.

'Mum! What are you doing?' hissed Autumn.

And then Levi turned towards them. He skipped across the road, waving at the boys he'd been walking with. He ran right in front of the car. Autumn instinctively ducked down and faced away. Laura froze, staring straight ahead. Levi darted between her car and the one in front and jogged down a side road. He was heading towards Montpelier, where they lived. Laura wondered if he knew someone there. Of course, he could still weave through the side streets towards Cheltenham Road and go elsewhere, she thought.

She waited a couple of minutes and then eased the car into the road and down the side street. Levi was in the distance, his twin shadows caused by the street lamps splayed out across the kerb.

'We're following him?' hissed Autumn. 'Mum, are you, like, totally insane?'

'Shush. Just watch him. See where he goes.'

Levi was no longer jogging, or walking with his former gangsta gait. He pulled himself erect, easing his rucksack over both shoulders. Before he reached the bottom of the street, he veered right and disappeared into the darkness.

'Where did he go? Can you see him?'

Laura drove a little faster. Forgetting to check her mirrors, she slammed on the brakes near where she'd last seen Levi. The car behind screeched to a halt and the driver blared his horn.

'Shit.'

She was about to pull over when she saw it: a tiny path running between the ends of the gardens, its entrance overgrown with ivy.

'Where does it go?'

Autumn shrugged.

Laura tried to take the next right, but the street had been blocked off to car drivers and she had to stop sharply. The driver behind honked his horn again. She backed up and swung the car around, heading the way they'd come. She turned left onto the road they'd originally parked on, and then took the first left. Just as she turned, they saw Levi, crossing the road in front of them. He started walking down the street opposite – a one-way street.

Laura swore and drove down the next road. To her consternation, instead of running parallel, the street curved and started to dip downhill. Laura took the first right, up a steep hill. She'd lost him.

But he was there, walking straight towards them. Laura was forced to drive past the boy. In the wing mirror she saw him open a gate and enter a garden.

'Which house is it? Look now and see which one it is.'

Autumn pulled the seat belt away from herself and knelt up to look out of the window. 'Got it,' she said.

At the top of the road, Laura turned left and parked the car.

'Do you want to come with me or would you rather wait here?'

'You don't know which house he went in to,' said Autumn sulkily.

'Well, you can tell me – or show me and then I'll take you back to the car. I'm sure the last thing you want to do is see Levi again.'

'It's okay,' mumbled Autumn, climbing out of her seat.

They walked back down the street until Autumn stopped.

'You're certain it was this one?'

Her daughter nodded. It was a tall, thin terraced house, similar to their own, but there the similarities ended. The gate that Levi had walked through was ajar, stuck fast on an uneven paving slab. The front garden was waist-high in brambles, a tangled mass that almost engulfed the path; thick, thorny stems arced out of the briar. The house had once been rendered with cream cement; in the vapid light of the street lamps, it seemed grey and was fissured with cracks. Parts of the exterior were coming away or had fallen off, to reveal uneven brickwork. The front door was streaked with mould and the paint had bubbled and peeled away. A greenish slime ran down the wall above the door all the way from a crack in the gutter on the roof, which was missing some tiles. The only light came from the window on the ground floor and they could see that the woodwork was splintered and rotting; the pane did not fit properly and a gap was clearly visible.

'Do you think this is his friend's house?' said Laura. She realized she was whispering.

Laura carefully stepped around the open gate and walked slowly towards the house, dodging the bramble tendrils. Autumn quickly followed her. When they were a few feet away, half hidden by the dense undergrowth, she peered into the front room. The curtains were hung haphazardly and didn't quite close. A desk lamp on the floor was lit. There was a sun-bleached sofa and a dining room chair piled high with school books. Balanced on the top was a plate, a fork and a glass, all unwashed. The TV was on in the corner, with the sound turned down.

In the centre of the room stood Levi. He had dumped his bag by the door and was wearing a tracksuit. He was moving gracefully, almost methodically, backwards and forwards and turning in a half circle. It was as if he was dancing in slow motion. She didn't know what he was doing – and then it came to her: he was practising Taekwondo.

There was something dreadfully wrong. She could feel it in her bones. There were no other lights on in the house. Even the door into the room he was in led into an unlit hallway. There was no sound, nor smells of cooking. She had a horrible thought: that this really was Levi's house, the one he lived in with his mother. And simultaneously, she had another smaller, nastier thought: now she could not, in all conscience, go inside and confront his mother, and for that, she was grateful. She felt sickened by herself, by her cowardice. She turned back towards Autumn, who was staring wide-eyed at the boy, spinning and circling and kicking an invisible assailant with stealthy grace in the dilapidated house. The two of them crept down the path and onto the pavement.

'I'm sorry, love, but there's one more thing we have to do,' Laura said when they were in the car.

Laura didn't know the address, but she'd dropped Jacob off once. He lived in Cotham, a genteelly fashionable suburb where professional couples and students were interspersed with independent film companies, edit suites and graphic design offices. Because of the traffic, it took much longer than she'd expected to reach his neighbourhood, and then she couldn't find his street. Swearing under her breath, she drove around for a few minutes, until she spotted it – wide, residential, but with a launderette-cum-café on the corner. Laura parked behind Jacob's Land Rover and, leaving Autumn in the car, walked across the small paved front yard, past a rose bush in a glazed blue pot. She was struck again by the incongruity of Jacob's flat. His basement bedsit was once a well-to-do person's parlour in a three-storey Georgian house; there were stone roses above the bay windows and the plaster cornice's were intricately patterned overlapping ferns. Now this beautiful, spacious room was cluttered by a bed, a sofa, a coffee-table, its surface covered with a stack of horticultural text books, empty beer bottles, and coffee mugs; an exercise ball looked as if it were escaping, and a pile of pads and boxing gloves were heaped haphazardly in one corner.

Her hands were clammy and her heart was beating irregularly. She wiped her palms on her jeans and knocked. When Jacob answered, he was still in his BMF kit: camouflage trousers and a blue vest. He crossed his arms and the muscles in his biceps bulged.

'You were right. I didn't tell you the truth,' she said.

'What do you want?'

'Levi cornered her. He tore up her—'

'I don't want your excuses.' He took a step back and seized the door as if to slam it in her face.

'I lost my temper!' she shouted.

Jacob paused.

'I know it won't change your mind, about me, or working together, or, or anything, but I wanted you to know the truth. What really happened. For the sake of our friendship.'

'Go on,' he said grudgingly and folded his arms again.

'Well...' She took a deep breath. She couldn't say she'd felt threatened; a little intimidated but not seriously threatened. It hadn't been self-defence. She hadn't been protecting her daughter. 'I pushed him. I wanted to hurt him.' She swallowed uncomfortably and felt the blush start to flame in her cheeks and rise towards her hairline. 'I pushed him and he fell. He hit his head on a stone and cut his cheek.'

Jacob's expression was unreadable. They stood staring at each other. Her face was burning. Eventually Jacob nodded, curtly. He shut the door.

Laura turned and walked back to the car. She and Autumn drove to Wolferton Place in silence. What had she expected, she wondered – absolution? Forgiveness? At least she'd told him. At least she'd finally been honest about what had really happened and how she'd felt.

AUTUMN

Autumn lay in the bath and shivered, in spite of the heat. Her mum was mad, following Levi. Suppose he'd seen them? She cringed in shame and her cheeks burnt.

And then she thought about where he lived and what they'd seen. It didn't make sense. Levi had always seemed so... she couldn't quite put it into words... He was always neatly dressed, his hair in even corn rows, his shirts clean and ironed, his skin shone. He wasn't one of those kids who looked like a nerd, or who came to school with their trousers too short because they'd suddenly grown an inch overnight and there wasn't enough money for a new school uniform. He looked cool, in control. Powerful.

Without consciously thinking about it, she ran her fingers through her shorn hair. She thought of all the horrible things he'd done. The slugs. The name-calling. Pointing out her scuffed, beat-up shoes, laughing at her unfashionable skirt that she hadn't even realized wasn't fashionable and the jumper her mum had shrunk in the wash so her bony wrists stuck out. Her tortured bike. Her paintings. The message scrawled on their house. The humiliation. The isolation. The fear.

And none of that matched the image she had of him now, rotating and pivoting, as fluid as a dancer, in that broken-down house in a cold and lonely room. It made her feel uncomfortable. Sorry for him. And she couldn't feel sorry for him. She *hated* him. He *was* hateful. She remembered the texts. Way beyond *your shit shoes, your emo hair* – the pure, unadulterated violence of them. And the Facebook page. Her cheeks flared scarlet again, even thinking about it, and she slid beneath the surface of the water.

She felt the pressure of all those messages building up, clamouring, crawling, seething through the Internet and scuttling across the page. Like insects, buzzing and vibrating with skittish hate. She'd left her mobile in the car on purpose and then her mum had found it and kept it as *evidence*. But she wanted to look at Facebook again, to see if Levi and all the others were still posting messages. And the thing she couldn't even bring herself to think about or tell anyone about. The most shameful thing of all.

Is it still there too?

Could her mum have seen it? What if she had to return to school? What if her mum couldn't keep her home or couldn't find a new school for her to go to and she had to go back? And face all of it. All over again.

She poured a large glug of bubble bath into the water and swished it about with her hands until it frothed. Her mum had said she'd got the Internet running again. She'd search for her phone tonight, she thought, after her mum was in bed, and take a look at Facebook. Just to see. Just to check.

LAURA

There was one message on the answerphone. Laura waited until Autumn was in the bath before she played it. She sat on the bottom stair in the hall. It began to rain, a few drops pattering against the window and then a deluge. It was so loud, she had to play the message twice.

It was from a woman with a thick Bristolian accent but her tone, rather than sounding warm, was that of a petty official, her speech peppered with unnecessary jargon. She said she was from Social Services.

'Myself and a colleague will be with you on Monday twelfth of November at 10.30 a.m. If that is not convenient, please call the office on the aforementioned number to rearrange our appointment.'

She wrote down the phone number, along with the time they would be coming on a pad by the phone. She pressed delete. She couldn't – she wouldn't – send Autumn back to school on Monday. She hadn't heard back from Mr George, so Autumn would be with her when Social Services arrived, which would not look good. And presumably this woman and her colleague would know about the court case. The interviews with the children – the witnesses to her crime – might even have been completed.

* * *

The rain beat against the skylight window in the attic. She'd loved the sound as a child: a reminder that she was back home after months in the Namibian desert. But now the noise no longer made her feel safe. She took deep breaths and tried to count them, but after two or three, her breathing sped up and she started thinking about Levi again, how he was terrorizing her daughter in such a calculated way. And yet she couldn't shake the image of him, alone in that run-down house, barely half a mile away from where they lived.

Unable to sleep, she rose to make herself a cup of tea. As she wrapped her dressing gown around her, she heard a sound. She wasn't sure what it was but after the previous night, she assumed the worst. She opened the bedroom door and listened. The house was still and silent around her. She tiptoed to the landing window but she could see little. The rain had eased and the clouds were beginning to clear. The noise had come from outside, she was sure. Perhaps it was Aaron, back to graffiti more Emily Dickinson on their house. That it had been Aaron — in spite of what Jacob had said — she was sure. She decided to phone the police immediately — and check on Autumn.

It was as she was walking downstairs that she heard a different noise. It was one so familiar that, for a moment, it was oddly comforting and then completely chilling. She stood motionless on the stairs, unable to believe what she'd just heard.

It was the back door opening.

The house was in darkness and she was standing at the top of it, the staircase spiralling downwards below her. She was wearing a thin white nightgown with a towelling bath robe. Her feet were bare. It was her lack of shoes that upset her more than her semi-nakedness: you couldn't run fast on soft Western soles. She had nothing she could use as a weapon. Her daughter was sleeping one floor below her. And someone had just broken into the kitchen.

It had to be Aaron.

As quickly as she could, Laura started down the stairs. She kept to the wall in case Aaron emerged from the kitchen and looked up and saw her through the banisters. Her instinct was to run to Autumn's bedroom. She forced herself to be careful, to tread gently so that the stairs wouldn't creak and give her away. She shouldn't jump to conclusions, she thought, trying to think logically. She didn't know for certain that it was Aaron – it could be a burglar. And if it was, it was better that he took what he wanted and left. Accidents happen when criminals are disturbed and feel trapped. Or find out that there is only a woman and a child alone in the house.

She was shaking by the time she reached the corner of the first flight. One more set of stairs and she would be on the same floor as Autumn. It was quiet below her. She wondered if she'd imagined the noise. It could have been her neighbour, or a fox knocking into a bin. She could feel a chill draught against the back of her neck from the landing window. She took another step and the wooden stair gave a shrill groan.

There was the unmistakable sound of someone moving about downstairs. Laura's heart started to race. She took the next few stairs quickly. As she reached the bottom, there was a much louder noise, a kind of squeak and a muffled thud, as if he or she were opening a cupboard in the kitchen or bumping into the chairs. So it was a burglar. Aaron wouldn't be looking through her cupboards. There was nothing of any worth in there, she thought. It wouldn't take whoever it was long to work that out. Her bike – and the mangled remains of Autumn's – were in the dining room, the TV and DVD player were in the sitting room. There was nothing valuable in the rest of the house – but then a burglar wouldn't know that.

At that moment, as she was poised on the bottom stair before the landing leading to Autumn's bedroom, the door swung open. Autumn stood in the entrance to her room, looking sleepy and confused, wearing her rose-patterned pyjamas. Laura froze, frightened that Autumn would come running towards her or speak. She held a finger to her lips and motioned for her to return to her bedroom. Autumn didn't move, but Laura saw the sleepiness vanish. She looked terrified.

She glanced over the banisters but she could see no movement in the stairwell or the hall. She darted across the landing, the elderly floorboards protesting. Autumn remained rigidly in place. Laura almost pushed her out of the way. Inside her bedroom, Laura held the handle down as far as it would go and slowly closed the door, then let the handle rise, millimetre by millimetre, until the door was soundlessly but firmly shut.

She turned to Autumn and hugged her tightly.

'Is it a burglar? Will he hurt us?' Autumn's voice was rising.

Laura put her hand over her daughter's mouth. She held her fast. Autumn was trembling. She could feel her ribs, the ridges of her spine. She tried to think, but her mind was blank. It was as if part of her brain was missing.

She needed to phone the police but her mobile was plugged in to charge in the kitchen. There were two handsets in the house – one of them she'd left lying around somewhere – either the hall or the kitchen. Why couldn't she be the sort of person to put them back? She'd been using the one in her office so hopefully she'd left it there. But to get to it she'd have to cross the landing and go down a flight of stairs, where she'd be in the open if the man or men came up. They might hear her. She couldn't risk leaving Autumn on her own in her bedroom, but if she brought Autumn with her, the two of them would make even more noise.

There was a scraping sound from the kitchen and Autumn gripped her mother even more tightly.

'Quick,' she whispered. 'We have to hide.'

Still holding each other, they looked around Autumn's plain little bedroom. The row of stuffed toys at the end of the bed contemplated them, their flat, fake eyes gleaming in the blue light from Autumn's clock. There was a bookcase, a chest of drawers and a small desk against one wall, some boxes they still hadn't unpacked and the wardrobe she'd assembled last week. It was tiny, the perfect size to hang a child's dresses in. Laura didn't think she'd fit inside. And, in any case, thanks to her shoddy DIY skills, the door didn't quite close.

She seized the blanket from the bottom of Autumn's bed and rolled it up loosely. She pushed it lengthways under the duvet and shoved George the lion on top, leaving his wispy mane poking out. In the darkness, it might look as if a small child were in the bed. She grabbed Autumn's hand and they ran across the bedroom to the Wendy house. She helped Autumn in and squeezed through the narrow door after her.

The Wendy house was made of wood. Laura had bought it second-hand on eBay for Autumn after they'd moved to Bristol. It was intended for the garden and Laura had thought it would be a project for the two of them – to paint the house and varnish it, make window boxes and a little path and a miniature garden for the house. Autumn, as indecisive as Laura, hadn't been able to choose a colour scheme, and because Laura's priority was to create a design for the garden, she hadn't got around to it.

Inside the house was a toy oven and a sink that Vanessa had bought Autumn when she was four. Laura had planned to find a table and some chairs from a second-hand shop but, like so many things, she hadn't done it. It did mean that there was room for both of them in the house since it was relatively empty. The one item that Laura had made was two sets of curtains. She pulled them across both windows and shut the door. They huddled together in the far corner, their knees to their chests. Autumn was shaking. Laura put her arms around her and pulled her close. They could hear the wind rattling through the Scots pine outside the window.

There was a click and a whine as if the man who'd broken in was opening the door from the kitchen, followed by a creak as he started to climb up the stairs.

It had to be a burglar, one man on his own, she thought, listening to the footsteps. Surely Aaron would not risk breaking into her house? He had too much to lose if he were found out: his business, his reputation, his son... But if it *was* him, and not a burglar, she had no way of predicting what he might do.

'Mum, I need to pee,' whispered Autumn, her voice rising.

Laura seized one of the toy pans from the top of the oven and helped Autumn pull down her pyjama bottoms and crouch over it. The child cried silently. The sound of her urine splashing into the plastic container was unbearably loud. Laura dug her nails into her palms to stop herself from telling her daughter to hurry. When she'd finished, Laura helped her up and moved the pan into one corner of the Wendy house.

They could hear the man taking one slow step after another. The stairs groaned as he gradually grew closer. Autumn whimpered and Laura put her hand over her mouth again. They waited. It felt as if hours were passing. Her left leg started to twitch and jump with cramp. Autumn's hot tears fell on her hand.

There was a loud crack, much louder than before. It came from the landing directly below them. She found she was praying, long-forgotten words from her childhood...

Forgive us our trespasses as we forgive those who trespass against us... Save my little girl...

There was the soft tread of the man climbing up the second flight of stairs. Towards her daughter's room. It seemed to take forever. Laura had her arms wrapped tightly around Autumn, her breath hot and wet against her palm, the smell of her hair in her nostrils.

There was another creak. Perhaps he'd head straight into the spare room – as a conventional burglar would do, looking for computer equipment or jewellery. But then the door to Autumn's bedroom started to open. One step. Two steps. He must be standing just inside the room, right by Autumn's bed, she thought.

What was he doing, leaning over her sleeping child? Why was he in the house?

Suppose he pulled back the duvet and realized that Autumn was not in the bed? Would he start looking through the rest of the bedroom? And what would he do when he found them? Their breathing sounded loud in the confined space of the Wendy house. Laura resisted the urge to lean forward and try and peek through the curtains. She buried her head in Autumn's hair. There was a long, slow creak. She couldn't tell if he had walked further into the room or was simply shifting his weight as he stood by her daughter's bed.

The alien blue light from the clock filtered through the cherry-patterned curtains in the toy house and strange shadows played across the walls: fragments of light and dark as the trees in the park tossed in the wind, splintering the light from the street lamp. Autumn's bedroom curtains were open a fraction – no doubt she'd been staring into the park as she so often was when Laura came to check on her.

She wasn't sure which direction he'd moved in, if he was now directly in front of the Wendy house or if he'd left the room. She allowed herself a fragment of hope. He was going to search each room for anything of value. Any moment now, he'd leave when he realized that there was nothing he wanted.

And then there came the sound that she'd been dreading since they'd been hiding. A ripping noise. The man was tearing back the sheet and duvet. There was a muffled howl and he kicked Autumn's bed. The wooden frame shook. They felt the tremor through the old floorboards. Whoever was in the room knew Autumn was not in her bed. Worse, they knew that she and Autumn knew there was an intruder in the house – only an adult, a mother, like Laura, would have thought to protect her child by hiding a stuffed lion in the bed. And then Laura realized that the man must have been searching – not for computers or gems – but specifically for her child. And right now, he was about to start hunting both of them.

Autumn put her hand on her mother's arm and whispered, 'It's Levi.'

Levi?

'Are you sure?' she mouthed back.

Autumn nodded. The room suddenly seemed to explode around them as the intruder kicked over Autumn's boxes of toys and flung open the wardrobe. It would explain the rage; she couldn't imagine Aaron losing control like that. Laura pushed the Wendy house door open by the smallest amount she could and peered through the crack. There was a dark silhouette in the centre of the room, shoulders heaving, smaller and thinner and narrower than a man's. A boy.

Laura crawled out of the small door. Her feet were numb with cold. Pins and needles shot through her toes and the arches of her feet. She hobbled towards him.

'What the hell are you doing in my house? In my daughter's bedroom?'

Levi said nothing. He was wearing a grey hoodie and tracksuit bottoms and they were dark with rainwater.

'I asked you a question.'

His breathing was loud and ragged. He still did not reply. Behind her she could hear Autumn clambering out of the Wendy house. She stood directly behind her mother. Levi gave a small smile when he saw Autumn emerge. A wave of heat prickled through Laura's scalp, flushing her cheeks: he was *enjoying* seeing how frightened her daughter was.

'I'm going to call the police,' she said, holding out her hand for Autumn and walking towards the boy.

He backed away from her until he was blocking the door. She stood directly in front of him. She could see the rise and fall of his rib cage. Autumn's hand felt fragile; her soft, small bones turning in her palm.

'Why are you here? What are you doing in Autumn's bedroom?'

When he didn't speak, she stepped forward to push him out of the way.

'I wanted to scare her,' he said, his words tripping over each other, the whites of his eyes glinting in the watery light from the street, 'as punishment, you know, for telling on me. And she wasn't in school...'

Laura felt anger surge through her. He wanted to *punish* her daughter? And what had he planned to do to her? How had he even got in – to the garden, never mind the house? She reached towards him and he flinched. She yanked his hoodie down so she could see him properly. He wiped the rain from his face and tried not to look at her.

'Telling on you?' she said, her voice rising.

'Yeah. You know. The Facebook page. Mr George called my dad. And he got mad.'

'Your father didn't know about it?'

Levi shook his head. 'Nah. He made me tell him.'

Laura snapped on the lights. 'Tell him what?' She leant towards him and he shrank from her. His eyes, that strange green of a quarry pond, widened.

'Everything.' He paused, his breathing laboured. Reluctantly, his voice fading, as if speaking was an effort, he said, 'I stole her pen and put it back so she'd look stupid – Dad borrowed the key to her classroom when he was fixing the computers and I copied it. Her bike, you know? Cutting off her hair. The garden where you worked. Painting on your wall.'

'That was all you? By yourself?'

'Yeah.'

'But... how did you know where I worked? Or the key code to get into our garden? Or what to write?' She thought of the words, *Bone by Bone*, scrawled in red across the wall of their house, a fragment of a poem that spoke of unendurable pain. 'How did you know it would even mean anything to me?'

'My dad's got a file on you. All the stuff he took off your laptop. Notes he's made about you. He's so angry with you for pushing me, cutting my face, complaining about me. He thought I hadn't done anything and you were being mental and it was his way of getting you back. Teaching you a lesson, he said – you know, the virus, and deleting all the photos of Autumn on your hard drive. He wrote a program specially.

'He was reading one of your essays. I saw the start of it. This weird poem. I didn't know what it meant but it sounded, you know, proper scary. Dad laughed about you having the same password for everything. He copied down the key code for the garden – he said how stupid you were to use Autumn's date of birth. He said you were the sort of person who'd have a spare key hidden in the garden.'

Laura closed her eyes.

'I'm still going to call the police, Levi. Get out of the way.'

The sound made them all jump. Incongruous in that small room, in the still of the night: it was a woman singing a catchy pop song peppered with expletives.

Levi fumbled for his mobile. 'It's my dad,' he said.

She hesitated. Should she speak to Aaron? She wondered why he was calling Levi at this time of night – he could hardly know the boy was here and she didn't want to risk angering him.

'Answer it. Put him on speakerphone.'

Levi shook his head.

'You either answer that phone now or I ring the police.'

Levi blinked. He looked smaller, frailer, not the malicious thug of her imagination. It came to her then that, in spite of what he'd done, he was only a child, a frightened boy who didn't want to speak to his own father. The ring tone continued, the music sweet, the words vengeful. Levi hesitated and then pressed a couple of buttons.

Aaron's voice barked, 'What in God's name are you doing in their house?'

'How do you know where I am?'

'I can track your mobile, you moron. Do they know you're inside?'

Laura stared at him. She couldn't believe a father – even a man like Aaron – would speak to his son like that. She thought of the suave way he'd spoken to her and the other mums when she'd first met him. Levi looked anxiously at her. She shook her head.

'No,' he said.

'Well, get out, now. Start walking. Head towards the school. I'm almost there. I'll pick you up.' There was a click as he hung up.

After a moment Levi said, 'Thanks.' He didn't look at her.

'For what?'

'For not telling him.'

'You'd better get going,' said Laura.

Levi didn't move.

'He'll be really angry, won't he?' said Autumn. Her voice was soft.

Levi nodded.

'Your black eye.'

His face twisted as if he was going to lash out at her, to say something hurtful and cutting, but then he stopped himself and his expression went blank. Laura thought it was worse than if he'd looked angry or upset, like a normal child would have done. There was a faint trace of a bruise on his upper cheekbone. It was the one she'd caused, she thought with a stab of guilt. And then she realized there was no scab where he'd cut his face on the rock when she'd pushed him – it was Levi's other eye that Autumn was talking about.

'Does Aaron *hit* you?' she blurted out before she could stop herself.

Neither of the children said anything.

'I'm going to call your mum. She can pick you up. Give me her number.'

'You can't. You saw his house,' said Autumn.

'What?'

'Yeah. We followed you yesterday.'

There was a pause as Levi took in this information. 'My mum is ill,' he said defensively. 'She's, like, tired all the time. It's a proper disease. ME.'

'Does Aaron know?' asked Laura. 'I mean, does he know how bad it is? That you're living like that – virtually caring for yourself?'

Levi shook his head.

'Then perhaps calling the police really is—'

'No!' He shouted so loudly, Laura and Autumn jumped. He held up his hands. 'I can take care of myself. I'll just leave, okay? I'll go through the garden, back to my mum's. She won't even know I've been gone.'

He opened the door and stepped out onto the landing.

'I can't let you do that. It's the middle of the night. You can't walk home by yourself in the dark.'

Levi snorted. She could tell he was about to make some kind of smart-ass reply, but then he looked at Autumn. His lips parted, his teeth blue-white, but he said nothing. He opened his hand, his palm pale in the moonlight filtering through the landing window, as if he were going to offer her a tiny gift, and then he laid his hand gently on her arm for a single second. He started down the stairs, his wet trainers squeaking.

She couldn't let him go, she suddenly realized – a twelve-year-old child, alone in the early hours, crossing the city in the darkness. It made her shudder just imagining it.

He was a couple of stairs below her. She put out her hand to stop him. And then the kitchen door opened.

Autumn, her eyes wide with fright, looked at her mother. Levi froze. The door squeaked and closed softly.

'I left the key in the lock,' said Levi. 'And my dad knows I'm still here.'

If Laura had felt frightened before, it was nothing to the terror that engulfed her now. It was overwhelming, like the emotional equivalent of white noise. There was something inevitable about this moment, crouched on the stairs in the dark with her daughter and her daughter's bully; her ex-husband, her mother, her father, her brother all on continents so far away they could literally be on other planets, on other stars. And, all the while, the man she feared the most had let himself into their house and was coming to find them.

She dug her nails into the thin flesh of her wrists and made herself speak firmly. 'Go to him. Pretend we're all still asleep. And then leave. Both of you.'

Levi shook his head. 'You don't know my dad.'

His face had become mask-like again, the skin waxen.

They could hear the slow, stealthy tread as Aaron started to climb the stairs from the kitchen to the hall. Levi pushed past them and ran back into Autumn's bedroom.

Laura and Autumn followed and shut the door. Levi turned off the lights and started fumbling with his phone, trying to prise off the back.

'He knows you're here already. He won't be fooled,' said Laura. 'If you won't go and speak to him, then I will.'

Levi ignored her, scowling as he was unable to open the phone. Laura reached out to snatch the mobile from him but it was too late. He sprinted to the other end of the room, hauled up the sash window and threw his phone out. A blast of freezing air hit them.

'We should hide,' said Autumn. She held the door of the Wendy house open for Levi and he clambered in after her.

In that instant, Laura spotted something, half hidden by the toys Levi had kicked over. It was Autumn's mobile.

What's it doing here? She must have gone through my office, searched the drawers in my desk.

Autumn had been looking at something on it. Laura snatched it up and quickly pressed the On button. It was still working. The screen opened on Facebook. She started back in revulsion when she saw the image – just about visible beneath the network of cracks. It was the same picture Aaron had sent her just before he destroyed her laptop, but this time the naked woman had a photo of another person's face crudely pasted over her own. Autumn's face.

She felt sick. But there was no time to think about it right now, to worry how Autumn was feeling. She quickly pressed a few buttons. There was no time to write a proper message. She slid the phone under a teddy. She wanted to keep the line free, in case he called back, so she ran down the next flight of stairs, her footsteps sounding unbearably loud, to get the phone out of her office. She could hear Aaron had reached the hall, one flight below her. She grabbed the handset off the desk, dialled 999 and pressed the call button. Nothing happened. She pressed it again. She dialled again. She put the phone tightly to her ear. There was no dial tone. She felt panic swell inside her. She should have kept hold of the mobile.

'It won't work. I cut off your landline.'

It was Aaron. He was dressed entirely in black: black boots, black trousers, a black jacket and a black woollen hat.

'A precaution.'

He was standing in front of the stairs leading up to Autumn's bedroom.

'I'm assuming they're both in here,' he said, looking up.

Aaron took the stairs two at a time. Laura ran after him. He burst into her daughter's room and turned on the light. He scanned the space – the boxes of upended toys, the bed covers tossed on the floor, the empty bed, the open wardrobe.

'Get out of the dolls' house. Now.'

After a moment, Levi pushed the little wooden door open and he and Autumn climbed out.

'Your son!' Laura shouted. 'You must believe me now! He broke into our house in the middle of the night to frighten my daughter.'

Aaron inclined his head. There was a long moment of silence. She could hear the rise and fall of Autumn's breaths.

'Well, now we have a real problem,' Aaron said eventually. 'Both of you are here. Both of you know what Levi has done.'

'God knows what he was planning on doing! He said he was going to punish her!'

'But no one else knows that. And no one else knows we're here.'

It was not what she expected him to say. She took a step forwards, stretching out her hands towards Autumn. Aaron moved in front of both children, barring her way.

'You know how important my son is to me,' he continued quietly. 'I love him. I want him. I want him with me. I want his mother out of his life. I have worked hard for this. I live in a slum and I work every goddamn hour, all hours of the fucking day and night, to try and raise the capital to pay blood-sucking solicitors extortionate sums to ensure I will get custody of Levi.' A muscle in his jaw worked and his voice rose in power and fury. 'And no one is going to fuck it up. Not my son, not your manipulative little girl, and certainly not you.'

Aaron's fists were clenched and Laura thought of those hands, hovering over her laptop, his fingers fine and strong, almost stroking the keys, and how he'd laid his hands in his lap, fingers intertwined, as he'd quietly spoken of stars and planets. She'd thought of touching those hands, of them touching her... Yet this was a man who abused his own son. And she had let him into her home, into her life. She had hurt his child and all that followed had been the result of that single, thoughtless action. Laura desperately tried to think of what she could say, how she could stop him. Autumn gave a tiny whimper.

'The thing is,' he said more quietly, rocking backwards and forwards on his toes and heels, as if warming to his topic, hooking his thumbs in his jacket pockets, 'the thing is, my son is a good, decent boy. He's just had a lot to deal with, with the divorce and so on. I must admit, I was surprised that he really was bullying her and it wasn't some racist little tale you'd made up to kick him out of school. But, for some reason, your daughter's a temptation for him. God knows why. He can't help himself.'

He took a step towards her. His eyes had not once left her face. She could see he was barely managing to control his rage and was trembling with the effort.

'I've tried to warn you. God knows how hard I've tried. I hoped you'd get the message.' A sliver of light from the street lamp outside sliced across his sharp cheek bones. 'I thought you'd back off, take your daughter out of that school. But you're too stupid. Too stubborn. I think it's you who needs to be punished. It's you who needs to be taught a lesson.'

Behind Aaron, Laura saw headlights breaking against the window through the half-open curtain.

Thank God!

Aaron saw the expression of relief on her face. 'Is this someone coming to see you?' He peered through the crack in the curtains and then stepped swiftly away. 'It's a Land Rover. Your Marine friend drives one.' He looked at her suspiciously. 'Did you call him?' He sounded incredulous. 'Your mobile is in the kitchen. I cut off your landline. I disabled your Internet. My idiot son has thrown his mobile out of the window.'

She felt relief wash through her. It was over. It was finally over.

'Sometimes he comes round, for a drink.'

'At this time of night?'

'He's lonely. And I can't go out. I don't know any babysitters.'

'Make him go.'

'You could leave now,' said Laura, her mouth dry, her voice harsh. 'Out the back, before he gets here.'

There was the sound of a door slamming and footsteps on the pavement below.

Aaron shook his head. 'And have you tell him what my son did? Risk him calling the police? I'd lose my custody battle. No. You have to get rid of him. I don't care how you do it. Make him go home.'

'And why would I do that?' she whispered.

'Because I have your daughter,' he said.

In one swift movement, he reached behind him and seized Autumn, dragging her in front of him. He put his hand over her mouth, forcing her chin up, her head back.

A spike of adrenaline hit Laura, turning her palms clammy, accelerating her heart rate.

'I could snap her neck,' he said, almost conversationally. 'Why take that risk?' The silver charm on his leather cuff glinted in the light; for a moment, it rested on his wrist bone: it was a small sword.

Autumn's eyes opened wide with terror, as she struggled to stand upright.

He has my daughter.

She looked at her child, the love of her life, and in that instant, she saw her as everything she had been and all that she might be: all that could be cut short here tonight.

She's two years old and she sees the sea for the first time. She shrieks with laughter as a small, foamy wave glides over her pudgy foot and then she cries. She's five years old and she tries an olive in a restaurant for the first time. Her mouth puckers up and her eyes water and she's saying, I like it, I like it. *She's just turned eight and she has a new pink bike and she's clapping her hands with delight and saying,* I love you, Mummy! *She's ten years old. She's standing in front of her paintings. She says she's going to be an artist when she grows up. She's fifteen and she's wearing a mini-skirt that's far too short and she's trying on silver eyeshadow. She looks unbearably grown-up and terribly young. She's at art college. She's showing Laura her final degree show. Laura's toasting her with champagne and she has her arm around a boy and her eyes are bright and soft.*

There was a knock at the door and then the doorbell rang.

Laura opened her mouth to speak, to protest. She looked at Levi. He was staring intently at her. Was he trying to scare her, to back up his father? And then she realized. The boy was beseeching her. He dropped his gaze. Laura backed away. She ran down the stairs. She paused in front of the door to try and collect herself. She unlocked it and opened it a crack.

Jacob was standing on the pavement outside. His jumper was rumpled, as if he'd dressed and driven here quickly, not even stopping to put on a coat. She made an elaborate act of yawning and said, as sleepily as she could in her wired state, 'It's the middle of the night, Jacob. What are you doing here?'

'I got a text from Autumn,' he said tersely. 'Is she here?'

She shook her head, still keeping the door only partially open. 'Everything is fine. She's in bed. I've just checked on her.'

Under the orange glare of the street lamp, his shirt seemed to fluoresce. Pools of rainwater lay on the road, black as Tarmac, an iridescent scum splintered across their surface.

'What's going on, Laura?'

Laura closed her eyes for a moment and saw Autumn, her neck like the stalk of a flower in Aaron's hands.

'Autumn was having a nightmare. She's okay, though.'

'Can I come in?' he asked.

'It's the middle of the night. I'm shattered.' She struggled to keep the high-pitched note of hysteria out of her voice. 'I've been woken by Autumn already. I really need to get some sleep.'

She leant out of the door and looked up at her daughter's window. As she did so, the light went out. In the darkness, something white flickered against the pane. Her heart trembled. It was the curtains. Only the curtains. She looked from the stone sill down to the ground. Such a long way to fall. There was no way they could jump. She shivered.

'There's nothing wrong. She's fine, Jacob. I don't know why she sent you a text. It must have been a mistake. She was just messing around. Checking her mobile was working. The screen is smashed to bits. It doesn't look like you could use the phone at all. But honestly, she's okay. Please just go home.'

She didn't know if he'd forgiven her. He'd said, *You no longer exist for me...* But she knew that he still cared about Autumn, no matter what he thought of her. Was there some way to tell him what was happening? Could she risk whispering to him? But then he would follow her inside and Aaron would hear him thundering up the stairs towards him and by then it could be too late... She wondered whether to retrieve her mobile, but Aaron would notice any delay returning to him. And she had nowhere to hide it. She couldn't do anything that would put her daughter's life at risk.

'She's in my bed now so hopefully we'll both get some sleep now. Goodnight, Jacob.'

She shut and locked the door. She thought of her one British Military Fitness class, the afternoon she'd spent learning self-defence skills with Jacob: a couple of hours punching a bag in front of an ex-Marine. It didn't amount to much; she was still a relatively unfit woman in her thirties with a small child. It hardly equipped her to confront a man in his prime with a black belt in martial arts. Jacob had been talking about some psycho in a pub, a mugger in a dark alley. He had not been thinking of this scenario, facing a man both skilled and deadly, whose reactions were faster than she would have believed possible. If she tried to kick him, or punch him in the face, he would block her blow and then he would be upon her. She'd never been hit or cut in her life; she hadn't even broken a bone. The thought of the pain Aaron could inflict made her feel ill. There was nothing she would not do to save Autumn – she would rather die than see her child harmed. But if Aaron hurt her badly, maimed her, even killed her, she would not be able to protect her daughter.

She had to do something to get Autumn away from him. She looked around for something, anything that could help her. Lying in the open living room doorway was her toolbox, the contents scattered across the floor, the Ikea instruction book open on the Chinese translation in front of a stack of wooden shelves. She raced up to Autumn's bedroom, praying that nothing had happened to her child.

She entered her daughter's bedroom. Aaron was in exactly the same position he'd been in when she'd left him, one arm resting on Autumn's throat, his other hand over her mouth. Self-defence was not an option, not as long as he held Autumn's neck between his hands. Levi was in front of Aaron though, slumped on the bed with his head hanging. As Laura entered the room, Aaron backed over to the window and watched through the crack in the curtains until Jacob's car drove away. Then he relaxed his grip on Autumn. Her daughter started to run towards her, but Aaron grabbed her arm.

'Not so fast,' he said, and pulled her back.

'Dad,' said Levi, standing up, 'let her go.'

Aaron moved so quickly, Laura didn't have time to react. He lashed out at the boy. Levi's head jerked back with sickening speed. He collapsed on the floor in front of her. Slowly, keeping an eye on Aaron, Laura stretched out one hand. She grasped the boy's wrist and then his forearm and levered him upright. He rocked on the balls of his feet, dazed, and wiped his face on the back of his hand, leaving a smear of blood.

'We have to establish some ground rules,' said Aaron.

'Please let Autumn come over here to me. You're frightening her. We're not going anywhere. Jacob has left. I told him I wasn't up for a drink. He's got no idea there's anything wrong, that you're here. What can the two of us do to you?'

As she was speaking, trying to make her voice level and soothing, her eye caught sight of Autumn's mobile, now half under her bed. Aaron must have knocked it there without noticing. She prayed Jacob hadn't abandoned them, that somehow he would realize there was something wrong. In the meantime, there was every chance Aaron would panic and do something rash. She had to get Autumn away from him – and fast. She stumbled as she was talking and looked back at him. Aaron was not fooled. He followed the direction of her gaze.

He yanked the bed over, still gripping Autumn's arm, and seized the phone. He threw it on the bed.

'Whose is this?'

'Autumn's.'

Aaron pressed a button.

'You sent Jacob a text,' he said, looking down at Autumn. '"Help."' He read it out loud.

'No,' said Laura. 'I did. Jacob won't abandon us. He'll call the police. You've got minutes to get out of this house.'

She had to get her daughter away from him. Autumn. That was what it was all for. She had sworn, since the day her daughter was born, that she would do anything and everything she could to protect her. She loved her. She loved her more than life itself. Aaron was a man who believed in a pure vision of the world, as rational and senseless as computer code. He'd hacked into her laptop and read everything; he thought he knew her in her entirety. But he did not know her. Aaron, she thought, did not understand love. The fierceness of it. The absoluteness of it. How all-encompassing love was. There was only one thing left that she could do, that she had to do, whatever happened.

She turned Levi gently towards her and took his hand. His fingers were cold. He stood level with her, a scared child, a boy with a split lip.

'Levi,' she said, 'there's something I need to tell you.'

'Get your hands off my son,' growled Aaron.

'I'm sorry I pushed you. I'm sorry you fell and you cut your face. I should never have done that. It was unforgivable. I can never undo what I did, or make it up to you. But I'm truly sorry.'

His mouth twisted in anger. She thought he was going to pull away. She pressed his fingers tightly between hers. He was about to spit at her, kick her in the shins. She squeezed his hand again and for a moment they stared at each other. Then she put one arm around him and hugged him. He stood rigidly in her embrace, resisting her. She expected him to shove her backwards as hard as he could. But then the child leant against her. He smelt of soap and rain. She could feel his heart-beat, his breath hot and uneven against her neck. Slowly he pulled himself upright and turned to face his father.

'Dad,' said Levi, 'you should go. That guy'll come back. You know he will.'

'*I* should go?'

Laura stretched out her hand to Autumn and this time Aaron, staring at his son, released the girl. She pulled Autumn towards her. Autumn pressed her face into her breast bone and wrapped her arms around Laura's waist. Autumn's shoulders were heaving, her heart vibrating in her frail body. She cupped her daughter's head with one hand, Autumn's short hair silken against her palm.

The boy spoke in a whisper; she could barely hear him. 'Yes,' he said. 'You should go.'

There was silence for a brief moment. It was quiet enough to hear the wind rattling the glass in the half-open window. Then Aaron roared with rage. Laura pushed the children behind her. As he sprang towards her, arms outstretched, she let the screwdriver slide down her dressing gown sleeve, the metal warm where it had been pressed into her skin. Aaron's hands closed around her throat and she staggered backwards as she caught the handle in her palm. She drove the blade into his chest with both hands and his weight, bearing down on her, helped ram it between his ribs until it was buried up to the hilt in his flesh. His blood was hot against her knuckles. He staggered, letting go of her, and fell to his knees. She gasped, drawing in a long, shuddering breath. She opened Autumn's bedroom door, her wet hands sliding on the door knob.

'Get out! Get out of the house!' she shouted, pushing the children through.

She was stepping over his semi-prone body when Aaron hauled himself upright and turned to face her, blocking her exit. His breath was wheezy and he clutched his chest with one hand. She stepped backwards, away from him, but not fast enough. She didn't even see his fist.

Right hook.

Some part of her brain registered what had happened, but now she was on the floor, aeons away from the safety of the door, her vision a blur of magenta, the pain in her jaw searing all the way into her skull and down her spine, a high-pitched singing in her ears. He was coming for her again. She grabbed hold of the edge of the Wendy house and used it to lever herself to her feet. Saliva slid from the corner of her lips. She couldn't close her mouth properly. The pain was excruciating.

Broken. Jaw.

As he pulled his fist back to strike her again, she remembered what Jacob had said: *You must retaliate with a pre-emptive strike: full intensity, all-out aggression.*

She held up her arm to deflect the blow. Her forearm, connecting with his fist, went numb. She grabbed hold of his shirt and pulled him towards her. He was still moving forwards with the momentum of his punch, so close she could feel his breath on her face. She swivelled on her heel, swinging him outwards, and then she was pushing him with all her might, with all her strength, one hand driving the screwdriver further into his chest, and he was screaming into her face before he smashed into the half-open window, the beautiful, old Edwardian window with its rotten wooden sash through which the wind whistled through.

EPILOGUE

THURSDAY 10 MAY

LAURA

Autumn gave a small, tight smile as Laura walked in. This was what money gave you, thought Laura, looking around. It always took her by surprise, visiting the school and seeing the polished wealth of the place. The floor was sprung wood and the equipment was new and it gleamed. There was no film of chalk, no dust balls or stray pigeons, no martyred saints encased in Perspex or sagging crash mats and soggy trampolines. The long windows set in one wall looked out over a gently undulating expanse of expensively maintained grass. A line of cherry trees flanked a gravel path that led to tennis courts, the blossom a froth of pink.

Laura had enrolled Autumn at a private school and talked the head into letting Autumn start straight away, instead of waiting until the beginning of the following term. Thursdays was Autumn's after-school gymnastics class and today the parents were allowed to stay and watch. The coach, a woman with highlighted blonde hair in a high ponytail, wearing a navy tracksuit, waved and jogged over. She shook Laura's hand firmly. She had freshly whitened, straight teeth and an almost horse-like face.

'I'm Tabitha,' she said. 'You're Autumn Wild's mum, aren't you? It's lovely to meet you. She's doing so well – you'll be amazed at her progress.'

When Autumn started at her new school, Laura had told Tabitha on the phone that Autumn would need to be gently coaxed into gymnastics again after her fall. A couple of weeks later, the coach had called her back and said that Autumn was refusing to participate in the classes.

'She's not distressed,' Tabitha had said. 'I don't think you need to stop the classes – she says she wants to be here. Her confidence had a real knock. She just needs time, poor love.'

And then, one day in early January, without saying anything to anyone, Autumn had joined in. Tabitha phoned Laura the same night to tell her, in case Autumn didn't. This was the first time she'd met Tabitha in person and she immediately warmed to the woman.

Laura sat on a bench at one end of the hall with the other parents. She knew a few of them and Autumn had already gone on play dates to their houses but, right now, she didn't feel like chatting to any of them: she wanted to concentrate on her daughter.

Tabitha clapped her hands and started the class warm-up. Autumn was wearing her school uniform tracksuit, which was a little large for her. Her cheeks glowed as she ran around the room, following the other children, sashaying from side to side and bringing her knees up to her chest. She'd filled out a little and grown a couple of inches since the winter and she looked healthy, robust, lightly tanned.

Laura tried not to think about what might have happened that night back in November. Even though it was nearly six months ago, she still had strange nightmares, brown and green, clouded with a muddy, underwater light, and in them she was searching for Autumn. She didn't know where her daughter was or even where she herself was. The two of them were alone, lost in the woods. In her dream, she felt the terror, glacial-cold, that had consumed her in real life, and she would wake, shaking and shivering, drenched in sweat.

Thank God she'd texted Jacob and he'd come round so fast. He said he'd been about to go home, he'd had it with her and Autumn, messing him around – but then, as he was driving away, he thought how frightened she'd seemed and he remembered what she'd said

– that she'd put Autumn in *her* bed. So why had the light gone out in Autumn's bedroom as they were talking? He'd gone to the lane at the back of the house to check if there was a light on in Laura's bedroom. The garden gate and the kitchen door were open. He'd been about to go inside, when he remembered what had happened in Northern Ireland. *Procedure. Always follow procedure*, he'd said. He'd called the police. And then he'd gone in.

A couple of days after that terrible night, PC Emery and PC Jones had visited her at home. They'd said that Levi's back was covered in bruises, he had a hairline fracture in a rib and a slight sprain in one wrist. Aaron had told them that Laura inflicted these injuries too. The boys who'd witnessed the assault all said Laura had 'only' pushed Levi and he'd hit his head and cut his face and, after that night, Levi changed his story and said that Laura hadn't seized his arm or punched him in the ribs. He said his dad had told him to say that.

As PC Emery was talking, an image of Levi came to her, the very first time she'd seen him, hanging from the yellow and red, paint-peeling climbing frame, and noticed his dangerous beauty, those strange tawny-green eyes with their thick lashes. She'd thought he was appraising her, assessing her vulnerability. And then the day in the nature reserve that had changed everything; she'd been so close to him she'd seen the rain glistening on his skin, smelt the take-away he'd had the night before. She hadn't seen him as a child. Only as a threat.

'I think it's safe to say that the charges against you for actual bodily harm against Levi will be dropped but I, or one of the other officers, will need to caution you formally in the station,' PC Emery said.

'What will happen to him?' asked Laura.

'He's been removed from Ashley Grove Junior School and he's currently in care,' said PC Emery gently.

'In foster care?'

'Yes – it's just a temporary measure. Social Services are trying to work out what support his mum needs. She's got chronic fatigue syndrome.'

Laura nodded. Emery must have seen her distress because she said soothingly, 'I'm sure he'll be back with his mum in no time. It's not like she's terminally ill or anything.'

Laura nodded again. 'Do you think I could visit him?'

She thought of those three short words he had spoken to his father: *You should go*. The bravery of the child made her want to weep.

PC Emery looked at her in surprise and then smiled. 'I'll speak to his case worker. I'm sure it can be arranged.' She laid her hand on Laura's arm. 'As for his father, Mr Jablonski... there will be an inquiry. I shouldn't really say it at this stage, but given your injuries, and Jacob Davidson's testimony, it's likely it'll be seen as self-defence.'

Laura closed her eyes. 'So I won't have to go to prison?'

She'd pushed Aaron backwards so hard he'd fallen through the half-open window, onto concrete, the screwdriver she'd rammed into his lung sticking out of his chest, and had hit his head on the pavement. He was still in intensive care.

'Let's hope not, eh?' said PC Emery.

The warm-up had finished. Autumn and the other children in her class discarded their tracksuits. She was wearing a leotard and T-shirt. Her hair, caught in an Alice band, had started to grow out and was in a short bob. She was bouncing on the trampoline, her toes pointed, her hair standing on end. There was a single moment, a fraction of a second, when she was stationary, suspended in mid-air, before she raised her legs into a piked jump, and then twisted to land on her front facing the opposite way. There was something so lovely and so fluid about it, the certainty with which she turned in the air, the long, lean lines of her legs, it brought tears to Laura's eyes.

After that Saturday in November, Laura knew that she would never take Autumn back to Ashley Grove Junior School. As soon as Vanessa reached Windhoek for supplies, Laura had phoned her and told her what had happened and asked her to pay for Autumn's school fees. Vanessa had said she and Julian would be delighted.

Vanessa was back in Namibia for the whole of the summer. Laura imagined that, right now, she would be in the place she loved the best: crouched by a fire interviewing the Himba women, asking them about their goats and their children, the heat of the day fading fast as the sun started to sink behind hills as dark as dragon's blood. It was a kind of half-formed thought, a feeling that perhaps she and Vanessa owed it to one another: that she needed to let her mother help them and her mother needed to pay for Autumn's new school. An atonement of sorts. She wanted her mother to know that she was forgiven. Or to understand that maybe there was nothing to forgive. Her mother had done the best she could, exactly as Laura had.

Autumn could have died that night, she thought. She couldn't imagine what her life would be like without her child. Sometimes, when she was working in the evening, she could hear laughter and it always took her a moment to realize it was her daughter and her new friends. She hadn't realized how much she'd missed the sound of Autumn's throaty laugh.

Over the winter she'd drawn up plans for her own business and she'd officially launched her company in February. She was confident she could make it work. Her first client was a wealthy woman with a huge house and garden overlooking Leigh Woods. She'd immediately recommended Laura to another two of her friends. Laura was sure she could pick up more work after she graduated and she no longer had to spend so much time on her dissertation.

Autumn was standing to one side of the trampoline now, watching one of the other girls. Tabitha stepped in to correct her position and show her pupil how to do the complex move again. The girl had another go – landing on her back, catapulting onto her front, lifting her hips and rising to her feet. Autumn smiled and clapped. She looked so happy – so pleased for this other child's success.

Autumn and the small group of children she was with followed Tabitha to the beam. Laura sat up properly and clasped her hands together. To her surprise, Autumn was first in line. Her daughter climbed onto the beam without hesitating and walked with ease along the narrow strip of wood, as Tabitha followed on the mat alongside, smiling up at her. And then, almost before Laura was aware it was happening, Autumn bent at the waist, planted her hands on the beam and lifted up into a cartwheel, effortlessly spinning through the air and rising to her feet at the far end, her face flushed. She looked up and smiled at her mother.

ACKNOWLEDGEMENTS

Every writer I know has a support system around them. In my case, it's my friends who take me out for prosecco, endless coffees or long hikes; my husband, who is a patient listener; my daughter, who is endlessly entertaining; and the rest of my extended O'Connell family. Sadly, my father, James O'Connell, isn't here to see *Bone by Bone* being published, but I know he'd be proud. My mum, Rosemary, and my siblings and their partners, Sheila and Simon, Dee and Ian and Pat and Em, have all been there for me when I've needed them, with Dad's favourite food: pizza and ice cream.

In terms of the actual nuts and bolts of putting *Bone by Bone* together, it has only been possible thanks to a grant from the Society of Authors' and Arts Council England. I'm grateful to Chris Wakling who read the plot synopsis and the first draft. I benefitted from his considerable expertise and belief in me. My sister, Dee, and Ali Griffiths read a later draft and made helpful comments. Ali and Joe Melia have been my constant and enthusiastic supporters, cheering me along what has sometimes seemed like a long road! Verity Otterbeck and her daughter, Halle, reminded me what it was like to be nine years old. Andy Torbet told me about being a Marine and what to do if you think someone is going to attack you (run like hell). Paul Whitehouse helped me with the police procedure (all technical errors are my own).

I'd like to thank my first editor at Corvus, Maddie West, for her useful insights; Margaret Stead, of Atlantic Books, for her faith in

330

the novel from an early stage; Louise Cullen and Sara O'Keeffe for steering *Bone by Bone* towards publication; Alison Davies, who ran the publicity campaign; Nicky Lovick for her careful copyediting; and the rest of the team at Atlantic Books and Corvus. Above all, I'd like to thank my agent, Rob Dinsdale, of AM Heath: for championing this book from the start, his painstaking editorial advice and reading more drafts than anyone should ever have to. Thank you.

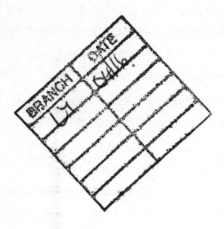